Praise for Her Pas

D1240532

"An engrossing tale about sexual assault that skillfully covers a tough and timely topic." —KIRKUS REVIEWS

"*Her Past Can't Wait* is a scathing commentary on how society treats women when they do something as simple as trying to set physical boundaries. Gut-wrenching, intriguing, and twisty, Boulden's thought-provoking story lays bare just how far we have to go as a society when it comes to believing and protecting women." —LISA REGAN, *USA TODAY* & *WALL STREET JOURNAL* BESTSELLING AUTHOR

"The World Health Organization singles out Eye Movement Desensitization and Reprocessing (EMDR) as one of the top 'evidence-based treatments of choice' for PTSD. In her fast-paced and absorbing novel, *Her Past Can't Wait,* Jacqueline Boulden illuminates the courageous and timely story of a woman facing her traumatic past and how EMDR eased her suffering. A must-read for all trying to live like the past is in the past, when it's actually still buried in their subconscious." —DONNA KNUDSEN, PSY.D., EMDR INSTITUTE FACILITATOR & CERTIFIED CONSULTANT

"An accomplished news journalist, author Jacqueline Boulden has applied her keen observation and reporting skills to telling a powerful story too many women know well, and one woman in particular must remember in order to live in peace." —RENÉE BESS, GCLS GOLDIE AWARD & ALICE B READERS AWARD-WINNING AUTHOR

Her Past Can't Wait

Jacqueline Boulden

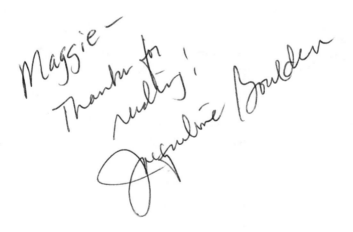

Maggie —
Thanks for
reading!
Jacqueline Boulden

PINE
PLACE
PRESS

Her Past Can't Wait

Copyright © 2022 by Jacqueline Boulden

This is a work of fiction. Apart from EMDR, which is a valid psychotherapy treatment, names, characters, and events are products of the author's imagination or are used fictitiously and are not to be construed as real. Any resemblance to actual events, or persons, living or dead, is entirely coincidental.

Library of Congress Control Number: 2022911804

Paperback ISBN 979-8-9860384-0-7

eBook ISBN 979-8-9860384-1-4

Printed in the United States of America

Published by Pine Place Press, Clifton Park, NY

Book cover: Lynn Andreozzi

Author photo: Kerensa Rybak Photography

For Helen

Chapter One

Late September 2018

All Emily Archer wanted to do was go home, collapse on the couch, and forget about the stressful week that saw her regularly reaching for ibuprofen or a glass of wine, depending on the time of day. But when she tried to skirt the perimeter of the dance floor in the Marriott ballroom, someone pulled her into the wriggling mass of people, whose inhibitions had been loosened by three hours of free alcohol and dinner prepared by one of Philadelphia's finest chefs. People smiled at her with such enthusiasm that she wanted to be a good sport, so she raised her arms and clapped her hands to the beat of the live band.

Then someone's hand pressed against her body. Not an accidental touch that was inevitable with so many people moving close together, but the pressure of someone's hand trailing down the middle of her back and groping her derrière. She swung her arm to brush away the offending hand and swiveled around to see who'd accosted her. There—a man starting to turn away, with a neatly trimmed goatee framing the smirk on his face. He slipped into the crowd and disappeared, but she was hemmed in.

A couple of minutes later, she worked her way off the dance floor and spotted her colleague, Martin Gilbert. She and Martin were guests at Clifton Pharmaceutical's annual gala because their agency led the company's advertising campaigns. Martin waved her over, but after seeing her expression, dropped his arm and raised his eyebrows. She pasted what she hoped was some semblance of a smile on her face and marched toward him.

"Emily, have you met Pete Shelby, Clifton's new Vice President of Sales?" Martin asked.

Shelby turned toward her and she swallowed a gasp. She instantly recognized his smirk, and every muscle in her body tensed. Every sexual innuendo or snide remark she had to endure, every story she heard about women who were physically or sexually abused, demeaned or marginalized, nudged or blatantly pushed aside in the workplace, all rose within her like a wave thrust up from the ocean floor. She glared at Shelby, reached out as if to shake his hand, then raised her hand higher and slapped him in the face.

"Emily, what the hell!" Martin's eyes were as big as the tabletops in the ballroom.

Shelby took a quick step back. He massaged his left cheek where a red splotch was growing and gaped at her. "Lady, what is wrong with you?"

He had a lot of nerve asking her that question. "There's nothing wrong with me," she said, trying to tamp down the anger in her voice, struggling to regain control of her emotions as tears welled in her eyes. "That was for grabbing my ass on the dance floor a minute ago."

"I didn't touch you." Shelby's eyes darted back and forth between her and Martin. "You have me confused with someone else."

"You're lying," she said, flexing the fingers on her right hand, surprised at how much they hurt. But she'd never slapped anyone before, so how could she know? It looked so different in the movies.

"Emily, please calm down," Martin said, his voice just above a whisper.

"Calm down? I'm telling you this man sexually assaulted me on the dance floor. Why would I make up something so disgusting?" She took a deep breath to soothe her shaky nerves.

"What's going on here?" Warren Painter, Clifton's CEO, asked as he walked up and joined them. Painter set his empty wine glass on a nearby table, took a white handkerchief from his pocket, and wiped beads of perspiration from his brow. His bright red face indicated he'd been enjoying the alcohol. It was his party, after all.

"This man," Emily waved her finger in Shelby's direction as she spoke to Painter, "just assaulted me on the dance floor."

Shelby looked at his boss and shook his head.

"Are you sure? Maybe it was someone else," Painter said.

"Oh, I'm sure. It was him." She thrust her chin up, daring Painter and Shelby to keep challenging her when there was no doubt in Emily's mind who had groped her.

Martin slid closer and took her elbow.

"When there's a lot of alcohol at an event like this," Shelby said, a smile spreading slowly across his face, "people make mistakes. I'm willing to chalk this up to mistaken identity and overlook what happened."

She scowled and glanced over his shoulder at the people watching them, whispering to one another, their curiosity piqued. Despite the noise level in the rest of the room, the four of them were attracting a lot of attention. Shelby was giving her a way out, but she was not about to take it. She'd done that for far too long with too many others.

"Emily." Martin's voice was soft and close. "Let's go. It's in everyone's best interest to step away. Please."

Martin wasn't just her fellow senior account executive at Barnes Advertising and Marketing, more commonly referred to as BAM; he was also one of her closest friends. She heard the concern in his voice, probably a little desperation, too. After all, she'd just slapped the new VP of sales for the company whose account helped make BAM one of the top five advertising agencies in the Philadelphia region. She willed her pounding heart to slow down, tried to take an emotional step back from what had happened, and see it through the eyes of others. It was like plodding through a reed-filled swamp. With ankle weights.

With one hand firmly holding her elbow, Martin put his other hand on her lower back, said goodnight to the two men, and spun her away from them. They pushed through the crowded ballroom, side-stepping chairs and people. The music faded as the heavy double doors closed behind them.

"Let me drive you home. We can come back and get your car tomorrow," Martin said as they stepped onto the escalator for the ride to the lobby.

"I am perfectly capable of driving, thank you very much." She didn't mean to take it out on Martin, but right now, any man who came too close could get caught in her wrath.

"It's just that you're so upset—"

"Yes, I'm upset." Exasperation dripped from every word. "Pete Shelby sexually assaulted me on the dance floor, then you shepherded me out of there like I was the one who was wrong." She winced at the pain in her fingers as she clasped her black clutch tighter in one hand and brushed her shoulder-length light brown hair out of her eyes with the other. Emily stole a glance at Martin as they stepped off the escalator and turned toward the exit. They'd navigated some tough times and unreasonable demands with difficult clients over the years, but nothing like this had ever happened. His jaw was clenched about as tight as she'd ever seen it.

Neither of them said another word until they got to her Outback in the parking lot across the street from the hotel. She flinched when he put his hand on her shoulder but didn't pull away.

"Em, what happened tonight was so out of character for you," he said as she turned toward him. "You've been subjected to vulgar behavior before; you've told me. But you lost it tonight. Plus, and don't get mad at me for saying this, you've looked tired a lot lately. What's going on?" His bright blue eyes bored into her dark brown ones with questions and empathy.

She thought about all the stories in the news and on social media—new ones almost every day—about women sexually assaulted or harassed by judges and generals, actors and lawmakers, Olympic coaches and Little League ones, business executives in companies large and small. She was so furious after watching hours of cable news that some nights she paced her bedroom until she was exhausted enough to sleep.

Of course she was tired. Most women were.

"Just a lot going on," she said, unable to confide even to Martin how Pete Shelby grabbing her on the dance floor had tapped into something deeper. Much deeper. "I'll see you Monday." She slid into the driver's seat and started the engine. With barely a glance around her, she put the vehicle in gear and steered toward the exit. Martin disappeared from her rearview mirror as she turned the corner onto 13th Street. She took a deep breath and tried to relax in the safety of her own space, but Shelby's words kept echoing in her head.

"You have me confused with someone else," she repeated in a mocking voice. "No, sir." Her voice grew stronger and louder as she flicked on her blinker and prepared to turn left onto Arch Street. "You have *me* confused with someone who would accept your self-serving comments and thank you oh-so-very-much for giving me a way out. Not me. I'm so *tired* of this."

The signal at the end of the block turned yellow and she stepped on the gas to beat the red light, eager to put the evening behind her.

Chapter Two

The minutes crept by, like cars on the highway inching toward the Jersey Shore on a late Friday afternoon during summer. Emily had been watching the digital clock on her laptop from the moment she arrived just after eight until one minute before nine. Then she stood and walked about forty steps to Chris's office. Chris Murphy, BAM's founder, had left a message on her cellphone Sunday asking—no telling —her to come to his office first thing Monday morning. She'd put off talking to him then, but avoiding the meeting was not an option.

"Is he ready for me?" she asked Joanie, whose desk was just outside Chris's office. Joanie was a recent hire, and Emily didn't know her well, but even a stranger could understand the eyes looking up at her with sadness. Joanie nodded toward Chris's door without uttering a word.

This might be worse than I thought.

Emily paused, threw her shoulders back, then knocked, stepped inside, and closed the door. She hoped they could have an informal chat around the small table in front of the bookcases, or in the comfortable swivel chairs against the other wall. Anything but Chris sitting behind his big oak desk and her across from him, like an insolent child called to the principal's office. He made no effort to move from behind his desk, so she sat in the chair opposite him and folded her hands in her lap.

Chris planted his elbows on the desk. He pressed his hands together with his pinkies and thumbs, then tapped his other fingers quickly and repeatedly. His lips were pressed together so tightly, they disappeared into his mouth. His tired eyes were shadows. His eyebrows scrunched together in a frown. She took it all in and tried not to squirm.

"Warren Painter was pretty upset when he called me yesterday morning. Can't say as I blame him when he told me what happened."

She couldn't remember the last time she'd seen Chris this angry. She wanted to tell him what had happened to her, not what happened to Pete Shelby, but instinct told her to wait.

"Painter wants me to fire you, Emily. He even threatened to pull his account and find another agency."

Chris's words hit her like a sharp jab in the ribs, and Emily took a breath that went in hard and fast. She concentrated on breathing slowly to stop sucking in loud gulps of air.

"I've known Warren for at least a dozen years," he said, tilting back in his chair. His elbows slipped to his sides, but his fingers kept tapping. "It took me two years to convince him to switch to Barnes Advertising and Marketing. Two years of long conversations and several marketing proposals before he signed on the dotted line. Clifton Pharma was my first big client—the one who gave me credibility in Philadelphia's competitive advertising and marketing field."

She listened and tried to remember to be strong.

"I know you've heard the story before, but under the circumstances, it bears repeating. I'd sure hate to lose Warren's account over a misunderstanding." He paused and looked at her for a few seconds before continuing. "What happened?"

She told him, from being intentionally groped on the dance floor to recognizing Pete Shelby as the man who accosted her. "And then I slapped him in the face," she finished.

"And he denied it?"

"He said I was mistaken. That it was someone else."

"Could it have been someone else?"

She didn't hesitate. "No." Her voice was confident, her eyes steadfast. "The smirk on Shelby's face when Martin introduced him was the same look he gave me on the dance floor after he groped me."

"And then Warren came over? How did he react?"

"He sided with Shelby. Of course."

Chris looked at her with less anger now, but there was plenty of disappointment in his eyes.

"Maybe the guy had too much to drink. Maybe everyone had too much to drink. Martin said there was free-flowing booze all night." He looked down at his hands, then back up at her. "I need to ask you, Emily. Did you have much to drink?"

She knew he would ask that at some point, and she fought the urge to be offended. Tried to modulate her voice. Stifle the anger and frustration. "Chris, I've worked for you for ten years. You've been to lots of client events with me. I almost never drink at them, and if I do, it's not much. Saturday night, I had half a glass of wine. With dinner. That's it. Ask Martin."

"I did already."

She nodded. She fully expected Chris would've asked Martin. "And what else did he tell you?"

"He said he didn't know you'd been accosted, didn't see it. Everything else Martin said corresponds with what you told me." He paused. Silence filled the air. The kind of silence that prompts people to hold their breath until someone speaks again. The kind of silence between two people when both know one of them is preparing to deliver bad news and the other is bracing for it.

"I'm in an awkward position, Emily. It's your word against Shelby's. What am I supposed to do?"

What kind of a question was that? She bit her lip and took another deep breath.

"You could say you support me. You could say you believe me." She leaned forward in her chair. "You've known me almost as long as you've known Warren Painter. Why would I make it up?"

"I'm not saying you made it up. I'm suggesting perhaps it *was* a case of mistaken identity. The dance floor was crowded, right? Martin said the lights were low and flashing. No one else came forward and said they saw it happen. He could sue you for assault. Have you thought about that?"

Yes, she'd thought about that. She'd also considered what it would be like to sue Shelby for sexual assault. But she didn't know if anyone saw him grab her ass and finding credible witnesses from the inebriated crowd could prove difficult. Unfortunately, more than a few people saw the slap.

"He wouldn't dare sue me." Emily's voice covered the twisting nerves in her body.

"Let's hope not." His eyes dropped to his desk while he fussed with the knot of his tie.

She could tell where this was going, and it would turn out badly for her. "So now you're siding with the guys from Clifton." There was a hardness to her voice that she didn't bother to soften. She'd never been in such a tenuous position at work before. It was upsetting and infuriating. So what if it showed.

"Careful, Emily." His eyes shot up and locked on hers. He put both hands up, tapping the air between them, warning her. "Look, I just promoted you to senior account executive because you're damn good at what you do. I'm not going to fire you. I'm not going to suspend you. But you know I have to take you off the Clifton account. And I need you to take a couple of weeks off."

"What?"

"You've been working hard. That's nothing new. I checked with HR. You haven't taken any time off in months. You've got six weeks saved up. Use some of them. Go sit on a beach somewhere. Drink rum cocktails with little umbrellas until the sun goes down."

"I slap a guy for groping me on the dance floor, and I'm the one who pays the price?"

"Most people would not consider a two-week paid vacation punishment."

"This isn't fair and you know it." Tears welled in her eyes, and she willed them to stop. She'd been strong so far and didn't want Chris to see the side of her that wanted to cry with frustration and yell out in anger. Neither would do her any good right now. She bit her lower lip to give the pain another place to land.

"Please don't make this an even bigger issue than it already is. I'm trying to save a twelve-million-dollar account. I am trying to appease our largest client."

"And what're you going to do to appease me, the victim of a sexual assault? Huh? Answer me that. What about me?" Her time for patience was over. She wiped a tear from her cheek, rose from her chair, and hurried out. She was in and out of her office in seconds, her leather bag slung over her shoulder, her footsteps hard and quick as she stormed out the front door.

Martin's text pinged her cellphone. Emily thought about answering it, but she wanted to get away from BAM. To get away from any connection to Clifton Pharma and Pete Shelby.

Back home, she walked back and forth between the living

room and kitchen until the anger subsided and laughter took over. A vacation? Really? Sit on a beach? Drink cocktails? Was Chris crazy? Did he really think she could enjoy a vacation right now? That she could sit still after what had happened? She shook her head. No, of course he didn't. He needed her out of sight so he could tell Warren he'd taken action against her.

She poured a glass of water and sat at the kitchen table, looking out the window at her little yard, at the plants trying to hold on to their blossoms a little longer before cooler autumn temperatures stole them away. What could she do for the next two weeks? She wasn't about to visit her parents in the Poconos. They'd love to see her and would be supportive, but she couldn't hide her pain and anger and didn't want her mom to worry. An impromptu trip away from Philly wasn't very appealing, not even to one of her favorite destinations. A week at the beach or someplace peaceful, no matter how many cocktails with little umbrellas she drank, sounded way too quiet when every inch of her body wanted to scream at someone or everyone for what had happened Saturday night. For what happened to her at work. For what was happening to women everywhere far too often.

Chapter Three

Emily changed into jeans and a T-shirt, then cleaned as if her house was about to be inspected by someone wearing a white glove. Not that her modest three-bedroom twin in the city's Mt. Airy neighborhood needed a deep clean. She'd moved in just a few years ago and was taking her time buying furniture. The third bedroom stood empty; the dining room had a table and six chairs, nothing else. The living room and master bedroom contained mostly oak furniture and the occasional antique. Her kitchen was on the small side, but with higher-end appliances and a table for two in front of the window. The house was a perfect fit for her.

The physical work helped quiet her anxious and angry mind, but the situation at BAM was never far from her thoughts. She took a quick break for lunch, and by late afternoon she was exhausted. She showered, put on a nice shirt with clean jeans, and was coming down the stairs when the doorbell rang.

"Hi, Em," Martin said, enveloping her in his strong arms, a chilled bottle of wine in one hand and a bouquet of bright orange and yellow mums in the other.

"Thanks for suggesting this," she said, holding him tight. "You brought me flowers? How nice. And wine." She laughed. "I am so ready for a glass of wine right now. Come on." She took the wine and put her hand in his.

"You've been cleaning up a storm, haven't you?" he asked, sniffing the air as they walked to the kitchen.

"I had to expend all this energy somehow." She put the flowers in an etched crystal vase and filled it with water. In the time it took her to take care of the flowers and place the vase at one end of the table, he'd opened the wine, poured some into two glasses, and sat down.

"What are people saying?" she asked as they touched glasses in a silent toast and sipped the wine.

"Who have you talked with from work today?"

"Are you avoiding the question?"

"No, just asking a different one first."

"Lily and I have spoken several times, as you know," Emily said, referring to her administrative assistant. "She's rescheduling my appointments and directing most questions to Tina, who's shouldering the load for me. I don't plan to answer any more calls from BAM."

She took another sip of wine, then set her glass down on the table, her hand shaking more from exhausted muscles than nerves. She was physically tired from cleaning all day, but her mind raced from one emotion to another. Anxious. Sad. Angry. Incredulous. It was like pulling pieces of paper out of a jar, and whatever slip of paper she picked out explained her tangled emotions at that moment. She couldn't remember ever feeling so disjointed. "So, what are people at work saying?" she repeated.

"You'll be happy to know people support you," he said. "Kevin even hinted at some unseemly behavior he saw from Shelby at a sales event a few years ago when Shelby worked for a different company. People are surprised Chris asked you to take a couple of weeks off. Some women say there's a double standard."

"*Told* me to take two weeks off," she said. "And there is a double standard. Women know it." The knot in her stomach returned and was as strong as it had been earlier in the day when she was sitting in Chris's office.

"Emily, I know this is hard—"

"Actually, Martin, you have no idea." Her voice shot out of her like a sudden burst of water from the tap. She clamped her lips together and rubbed the tops of her legs. "I'm sorry. I didn't mean to lash out. It's just that you might understand intellectually, but you're not a woman. You can't relate emotionally. This is wrong. On so many levels."

They sat in silence until Martin cleared his throat and began speaking softly.

"Em, this isn't a perfect analogy, okay, but it's what popped into my mind. Do you remember when my sister died?"

She glanced back up at him. "Of course." Like she could ever forget the day Martin was shattered by unthinkable news.

"One day, Sara called to tell me she was heading out on a hiking trip with some friends. She was so excited, so full of life." He paused with the pain of the memory before he could continue. "The next day, I got a call from a trooper with the Colorado State Patrol telling me Sara had fallen into a ravine and died. Just like that, she was gone."

"You were inconsolable for weeks." She reached out and touched his hand.

"I was so angry at the world for taking Sara from me. She wasn't just my little sister; she was one of the most important people in the whole world to me. I couldn't think straight for a while. Remember? I was angry. A lot. I shouted at other people. A lot." The muscles in his jaw looked like rocks.

"Everyone felt so bad, but we couldn't figure out what to

do for you, other than to give you our love and support." Her voice was barely above a whisper. "No matter how much we listened and tried to understand the depth of your pain, none of us could help you."

"No, you couldn't, even though you tried. Ramón convinced me to see a therapist. I could not have found my equilibrium again without Mandy and all those hours of therapy."

"I remember how much Mandy helped," she said. "She brought you back to your old self."

"I'm saying this as your best friend, someone who loves you very much. I don't know what's going on, and I mean going on deep inside of you. But I know something is, and I think what happened Saturday night was the last straw."

Emily stared at the table and didn't try to deny it. Her fingers spun the wine glass around several times while she thought about exactly what to say. "Remember last Friday when I blew up at the guys for making a sexually offensive joke during our meeting? It's not the first time they've said something inappropriate, but usually I'd just tell them to zip it. That time, I couldn't stop myself from shouting at them." She shook her head in disgust. "And did you hear about the latest slap in the face to women everywhere? About the college athlete who was given probation for raping a fellow student?" She stopped spinning the glass and gripped it with such force her knuckles turned white. "He got probation because the judge said he's a star athlete with a promising future, and why should the young man's life be ruined by this girl's claim? His words, not mine. He's a star athlete and a young man. They called her a girl. She's not a girl. She's a young woman. She also has, or had, a promising future until the guy who raped her gave her a lifetime of anxiety and fear of the dark."

She took a gulp of wine, then poured more into her glass.

Martin nodded. "I agree. The judge should be reprimanded, maybe even removed from the bench. But that was recent. Whatever's bugging you seems like it's been going on much longer. What else is it?"

"I don't know how to explain it. I keep having a sense of— I don't know what you would call it—dread, I guess. I've had some bad dreams and something that felt like a flashback. Of what, I don't know." She tried to push the heaviness out of her body. Tried to replace the flat air in her lungs with fresh air. Tried to stop her feet from bouncing on the floor.

"But it built up so much you felt compelled to slap someone?"

Emily looked at him, shook her head, and shrugged. "I get it. I'm one of the strongest people I know. At least I used to be. I used to be funny, too. I used to have more fun in life. Too often now, I feel shaky, scared, and angry, like something has been bubbling up inside of me. It started getting worse with the misogynist and racist and anti-Semitic attitudes that have dominated Washington for so many years. A lot of men treat women as second-class citizens. I've felt like when the pressure inside a volcano builds up and finally blows—I've been like a simmering volcano. And Shelby shot me over the top."

"I don't think your friends and colleagues can help you any more than they could help me after Sara died," Martin said. "But I think Mandy could." He stood, took a business card out of his wallet, and put it on the table. "Call Mandy. Please. Now, I've got to go. Ramón is waiting with dinner." He kissed the top of her head and whispered, "By the way, the place looks great."

She started to get out of her chair.

"Stay put. I'll let myself out."

She stared out the window thinking about their conversation, then picked up the business card. Held it in her hands. Ran her index finger over the embossed lettering. Mandy Weston. She had an office in Center City. Emily took a sip of wine for courage, picked up her cellphone, and tapped in the phone number.

"Mandy Weston," a soothing voice said.

"Oh, hi. I didn't expect you to pick up."

"I'm between clients. How can I help you?"

Emily pressed her right hand against her chest. The action reminded her of when she recited the Pledge of Allegiance in Girl Scouts. Only now it was to keep her heart from popping out of her body. "I'm a colleague of Martin Gilbert's. He gave me your number."

"Why don't we begin with your name?"

Emily laughed. At least she thought it was a laugh. "Emily Archer. I work with Martin at Barnes Advertising and Marketing. We're best of friends. Which is why I'm calling. Well, not because we're best friends." She must have sounded like someone who'd just come out of anesthesia and was incapable of putting together sentences that made sense.

"Okay, Emily, so you're interested in coming to therapy?"

"Martin thinks it would help. I slapped the vice president of sales for a major client of our advertising agency, and I've been told to take two weeks off."

"It sounds to me like you're going through a rough time. I have an opening tomorrow afternoon at one o'clock. Would you like to see me then?"

Emily gulped, and her heart started racing again. "I'm still trying to absorb the fact that I called you. I didn't expect to get an appointment so soon."

"You can wait if you need to give it more thought. I don't have many openings, but if you prefer, we could try to schedule a time later in the week or next week."

"I have nothing *but* time right now," Emily said after a short pause. "Okay. I'll see you tomorrow."

Chapter Four

E mily expected to be nervous. She'd never seen a therapist and wasn't sure how she would react. During the drive into the city, she thought about scenes with therapists in movies, on TV, and in books. She tried to recall some of what Martin described when he saw Mandy years ago. None of that helped settle her down.

Before she realized it, she was parallel parking into a tight space on Pine near 22nd Street and walking the few blocks to Mandy's office. After entering the security code to the building on the keypad, she walked inside, strolled down the hallway, punched in another code, and opened the door to a cozy waiting room. The lights were as soft as the classical music wafting from the Bose sitting on the bookshelf. The couch and chairs were two shades darker than tan—a good dirt color, her mother would say. The walls were painted beige and decorated with a few pastel paintings framed in white. The room was easy on the eyes and ears and loosened the knots in her stomach. She picked up a magazine on the coffee table and plopped into a comfortable chair.

A few minutes later, the door to Mandy's office opened.

Emily kept her eyes lowered until she heard the click indicating the previous client had left the waiting room.

"Emily?"

She looked up and nodded at the woman standing in the doorway to the inner office, who was about her height, older, maybe in her late forties, with silver streaks in her short-cropped black hair.

"Come on in."

She and Mandy made idle conversation about city traffic and the never-ending hunt for on-street parking while settling in, Mandy into the overstuffed beige chair and Emily on the couch opposite it. Small tables on either side of the couch held boxes of tissues. Another box sat on the narrow coffee table between them, with small bottles of water on the shelf below. It was her first trip to a therapist's office and her first thought was that crying was either expected or encouraged.

"I'm going to ask you a lot of questions," Mandy said. "And I want you to ask me any questions you have. Why don't we begin with you telling me what brings you here?"

Mandy's eyes were inviting and her voice calming, but Emily's heart raced, and her voice caught in her throat when she tried to speak. After a cooling sip of water, the words finally came out, flowing so fast her brain almost couldn't keep up.

She told Mandy how a man groped her at his company's annual dinner, and she recognized him when he was introduced to her. Her hands squeezed into tight fists, and her hunched shoulders edged up. "I reacted without thinking about the ramifications to my job. I slapped him." Then she explained how the company was one of BAM's largest clients, and her boss didn't fire her, but he told her to take two weeks' vacation.

"Has anything like this ever happened to you before?"

"The groping or the slapping?"

Mandy smiled gently. "Either. Both."

"You're a woman," Emily said. "So you know how men leer and make jokes and snide comments, and they don't even try to hide it a lot of the time. Yes, I've been groped before, but not as thoroughly as Shelby did on the dance floor. I've pushed men's uninvited hands away from my body before, but this is the first time I've slapped a guy. I think Shelby's boldness, how he stroked my behind, then his smirk ..." She sighed. "I've never gotten so angry so quickly before." She pressed her shaking hands between her knees.

"What are some other incidents where you've been groped or verbally offended, and how recently did they occur?"

"Last Friday, I snapped at a couple of coworkers after they made a sexist comment. I'm so tired of that kind of talk." She collected her thoughts and Mandy didn't rush her. "And last Tuesday, I was spooked by a man who leered at me in a bar. His eyes were dark and threatening. I was scared to death when I thought he had followed me to my car. I saw the glow of a cigarette in the shadow of a bridge, and I was sure it was the guy. As soon as I got home, I had a meltdown."

"A meltdown?" Mandy paused from taking notes and looked at her over her turquoise reading glasses. "What kind of a meltdown?"

"After I made sure to set the security alarm, I collapsed on the floor in tears. I couldn't stop crying."

"Those are three intense incidents in just one week. No wonder you're at your limit."

Emily nodded, grateful Mandy understood. "And it's so many other disgusting attacks against women who've faced sexual harassment at work or sexual assault and abuse in their own homes. It's happening so much without any retribution or punishment that a lot of men think they can get away with almost anything. I feel so vulnerable so much of the time. I'm so tense that when I'm driving and get to an intersection, no matter how many times I look both ways to make sure it's clear, as soon as I step on the gas, I brace myself as if I'm about to be hit. Sometimes I feel like I'm walking around like that too."

"Bracing yourself so much for the unexpected is physically and mentally exhausting." Mandy set her notepad on the table next to her chair and removed her glasses.

"I know. I've felt this anger and tension building inside of me, like I said, and a growing fear that something bad is about to happen." She squeezed her eyes shut and opened them again several times. "I've also had some feelings, flashbacks, I guess, but maybe snippets of dreams. I can't see a full picture in my mind, but there's darkness and fear."

"Does this sense of fear and foreboding connect back to anything you remember when you were a child, an adolescent, or any other time in your life?"

Emily had already searched her memories for an incident or event that could be triggering her current angst. "No, it doesn't."

"How do you handle this anger and tension? Do you meditate?"

"No, I tried it once but couldn't sit still that long."

"Do you use alcohol or drugs?"

"I don't use any drugs. Smoked a little pot in college, but that was it." She didn't want to get into her drinking habits, but after all, she was sitting in the therapist's office to deal with what was going on in her life. She should probably be honest. "I drink some wine most evenings. Around dinner."

"What does some wine mean? One glass? Two?"

"One. Sometimes two."

"Do you ever drink more than a couple of glasses?"

"No, not really. Not now." She looked at her hands, held them in front of her chest, and rubbed them together. "A few years ago, I was under a lot of stress. At the time, I thought it was about work, but then I realized it was because I wasn't sleeping well. I often woke up with nightmares that had nothing to do with work. I couldn't figure out what they meant. I started having a little more wine before bedtime to help me sleep."

"How long did this go on?"

"A few weeks. Maybe a month."

And do you still have a little more wine before bedtime?"

"No, those nightmares went away. Mostly."

Mandy was quiet for a moment, so Emily took a sip of water and leaned back, settling into the pillows on the couch.

"Let me tell you about EMDR and how we can use it to work through these events, these traumas, to address your anger and tension."

"I know a little bit from Martin, but not enough to feel comfortable doing my own therapy, so I'd love to hear more about it."

"EMDR stands for Eye Movement Desensitization and Reprocessing. This type of therapy helps people overcome anxiety from traumatic events, and address the aftereffects of these events, or PTSD, Post-Traumatic Stress Disorder. We use bilateral stimulation to connect to unprocessed memories stored in the brain and work through the trauma. That means accessing both the right and left sides of the brain. Sometimes we use eye movements, such as moving the eyes back and forth, right and left without moving the head, and sometimes we use tapping." Mandy picked up a little black contraption with two oval discs attached by thin wires. "You hold one of these in each hand, and the tappers send a pulse to one hand, then the other. That's the bilateral stimulation. Are you with me so far?"

"Yes, I am," Emily said, remembering Martin's explanation of how his eyes followed Mandy's hand as she moved it from right to left during his sessions. This was the first she'd heard about a tapping device.

"But before we do any actual EMDR," Mandy continued, "I'm going to ask you a lot of questions about your childhood, any traumas you remember, get a little more background. We call it taking a history, and it's an important first step in EMDR."

"Okay. How many sessions do you think this will take?"

"I can't say for sure," Mandy said with a reassuring smile. "It depends on how many traumas are bottled up inside you. EMDR is intended to work through these memories in a process that won't overwhelm you." Mandy picked up her notepad and put on her reading glasses. "Shall I begin asking questions about your history?"

They covered a lot of ground over the next thirty minutes. She told Mandy about her family, that she had an older sister, a niece and nephew, and parents who lived part of the year in the Poconos and spent the winter in Florida.

"Are you close to your sister?"

"Yes, I am."

"And your parents?"

"Yes."

"Are they supportive of you, in your life, in your career?"

Emily nodded.

"What about your love life? Husband? Boyfriend?" Mandy paused. "Girlfriend?"

"None of the above currently," she said. "I dated a guy for a couple of years and thought we might get married, but one day he said he'd found someone else and that was the end of that."

"Did he ever abuse you? Hit you?"

"Trevor hit me? No never," she said, shaking her head emphatically. "Never threatened me. He was not a reactive kind of guy. At least he wasn't until he left me."

"Have you ever been in a bicycle accident, car accident, boating accident, had any medical traumas? Anything that caused you physical and emotional trauma?"

"No."

"Are there any distressing memories that come up for you when you think about your childhood?"

She closed her eyes and did a quick scan of her life growing up. "I think I had a pretty good childhood," she told Mandy. "I honestly don't remember anything that would be considered distressing or traumatic."

"What are your ten worst memories from childhood?"

"I don't think I have ten worst memories."

"Then tell me as many as you can think of," Mandy prodded.

After considering Mandy's question a little longer, she told her about the time a boy pushed her at the school playground and she fell and broke her wrist, and when a girl called her stupid in algebra class because she couldn't understand a complicated equation. The girl called her stupid for the rest of the school year, and every time she did, Emily had fought back tears.

"Are those the kinds of painful or distressing memories you mean?"

"Yes, they are. What else?"

"I don't know. I really can't think of many that still bother me." She shrugged her shoulders and shook her head.

"Okay, what about your ten best memories from childhood?"

A smile erupted so wide, it pushed her cheeks up against her eyes. "When I learned I could borrow five books at a time from the library. The first time I had an ice cream sundae with chocolate syrup and peanuts. Making snow angels with my sister every winter until we graduated from college. We still do that sometimes after a big snowstorm, only now we do it with my nephew." She paused, smiling at the memories, then continued. "Sunday mornings in the kitchen learning how to cook with my mother. Christmas mornings, especially the year I got my first bike. Happy memories I could go on and on. Like I said, I had a happy childhood."

"Before we meet again, I'd like you to think more about any distressing memories from your childhood."

Emily shrugged her shoulders. "Okay, I'll try."

"You have some traumas from childhood in addition to some of the more recent ones that are troubling you. We can use EMDR to help ease the distressing memories and minimize those anxious feelings." Mandy glanced at the clock. "But we can't start today. We're almost out of time. Do you want to schedule our next session for next Tuesday at this time?"

"Can't I see you again before then?" Emily asked. "As I told you, I'm on a forced vacation, so I have lots of time on my hands. I'm eager to begin working, and I've got so much tension I can't wait to get it out of my body."

"Let's talk about dealing with the tension before we get back to scheduling." Mandy rested her hands on her knees. "Here's what I'd like you to do whenever you have disturbing or upsetting thoughts or memories. Think of a container."

Emily tilted her head in surprise. She thought Mandy would make suggestions about breathing exercises, trying meditation again, recommend she listen to soft music, maybe soak in a warm bath. She'd never have guessed Mandy would ask her to think about a container. "What kind of container?"

"It could be a big tub like a rain barrel in a garden, but it must have a lid. It could be bigger, like an enclosed railroad car, a big, boxy cargo car, as long as it has a door. It could be smaller, like a jewelry box with a metal latch. Then whenever something upsets you, open up the container. Put the upsetting thought or memory in there. Close the container tight, and don't open it until we meet again."

She tried to envision dumping her problems into a container. It was a stretch, but she was willing to do just about anything. "Okay, I'll try that," she said quickly, still anxious to set up another session. "Can I see you again this week?"

Mandy eased back in her chair and picked up her brown moleskin scheduler. Opened it to the page with the paper clip. "I could see you Thursday at nine."

Ugh. Rush hour. A category nine on the ten-point scale for headaches driving in the city. But she was desperate to feel happy again.

"That works." She wrote Mandy a check and took the appointment card. "Martin was right. He said I would like you. Thank you, and I'll see you Thursday morning."

Her step was lighter during the ten-minute walk back to her car. Later that evening, she logged onto the internet and read how EMDR's creator, psychologist Francine Shapiro, took a walk in the woods and discovered that disturbing memories dissipated when she moved her eyes from side to side. Dr. Shapiro tried this bilateral stimulation with clients and found their distressing memories also eased. Her discovery was more than thirty years ago, and according to reports, EMDR had helped thousands of people deal with emotional trauma since then. Veterans. Everyday people. Famous people like Prince Harry and Sandra Bullock. All were healing through EMDR.

Emily thought about her next session with Mandy with a mixture of excitement and anxiety: excited to finally get rid of the anger and tension taking up residence in her body, and afraid of what disturbing thoughts and negative feelings might be hiding in the recesses of her mind.

Chapter Five

"I goofed, Emily. I'm so sorry." Lily said.

Emily rubbed her right temple and tried to figure out what to do. Lily, her administrative assistant at BAM, had called and left a message late the day before about a scheduling issue, but Emily didn't have the energy to deal with the problem then. So she called Lily back first thing Wednesday morning.

"I thought I had everything in order on your schedule, but somehow I missed this one," Lily continued. "I considered canceling, but then decided I should check with you before I call the school."

"I'm glad you reached out to me," Emily said. "I try to be there every time Central High asks, and I was looking forward to career day again. It slipped off my personal calendar as well."

Every year, half a dozen alumni from Philadelphia's Central High School spoke with junior and senior class students about their career paths, the colleges they'd attended, and the challenges they'd overcome. The morning panel was followed by lunch where students could talk informally with the presenters. Each panelist sat at a different table; students filled their lunch trays, then joined them. Lunch with students was Emily's favorite part of the day.

"Maybe you could get your sister to go in your place," Lily said, suggesting an option Emily had also considered but ruled out. Normally she wouldn't hesitate to ask Cara to fill in for her, but not this time.

"I think that would be complicated. I haven't told Cara what's going on at work, and I don't want to make up some excuse why I can't participate. Besides, with two young children and a heavy production schedule at Flagstone, she probably wouldn't have time."

"Is there anyone else you could ask?"

"Not comfortably." Emily had spent half the night thinking about what she would say to her sister, to anyone else she might ask to fill in for her, but she couldn't figure out how to have a conversation that didn't include discussing how her life was currently in flames.

"Do you want me to cancel then?"

Emily shook her head even though Lily couldn't see her. No, she wouldn't cancel on such short notice. It didn't feel right to back out. It was easier to show up.

"What time Friday morning?" Emily asked, thinking she could make it through a few hours. After all, she had an interesting career, mostly wonderful stories to tell, and could advise anyone thinking about going into advertising and marketing what colleges to consider and what courses to take.

"You need to be there by 9:45," Lily said. "The panel is from 10:00 until 11:45, followed by lunch. They promise to have people out of there by 1:30 at the latest."

"Did they send you any written materials?"

"Yes. I'll email them to you right away. There's a new person overseeing career day this year. She's very nice. Her name is Lacey Hargood."

"Did you say Lacey Hargood? What happened to Mrs. Chambers?"

"When Ms. Hargood called to confirm, she said she stepped in at the last minute, but she didn't elaborate. I didn't feel it was appropriate for me to ask. Perhaps she'll tell you more on Friday."

Ms. Hargood. Lacey. She was back in Philly? Since when? And why hadn't she reached out to Emily to let her know? A series of scenes played out in Emily's mind: She and Lacey riding bikes in their Mt. Airy neighborhood, the two of them competing to see who could read the most books from the library at Jenks Academy middle school, both of them squealing and squirming as they struggled to dissect a frog in biology class.

She closed her eyes and heard the familiar laughter of the girl who had become one of her best friends in elementary school. And who had disappeared in the middle of their sophomore year without a word.

Chapter Six

Cara Levner had plenty of work to do at her desk—finalizing the upcoming video production schedules and reviewing several scripts—but she had a more pressing task, one she shouldn't put off any longer and would take her out of the office for the better part of the afternoon.

"Where is the *Fix It or Ditch It* crew working today?" Cara, the program's executive producer, asked her production assistant as they wrapped up their meeting. *Fix It or Ditch It*, the nationally broadcast home renovation series, was one of Flagstone Productions' most successful programs.

The young woman ran her fingers over the tracking pad on her laptop a few times and studied the screen. "Looks like they're out in Villanova. Do you want me to text you the address?"

"That's okay. I'll grab it off the schedule later," Cara said. While she didn't often attend video tapings in the field, it was time to pay this crew a visit and watch them interact, especially because of the complaint that recently crossed her desk about the new cohost. It was the second grievance about him in as many weeks, and she needed to find out if there was a problem. If *he* was a problem.

Villanova was an affluent Main Line community in neighboring Delaware County. It was home to Villanova University, a Catholic institution well known for many reasons but especially its 2016 and 2018 winning men's NCAA basketball teams. The community itself was graced by grand old multi-million-dollar homes and some choice smaller places. The current project for *Fix It or Ditch It* was a $945,000 four-bedroom home that hadn't seen much maintenance in more than a decade. The video crew was examining the property with a construction and restoration company to determine whether the owner should make repairs or put it on the market "as is."

Cara left Flagstone Productions right after lunch. Almost an hour later, she turned off a main road and into a small neighborhood of homes built in the 1940s. She parked on the street, unplugged her cellphone from the dashboard, got out of the car, and walked up the driveway past several production and construction vehicles. She followed the sound of voices through a gate on the left side of the home and into a backyard. Standing on the large slate patio, *Fix It*'s cohosts and construction expert were assessing the pine siding directly behind them.

"There's no question some of the siding will have to be removed," Drew Reston said, pointing to a section of the wall, "to determine whether this peeling paint is an isolated problem or indicative of a bigger issue. We've seen a lot of situations where sweeping rains pushed in behind the siding." He made a sweeping motion with his arm to emphasize his words. "The wood can't dry out, so it starts to rot."

"How big a price tag would it be?" Stan Hester asked. "To fix that kind of a problem?"

"I couldn't say until we got in and looked at it," Drew

said. "But we recently had to remove, replace, and paint a twenty-foot-by-ten-foot exterior, and that small project cost more than ten grand."

"The renovation numbers for this home are adding up in a hurry, aren't they?" cohost Suzie Ackerman said, leaning in toward Drew.

"Cut. Cut. Don't anybody move!" producer Laura Stricker yelled, coming from behind one of the cameras. "Suzie, you leaned into the shot and the camera couldn't see Drew. Let's pick it up with your question, but please don't lean in." Laura took Suzie by the shoulders and stepped her back about three inches.

Cara watched from behind the cameras. She wasn't spying exactly, but she wanted to see Stan interact with others without knowing she was there. Having the executive producer in the field often made the crew and hosts nervous; it also put them on their best behavior.

At a glance, the complaints she'd heard were not a big concern—yet. One of the videographers said Stan kept getting in her personal space, leaning in so close she could tell what brand of mouthwash he used. A more serious complaint came from Shelley, a young staffer on the show, who said Stan had a habit of putting his arm around her shoulder and pulling her toward him when he wanted to talk. Shelley told Cara she kept removing his arm and stepping away, but he didn't seem to take the hint. The schedule indicated Shelley was on location today.

"Okay, those last two takes were good," Laura told everyone after another ten minutes. "Let's take a break." She consulted the notes on her clipboard. "Next, we'll set up outside of the garage. We've got a few more locations around the house to shoot today and clouds are moving in, so this good light won't last forever. Let's hustle, everybody."

Stan walked over to Laura and said a few words. Laura

blushed, but she had a broad smile on her face. Then, just before Stan turned away, he patted Laura's back. *Or did he stroke her back?* Suddenly Laura looked uncomfortable, her laugh forced.

After Stan walked away, Cara sauntered over. "Hi, Laura. I love this house. What a great property for the show."

Laura's head shot up. "Cara, I didn't know you were coming out today."

"It was a spur-of-the-moment decision," she said. "I haven't seen Stan in the field, and I wanted to check on how things are going."

"He's a natural on camera," Laura said. "He's got great energy. Sometimes he dominates the shots with Suzie, but we're working on making sure she doesn't get lost in his big presence."

"I couldn't help but notice he seemed pretty friendly to you a minute ago. Overly friendly?" she asked with raised eyebrows.

"That's just Stan. Like I said, he's a big presence."

Laura searched her eyes, perhaps for another question, but Cara didn't want to push.

"Laura? I need your input over here," one of the crew called out.

"I better let you get back to work," Cara said. She watched Laura for a moment longer, then made her way to the garage, where people were setting up tripods, cameras, and reflectors. Drew chatted with one of his construction workers, and the two hosts reviewed their scripts.

"Hey, Stan, Suzie. How's it going?" Cara said, walking up to them.

They looked up in surprise and said hello.

"Are you two getting comfortable with each other on camera? I know chemistry can take time to build."

Suzie laughed. "I have to battle Stan for the camera sometimes, but I can handle him. Remember when he was here for the job interview, and we taped our demo? I could tell what we'd be getting into, but I know how to fight for airtime."

Stan's face filled with a thousand-watt smile, directed first at Suzie, then Cara. "Suzie's a breeze to work with. In my last gig, I cohosted one show, but I also did another show solo, so I may tend to take over once in a while. We're working it out."

"Let me know if you need any input from me," Cara said, paused, and added, "about anything."

Just then, Laura and Shelley walked around from behind the garage and came over. Cara lingered as Laura explained what she wanted from everyone in the next sequence, then she moved off to the side again.

"Is everyone on the same page now with what we're doing?" Laura asked, looking from Stan to Suzie to Drew. After all three nodded, she motioned to Shelley to walk with her to where the video cameras were set up.

Stan's eyes danced over the backs of the two women as they walked away, giving them the once-over more than once. His smile revealed the pleasure he found in scrutinizing their bodies.

Cara was embarrassed watching him.

"What did you say?" Stan asked. As he turned to Suzie, he noticed Cara. The look on his face indicated he probably knew she'd seen him eyeball Laura and Shelley. Most men would have been embarrassed at being caught visually undressing women. But apparently not Stan. His smile barely faded as he turned his attention back to Suzie.

Cara shivered and rubbed her arms.

During her drive back into the city, Cara couldn't stop thinking about how Stan looked at her when he realized she'd been watching him, the way he casually looked away as if she were as inconsequential as a piece of lint he needed to brush off his sleeve. If he was unconcerned about getting caught *looking* at women that way, what wouldn't he dare do?

Chapter Seven

Cara walked into her office mentally reviewing Flagstone's process of hiring Stan from a TV station in Tampa. Everything she and other management at the production company had learned about him had pointed to a talented host and a team player who carried no unwelcome baggage. *Well, everyone has baggage of some sort*, she thought. *But did Stan have any skeletons in his closet I should have been told about when we checked into his background and his references? Maybe a call to our human resources office would give me some answers.*

"I have a question that I'd like to keep between the two of us."

Cara quickly told Flagstone's HR director, Jessica Naylor, what she'd seen on location with Stan, and about the complaint Shelley had voiced a few days ago. "I know we're in a gray area here about confidential records of an employee at a previous job, but I need to know if Stan was accused of inappropriate behavior or sexual harassment, anything like that."

Jessica hesitated. "If anything happened, and I emphasize *if*, it may be confidential. Unless there was a formal reprimand. That likely would have been in his personnel file and his former employer would have been duty-bound to share that with us when we checked with them during the candidate vetting process."

"I understand, but I want to know if maybe there was a pattern of behavior or actions or accusations that weren't followed up on for whatever reason." Cara blew the tension out of her chest with a blast of air between her lips. "I need to know if there was something, anything out of line with how he dealt with women. This couldn't have come out of the blue."

"If there is a problem," Jessica said, "I think we'd all want to know."

"Can you make some calls? Discreetly?"

"We don't want to contact his old station again, not unless we learn something they should have conveyed to us. Someone else in the Tampa media may be aware of inappropriate behavior, if there was any. I don't know anyone in Tampa, but I do have contacts in other parts of Florida. I'll see what I can do. Do you want to say anything to Jim or Aaron?" Jessica asked, referring to Flagstone's two owners.

"Not yet. I don't want to question someone's reputation if it's not warranted. That's why I want to do this very quietly. If this turns into a problem, then we'll bring them into the loop."

Jessica agreed and hung up.

A couple of hours later, the crew and cohosts from the Villanova video shoot streamed into Flagstone's open office space filled with low-walled cubicles. Private offices like Cara's ran along the side of the room with glass windows allowing her to look into the room, and shades when she needed privacy.

Laura waved as she walked by and sat at her desk about

twenty feet from Cara's office. A minute later, Shelley passed by.

"Shelley, come in a minute, will you?" Cara called out. As the young woman walked into her office, she motioned for Shelley to close the door.

"How was the taping at Villanova? I was there for a little while, and it seemed to go well. You like working with the video crew in the field, don't you?"

"I love going out with the team," Shelley said with uninhibited youthful enthusiasm. "There's so much going on behind the scenes, watching camera operators setting up the shots, and then seeing the hosts do the interviews and tape other on-camera segments. I can get a little overwhelmed at times, but I do love it." Shelley bounced from one foot to the other. She was a relatively new hire and Laura had once mentioned that Shelley was a quick study, ready to take on more responsibility.

"I noticed you kept your distance from Stan today, and I recall what you told me a few days ago. Have you had any other problems with him being too friendly?"

"No, it's fine." Shelley stopped bouncing on her feet and laughed, a shallow laugh that failed to hide her nervousness. She tugged at the hem of her blouse and eyed the floor. "I think he's one of those touchy-feely people, always reaching out to touch your arm or shoulder or hand. Maybe I over-reacted."

"Constant touching from someone you don't know or don't know well is not appropriate if you don't want to be touched," Cara told her. "And it is not overreacting if someone makes you uncomfortable. Remember that. Okay?"

"Sure. Okay. Thanks." Shelley spoke quickly and darted out the door.

A short time later, Laura sat at her desk going over a document with Stan, who stood behind her with both hands on her shoulders. Laura took Stan's left hand off her shoulder and swiveled her chair around to face him.

Cara kept her gaze down while she pretended to work on her computer. As she discreetly watched the two of them, Laura rose and forced Stan to step back. He almost lost his footing. With a hard set to her jaw, Laura said a few more words, then sat back down.

Stan turned away from Laura, and as he did, he spotted Cara watching him closely for the second time that day. His smile disappeared and he glared at her. Cara dropped her head back down at her desk and swallowed the lump in the back of her throat. Stan's look was unsettling, if not outright threatening.

When Cara came to work the next morning, the red button on her desk phone was flashing. She listened to her messages, made a few notes, and punched in some numbers.

"Hi, Jessica. You didn't say much. Do you have some info for me about that inquiry I made yesterday?"

"Yes, I do. Could you come to my office?"

"On my way."

Jessica got right to the point after Cara sat down. "I'm not going to say who I got the information from because it was given to me in strict confidence, except to tell you that a friend of mine who works in HR in an Orlando station called a contact of hers. She asked if there was any knowledge about Stan Hester and sexual harassment claims when he was working in Tampa. What I can tell you, *off the record,*" Jessica stressed, "is that there were a couple of complaints, but they never rose to the level of actionable punishment."

"Is that HR lingo for saying he was never reprimanded?"

"Yes, after the women—both junior staffers, by the way—

backed down and said they did not want to proceed with any formal action."

"He got his hand slapped and nothing in his file?"

Jessica pursed her lips. "More or less, which is why no one could share those details with us when we asked about his employment history. Technically, there's nothing to tell. In Tampa. But something did happen when he was a news anchor in Jacksonville."

Cara realized she was holding her breath and forced herself to exhale.

"I also got this information off the record, so you can't share it with anyone." She waited for Cara's assent. "A female reporter at the station where Stan worked in Jacksonville accused him of sexual assault."

"Rape?"

"No, it wasn't rape. The reporter filed a complaint with the station's HR director, then went to the police, claiming Stan repeatedly made advances toward her, and one time slid his hand under her dress and almost up to her ..." Jessica's voice trailed, not needing to finish the sentence.

"Are you serious?" Cara swallowed hard. "What happened?"

"There was an investigation by the station and Jacksonville police. I wasn't given the details, but it seems Stan talked his way out of it, said the woman indicated she was attracted to him. Then the woman was apparently embarrassed that things had gotten out of control, and after Stan apologized to her, she chose not to pursue any further action."

Cara stared at Jessica for a moment, thinking about the power dynamics where a high-profile on-air talent could intimidate other staff, especially impressionable young men and women. So many organizations had heard the stories about young females and the powerful men who supervised them, intimidated, and took advantage of them, that they made sure another person was in the room whenever the two of them were together. Or they assigned female junior staffers to women executives. Of course, with glass ceilings covering the business world, top female executives weren't easy to find.

"Didn't management in Tampa know what happened in Jacksonville before they hired Stan?"

"Because no formal charges were filed against Stan in Jacksonville, there was no record." Jessica referred to a yellow notepad on her desk. "I was told there was a letter in his HR file warning him about inappropriate behavior and requiring him to attend a sexual harassment seminar. I can't say if station management in Tampa knew about any of this. If they did, they hired him anyway."

"And didn't share it with us."

The two women stared at each other across the desk. Cara was grateful for the information but unhappy they hadn't learned it sooner.

"Well, if someone had given us hints about his behavior, formally or off the record, it might have saved us a problem."

"Perhaps he's cleaned up his act," Jessica said hopefully.

"Maybe he's less physically aggressive but judging from a few interactions I saw with him and Shelley, as well as with Laura, he still has an issue respecting women. And boundaries." She gazed at the navy-carpeted floor to collect her thoughts, then looked back at Jessica. "Now what?"

"Watch and take copious notes of anything you see or are made aware of that is inappropriate behavior." Jessica paused and tapped her pen on her desk. "It's been a while since we've had any employee meetings about sexual harassment. Perhaps now would be a good time to be proactive and gather everyone together to remind them about proper behavior in the workplace."

"I'm all for being proactive," Cara agreed. "Like I said, I'm not trying to make trouble, I'm doing what I can to avoid it."

Chapter Eight

"During our first session, you mentioned two upsetting memories from your childhood," Mandy said as she reviewed her notes. "One was when the boy pushed you and you broke your wrist, and the second was when a fellow student ridiculed you about a math equation." Mandy flipped over a page. "You also talked about some recent events, including the night in the bar."

Emily listened and sipped the coffee she'd brought from home. The caffeine calmed and invigorated her at the same time. She was about to experience EMDR for the first time and was wondering what to expect, what the bilateral stimulation would reveal about her past traumas—the ones she remembered and maybe others she'd forgotten.

"Did you think of any other distressing events from your childhood?"

"Not really. The typical sibling squabbles with my sister, times that high school was more stressful than fun, but nothing that rises to the level of traumatic. I think I let things roll off my shoulders pretty well. I used to, anyway."

"Okay, then, let's talk about the recent evening a man

unnerved you by staring at you in the bar, and how you were afraid he had followed you. What picture do you see in your mind that best represents this?"

Emily responded without hesitation. "Seeing the man's eyes locked on me, the dark streets when I was walking to my car, and spotting a shadow under the bridge near where I'd parked."

"Let's start with the man in the bar. What negative belief comes up when you think about that picture?"

"I guess it would be that I can't protect myself."

"What emotions are you feeling?"

A little slower response this time. "Unnerved. Scared."

"And what would you say your level of upset is when you think about him? On a scale of zero to ten, zero being the least upset and ten the most?"

"My level of upset? What is my negative belief? I've never heard of these kinds of questions. How do they relate to trauma, to the work that we're doing?"

"These questions are an important part of the EMDR protocol, Emily. Remember when we talked about memories during our first session? You found it easy to come up with several happy memories, but even when I pressed you, you had a difficult time recalling many upsetting or traumatic childhood memories."

Emily shrugged her shoulders. "My parents weren't big drinkers, they rarely fought, they never hit us. I had a happy childhood."

"Well, yes, and maybe no." Mandy set her clipboard down and collected her thoughts. "You found it easy to recall happy memories because you've probably thought about them many times. And every time you thought about them, you processed those memories. They stuck with you. Traumatic memories are different because you don't process them. They're so upsetting, you push them out of your mind, out of your memory. You could say those memories are scrambled, frag-mented. And these questions I'm asking about determining your level of upset or your negative belief are designed to pull information from different areas of your brain. In that way, we find those traumatic memories, pull the pieces together, and process them so they don't stay stuck in you."

Emily looked down, put her hands together, and pressed her fingertips to her lips. Processed memories. Scrambled memories. This EMDR was a lot more complicated than she'd realized or understood.

"Did I lose you?" Mandy asked.

"Close, but not yet." Emily tried to smile.

"Do you want to talk about this some more, or are you ready to resume with the questions?"

"I'm ready to go back to the questions, but I probably want to talk about this again, after I've had more time to think about it."

"We can discuss it further anytime you want." Mandy glanced at her notes. "Okay, the last question I asked was about your level of upset when you think about the man in the bar staring at you. On a scale of zero to ten, zero being the least upset and ten the most, what is your level of upset?"

She pushed out a breath between her lips. "A week ago, when it happened, it probably would've been an eight. Now it's about a seven."

"Where do you feel it in your body?"

"In my chest. My arms. A lot of tension in both areas."

"Take the tappers and put one in each hand. The gray one in your left hand, the black one in your right. Close your eyes and think about the man staring at you. I'm going to turn on the tappers. Just let your mind free-associate as thoughts come to you. In a little while, we'll talk about what you experienced."

Electronic pulses vibrated in her left hand, then the right, and back again. Her palms were sweaty, and her first thought was about how many times a day Mandy had to clean the devices. She shook that off and forced her mind back to having drinks in the bar with her two colleagues. They were laughing. Emily raised her glass of wine to take a sip and froze when she saw a man at the end of the bar staring at them. At her. With hard, cold eyes.

Her breathing increased and came in short gulps. She sat on the couch reliving the memory and struggled to slow her breathing. Her arm twitched, and then the tapping in her palms ceased.

"What's happening?" Mandy asked. "Take a deep breath and tell me what you got."

She opened her mouth, sucked in some air, and pushed it out of her lungs. "One of my colleagues made a joke and we were laughing. Then I saw the man staring at us. He kept staring. He took a sip of his drink, but his eyes never looked away." She shivered and rubbed her arms. "Thinking about it again gives me shivers, just like it did that night."

"What emotion do you feel as we talk about this?"

She winced and opened her eyes. "Scared. Threatened."

"I'm going to turn on the tappers, and I want you to bring up that image again. Think about the man staring at you. Notice what comes up."

Mandy didn't ask her to tell her what she saw, but as soon as Emily closed her eyes again and felt the tapping, things began to happen. She just naturally began speaking. "My colleagues wanted another glass of wine, but I was too spooked by the guy at the bar. The two of them were driving back into the city together and offered to walk me to my car, but I told them I'd be fine." Her eyes were closed. Squeezed tight. "We said goodnight, and I walked in the other direction. I was comfortable enough on Main Street, but when I turned the corner, it was a little darker, a little quieter. My heart skipped a beat. I started walking faster."

Her arms shook and her heels bounced on the floor.

"Stay with it," Mandy said softly. "Just watch it go by."

She took short, fast breaths and watched the memory of her walking on the sidewalk, hearing footsteps. Coming up behind her faster. A man's heavy breathing. She turned around. It was only a jogger, who apologized for startling her. Up ahead, she saw her car and used her key fob to unlock it. Then she spotted the red glow of a cigarette. Her pulse raced. Someone was standing in the shadows of the bridge, not far from her car.

"He's too close," she said. "I have to get in the car quickly because he's too close." Her feet bounced faster on the floor, almost as if she were running. Her head twitched from side to side. A moment later, the tapping stopped. Emily opened her eyes, her vision slightly blurry, her thoughts racing.

"Tell me more about what you saw and felt," Mandy said.

She blinked a few times, then explained the images and feelings that came up when she thought about the man, the threat his presence implied.

"What is your level of upset now when you think about what happened?"

"It's still at least a six," Emily said, flexing her fingers and sighing.

"Where do you feel it in your body?"

"My arms and hands." She looked down at her fists holding the tappers. "When did I make such tight fists?"

"When you said you squeezed the key fob to unlock the car doors."

They talked more about what she saw in her memory, then Mandy asked if she was ready for her to turn the tappers back on.

"How many times do we do this?" Emily asked.

"Until your level of upset over the memory is a zero, or at most a one."

She nodded, heard Mandy tell her to just follow her thoughts, and disappeared into the past as the tapping passed from one hand to the other. She silently watched the scene play out again in front of her eyes. The bar. The sidewalk. The glow of the cigarette someone was holding. Images came and went. Then she was in her car. Safe. The tension in her hands, arms, and chest gradually eased, and her breathing became more regular with occasional deep breaths.

She sighed and dropped her shoulders, tilted her head down. "I was surprised at how upset I was. I've been watched in bars before. But this guy really got to me."

"Did the man come out of the shadows when you reached your car?"

"No, he didn't, but I was still spooked by him, especially when I saw the red glow of a cigarette."

"So, nothing happened? No one hurt you?"

"No, they just scared me."

"Let's revisit your negative belief. You said you felt like you couldn't protect yourself. What would you rather believe?"

"That I'm strong. That I can feel anxious, and everything will still be okay. I could push the panic button on my key fob and make a lot of noise. I could cause a commotion and keep him away from me. There are things I *can* do to protect myself."

"Go with that for a few minutes."

After a short while, the tapping stopped. She opened her eyes.

"How do your arms and hands feel now?"

"I don't feel like I'm going to squeeze the tappers so hard they'll break." She smiled again. "That's better."

"Okay, let's go back to your picture of the man in the bar. What is your level of upset now?"

"Still about a four, I think."

"Go back to that image and let's work on that some more."

She closed her eyes again. She and her colleagues laughed. She took a sip of wine. He stared at her. She and her friends left the bar. Then she saw the shadow under the bridge. She pressed the panic button on her key fob. All at once the street disappeared. Her car was gone. Blackness filled her vision. She drew in a sharp breath through her nose.

"What's going on?" Mandy asked.

"I was almost to my car. I pressed the panic button on the key fob, but the street, the car, they disappeared. Everything went black." Her eyes popped open and she gaped at Mandy. "And I got scared. I had this terrible feeling, like I was in danger and something bad was about to happen."

"Where do you feel that in your body?"

"In my chest," she said without hesitation. Her right hand clasped the tapper hard against her chest. "My chest feels so tight right now."

"Go with that," Mandy said.

"I'm scared of the blackness."

"Remember what I said, Emily, you have to *go* through it to *get* through it, to get over it. We need to unscramble your memory. Take a deep breath. Focus on what you feel in your chest."

She hesitated, sighed, then closed her eyes. The vibrations passed back and forth between her hands. Then someone or something pressed down on her chest so hard, she struggled to take a breath. She focused on the tightness in her chest and searched the black for answers. A face flashed before her eyes. And just as quickly disappeared. She jerked her head from side to side, searching for the face, but it was gone. Then she was back in the bar, drinking her wine, leaving with her friends, and walking to her car.

Mandy stopped the electronic tapping and was watching her when she opened her eyes. "Tell me what's going on."

"I focused on the tightness in my chest, and all I could see was darkness again. Then a face flashed before my eyes for an instant."

"Do you know whose face it was?"

"No."

"Then what happened?"

"After the face disappeared, so did the blackness. I was on the sidewalk, about to get into my car."

"What is your level of upset now about the incident we started with, the man staring at you in the bar and you thinking someone was following you to your car, seeing someone smoking a cigarette in the shadows?"

She thought for a moment before answering. "It's maybe a three. I may think I'm strong enough to protect myself, but when I saw the shadow under the bridge, I still got spooked."

"Anything else?"

She let out another long sigh. It felt good to let go of the memory and the tightness in her body. Most of the tightness. She pressed the tappers on her legs and wiped her sweaty palms on her jeans. "I'm upset about the blackness and the face."

"I think that may be a different memory, and I'd like to work more to lower your level of distress about the incident at the bar before we tap into a new memory," Mandy said. "But we're almost out of time for today. Remember what I told you last week about putting upsetting memories into a container? What kind of container do you have?"

"An old jewelry box." The jewelry box her grandmother had given her, about a year before she'd passed, was one of Emily's favorite possessions. The top of the beautifully carved cedar box was accented with a laminated forest and lake scene, surrounded by a decorative carved border. The inside of the box was lined with black velvet and gold trim. When she was a child and visited her grandmother, she'd run her fingers over the box, feeling the texture of the wood and the softness of the laminate. Sometimes she and her grandmother would make up stories about who owned the land, who would visit the forest and lake, and what animals lived there. At first, Emily balked at using the beloved jewelry box to store upsetting thoughts or images, but then she decided perhaps it was actually the perfect place to begin letting go of things that upset her.

"I want you to open that jewelry box and put that memory with the blackness and the face inside," Mandy said. "We can talk about that during our next session."

"It was so ominous," she said, rubbing her hands on her legs over and over again. "I was so scared something bad was going to happen."

"Open up that jewelry box right now," Mandy said again, leaning toward her. "Take the memory of the darkness and the face and put them in there. Can you do that?"

"Yes," she whispered.

"And put the memory of the man in the bar and standing in the shadows in the container as well. Close it back up tight. Lock it with a key. Leave it that way until our next session on Tuesday."

She heard the firmness in Mandy's voice and shoved the blackness into the container. She put the flash of the face in the container, the man in the bar, the shadows. Then she closed the jewelry box and locked it. But the dark memory called to her so strongly she didn't know whether she could keep it locked away for all the days between Thursday and Tuesday. Tuesday was so far away; the darkness lingered before her eyes.

They said their goodbyes. Emily stepped out of the building, down the half-dozen steps, and onto the sidewalk. The fingers on her right hand were pressed together so tight her nails dug into the palms of her hands. She clung to the imaginary key to the imaginary lock to the imaginary container. The darkness was frightening, but her desire to know where it led was impossible to ignore.

Chapter Nine

It was barely past ten. The entire day lay ahead of her with no commitments. She struggled to pull her thoughts together, walking down one street, then another, following wherever her feet took her. The sky overhead mirrored her feelings: gray, flat, darkness closing in quickly on a biting wind. Her pace quickened when the first drops made little polka dots on the sleeve of her light blue blazer. She hadn't thought to wear her raincoat or bring an umbrella, so she looked for someplace to tuck into until the showers passed.

The storm intensified, and a sharp clap of thunder pushed her closer to the storefront windows. A strong wave of coffee hit her nose like a jolt of smelling salts. A door opened ten feet in front of her, and a man clutching a cup of coffee walked out of Beans & Brews Café. She grabbed the door and hustled inside to the comforting sounds of chattering voices and the swoosh of the espresso machine.

"Large coffee, black," she told the barista when she reached the front of the line. "Make that with cream. No, wait." She looked into the face of someone who was doing her best to be patient despite the growing line behind Emily, then glanced up at the menu board behind the register. "Sorry. I've had a weird morning. Could I please have a latte with whole milk? No, make that skim milk. Grande. Large, right? Sorry. My brain. Not really connected."

The woman behind the counter raised her eyebrows as if asking Emily if she was sure of her order. "Name?"

There were only a couple of empty tables in the coffee shop, and she grabbed one of them after picking up her drink. She stared out the window and into the rain, seeing the memory she'd just relived. She sipped her latte and thought about the night in the bar. Why did that guy stare at her? Had he followed her? Maybe not. Maybe it was someone else under the bridge. Snapshots of memories flew through her mind like dry leaves falling from the trees and carried away on a brisk wind. Trying to make sense of her thoughts was as successful as trying to glue leaves back onto the trees.

Outside of her window, people hurried on their way, holding umbrellas over their heads, clutching bags and brief-cases close to their bodies. They faded out of focus, and her glazed eyes stared past them into nothingness. Then blackness came. The flash of a face. Then it was gone.

"Go away. Get back in the container," she whispered, her hands trembling. She forced herself to take several deep breaths, and bits of tension released from her shoulders and neck. People on the sidewalk came back into focus, and the café door blew open and closed with new arrivals. The last sip of her latte was cold. The rain had stopped. She stepped outside and took a moment to remember where she was, to figure out how far she had walked from her therapist's office. And how far her memories were taking her, on paths veering out of sight to endings she could not yet see.

～

Later that afternoon, she sat on her couch, her laptop resting on her legs. She opened a Google window and typed "EMDR." She reconnected to the EMDR website, where she had researched the trauma therapy before her first session with Mandy. The EMDR info link gave a detailed explanation about the therapeutic process and cited many articles and academic papers validating bilateral stimulation for successful treatment of trauma. It appeared the site was mostly a resource for therapists, especially those interested in taking the training. However, it also contained a directory of EMDR therapists for potential clients to find someone near where they lived.

She stared at the EMDR home page, at the Resources section, then clicked on a link to "Getting Past Your Past." *Getting Past Your Past: Take Control of Your Life with Self-Help Techniques from EMDR Therapy,* written by PhD psychologist Francine Shapiro, was required reading for EMDR therapists. It was also described as a user's guide to help people learn ways to facilitate their own emotional healing using self-help techniques based on EMDR therapy. She opened a link to Amazon and ordered the book for next-day delivery.

Emily returned to the EMDR website. All of the EMDR info was helpful, but she wanted to see examples of therapists and clients actually doing it. She couldn't watch herself processing memories with Mandy, and she wanted to see what it looked like, what *she* looked like when she held the tappers and recalled an upsetting memory.

She clicked back to her original search. Under the official sites that populated the list, she saw video thumbnails of people talking about EMDR. The first video was an explanation about bilateral movements, but she was a quick study and had already learned that much. She clicked on a video from NBC, but it was also more of an overview. Hungry for more, she kept scrolling until she found a video of a therapist doing

EMDR with a client who had given her permission to have the session taped and posted on YouTube. The woman's face was blurred and her voice digitally altered to protect her identity.

Emily sat back and watched the woman—called Jane—explain how her boss repeatedly harassed her with sexual innuendos and inappropriate touching. Jane said she felt powerless to do anything because she was a single mother and needed the job. Jane and her therapist faced each other on camera. Emily had a front-row seat to their session. She watched for almost an hour, following the familiar steps in the EMDR process. She'd wanted to see someone processing their difficult memories but sitting in on this session tapped into her own pain.

Emily's eyes filled with tears again, and she hit the pause button on her laptop so hard, it fell to the floor. A face flashed in front of her eyes and disappeared. She quickly unlocked her container and put it inside, then locked the container again.

Loud chirps from her cellphone shot Emily to her feet. She glanced at caller ID. Martin, the only person she could confide in at the moment. Even then, she wasn't sure she wanted to talk. Her hand paused, then she swiped the glassy front of her phone and said hello.

"I called to see how your session with Mandy went," he said. "That is if you want to talk about it."

"My brain's a little scattered, trying to put the pieces together." She strolled into the kitchen for a glass of wine, glancing at the clock to make sure it wasn't too early. But she wasn't working. Was there a rule for the appropriate time to have a drink if you weren't working? She pulled an open bottle of Chardonnay out of the fridge, filled a glass, and set the bottle on the kitchen table.

"I was struck by how vivid my memories were," she said, picking back up on the conversation. "I thought about the events with men lately that have upset me. The two guys in our meeting. The man in the bar last week. The guy standing in the shadows with a cigarette. I was working on that memory when everything went black, and I got really scared. Mandy said it was probably another memory that came out of my subconscious. I struggled to follow where images were coming from, where they were going. It was like watching a play with too many actors on stage, moving in different directions, talking to no one and everyone all at once. The only word I can use to describe it is weird." She paused. "It was a ten-sigh session," she said, sighing.

"Pardon me?"

"A. Ten. Sigh. Session. I sighed, deep sighs reaching into the bottom of my lungs or deeper, to the core of my being. I must have sighed at least a dozen times during the session. I expected to cry during therapy, but I didn't know I was going to sigh so much."

"It's your body letting go of the pain," he said, reassuring her. "It has to come out somehow. I recall sighing over memories of Sara. Good and bad memories. I suddenly heard snippets of conversations I'd long forgotten. Sometimes they made me smile ..." His voice broke, and he cleared his throat a few times. "And sometimes I heard words I wished I'd never said."

She leaned against the kitchen counter and sipped her wine, waiting for him to come back to her.

"Aside from the therapy process," he said after clearing his voice again, "are you comfortable with Mandy?"

"I am. I like her a lot."

"That's great. So, what are you doing to fill the rest of your time?"

She laughed. "I put in my earbuds, created a music list with Pink, Beyoncé, Adele, Cyndi Lauper, Madonna, all strong women, and got lost in the music, in their words. And then I cleaned. Again. You could eat off my kitchen floor. It's as spotless as the counters and the stovetop. I even found places I didn't know were dirty. The window into my backyard no longer has a layer of film dulling the sunlight. It's so bright in here, I need to wear sunglasses. The entire house is probably cleaner than it's been since the day I moved in. It's been tiring, physical work, and just what I need to occupy my time."

"I'm impressed," he said. "Are you ready to come out of your safe space for a while? Do you want to join Ramón and me for dinner tomorrow night? He's promised to make your favorite black bean, mushroom, and caramelized-onion enchilada, and for dessert, chocolate hazelnut churros."

"Oh, sweetie, that's such a nice offer, and it makes my mouth water, but I can't even imagine carrying on a conversation with anyone other than you."

"I understand. Call me if you change your mind. We'll be around all weekend."

"You're the best."

After walking back to the living room, she crouched down and picked up her laptop. She studied it as if it were a complicated document she couldn't decipher, trying to decide whether to watch another EMDR video with a different client and therapist. Then she put the laptop on the coffee table and curled up in her favorite spot on the couch, deciding she'd had enough pain for one day.

Chapter Ten

E mily stepped into Central High School's auditorium and fell back in time. She closed her eyes and took a deep breath, smelling the mustiness of the old velvet curtains and the matching velvet-padded seats. Those old curtains in this worn auditorium were full of wonderful memories. The familiar music from *Grease*, the drama club's production during her freshman year, played in her head. She and Lacey had helped paint the play's backdrops for weeks, joined two other students poking around used clothing stores for the perfect outfits for the cast, and worked backstage helping with props and scene changes. They loved the energy of participating in a live musical production and backstage suited them.

Then there was orchestra. Emily played violin and Lacey the clarinet. Lacey breezed through her audition, but Emily had failed hers, leaving her in tears and apologizing to her friend. Lacey pushed Emily to practice frequently, even joining Emily with her clarinet most days because Lacey didn't want to be in the orchestra without her best friend. Thanks to Lacey's encouragement, and her guidance during the practice sessions, Emily succeeded in her second audition.

It had been that way with the two of them ever since elementary school, each prodding the other to join the same clubs and participate in the same activities. Until the day Lacey simply didn't show up. Emily stuck with the orchestra because she loved music, but she dropped out of drama club. It wasn't nearly as much fun when she couldn't share it with her friend.

A screech pierced the air. Emily's eyes popped open, back in the present.

"Everyone please be seated. We'll begin shortly." The voice came from the overhead speakers, followed by another screech, then silence.

She paused a moment longer in the back of the auditorium, listening and watching the chattering students who filled the rows in the front half of the room. On stage, several people gathered to one side, talking quietly, sometimes glancing out into the crowd. Emily recognized a few of the faces but didn't see Lacey among them. Just to the right of the people, and in the middle of the stage, sat a couple of long, wooden tables, notepads, and pens placed in front of the seven chairs. The event planner in her assessed the setup: moderator and six speakers; one microphone for the moderator, and two mics, one on each side of the moderator, for the speakers.

Emily shook off the past, quickly crossed the back of the auditorium, and strode down the left aisle. When she reached the stage, she hurried up the stairs.

"We were starting to wonder whether you got held up in traffic or something," said the man standing closest to the stairs.

"Just running a little late this morning," Emily said, greeting those she knew and introducing herself to those she didn't. She'd barely had time to catch her breath when a woman appeared from behind the curtains, blonde hair falling past her shoulders, running her eyes quickly over the group and coming to a stop when she saw Emily.

"Emily Archer. Gosh, it's been forever," Lacey said, folding her into a hug. "I'm so glad you could join us this morning."

"I wouldn't miss it for anything," Emily said. "I was surprised to see your name on my handout materials."

"I took over responsibility for career day from Shawanda at the last minute," Lacey said.

"That's not exactly what I meant," she said softly, blinking back tears that came on suddenly.

Lacey held her eyes for a moment. "I know. We'll find time to chat later." Lacey patted her arm and turned away. And then, Lacey was all business. She motioned everyone to the tables and asked them to sit behind the tented signs where their names indicated. Lacey remained standing behind her chair in the middle of the group, the microphone in her hand.

"Good morning, juniors and seniors," Lacey said, a smile on her face that carried over into her voice and echoed throughout the auditorium. She greeted students one more time before their chattering quieted enough to continue.

Emily watched from her spot at the left end of the table. Did Lacey put her as far away from her as she could on purpose? Lacey had certainly been warm enough when she had greeted her, but that moment of connection between them dissipated in a wisp, like a warm exhale of breath on a brisk, winter morning. Lacey told her they would find time to chat later. Maybe then she would learn what had happened, why Lacey was in school one day and gone the next. Emily didn't know if she'd done something wrong, why Lacey never called or texted her again.

Central was one of the best high schools in the city, and the students showed why. They were engaged in the conversation and asked interesting questions. The weekend anchor

from Channel 6 fielded the most questions. No surprise—
high school students were always intrigued by local TV news
personalities. But Emily handled her share of questions, as did
the others, and the panel discussion wrapped up before she
knew it.

"Join me in a round of applause to thank our guests for
giving us such helpful career advice," Lacey told everyone,
putting the microphone down on the table as she stood and
joined the applause.

Most of the students filed out of the auditorium, but a
dozen of them came on stage and stood in front of the table.
They must be the luncheon escorts. She greeted the young man
and woman in front of her and joined them weaving their way
through crowded hallways toward the smell of meatloaf and
mashed potatoes.

She answered more questions over lunch and watched
from the corner of her eye as Lacey visited each speaker's table,
apparently saving Emily's group for last. With just five
minutes left in the lunch period, Lacey found an empty chair
at Emily's table and sat, listening to her answer one last
question.

"Okay, everyone, lunch is over," Lacey told the students.
"On to your next class."

Emily stood and shook hands as the students walked away,
then Lacey came to her side.

"Thanks again for coming today," Lacey said. "I can't
believe how good it is to see you."

"It's great to see you too, but where on earth have you
been? I don't think you've been teaching here, or I would have
heard something from you, wouldn't I?" Emily's voice grew a
little louder as she took in Lacey's presence.

Lacey opened her mouth to speak but was interrupted by
sneakers hitting the linoleum floor and growing louder. She

turned toward the young man approaching them. "Timothy, why aren't you on your way to class?"

"I just wanted to say hi," he said.

"Is this your son?" Emily looked at the teenager, studying his face for a hint of Lacey and not seeing much resemblance. There was so much she didn't know about her former friend. So much she wanted to learn.

"No," Lacey said, smiling and putting her arm around his shoulders. "This is my nephew. Timothy, say hi to Ms. Archer."

"Aunt Lacey mentioned she was going to see an old friend today," he said, shyly shifting his eyes to the floor. "Nice to meet you."

Then Lacey gave him a gentle nudge, suggesting if he left right away, he wouldn't be late for class.

"He seems like a nice young man." Emily watched him hurry out of the room. "Good manners, that's for sure. Timothy's your nephew?"

"Yes, my sister's son." Lacey followed Timothy with her eyes as well.

"Right, I remember Angela. I saw her a lot when I was at your house. I remember when Cara and I came over, or you and Angela visited us, the four of us playing together for hours on the weekend or in the summer when we were younger. I think we drifted to different interests as we grew older, especially in high school, even though we were all at Central."

Lacey's expression didn't change as Emily reminisced about their youth. "Angela is about the same age as my sister isn't she. How is she?"

"Angela? You don't know?"

"Don't know what?"

A deep voice reverberated in the overhead speakers before Lacey could answer.

"Ms. Hargood, you're needed in the principal's office. Ms. Hargood to the principal's office right away, please."

"Sorry, Emily. Terrible timing." Lacey picked her papers and cellphone up off the table. "There's no short version to tell you about what happened to me and my family, especially to Angela, and I've got to run. I promise I'll call soon and we'll talk."

Emily stood in the cafeteria, alone except for a few people wearing aprons, who swept into the room and began wiping down tables, tossing trash into the big, gray receptacles they dragged beside them.

Lacey's words bounced around inside her head. That was quite a comment to drop and walk away. What didn't Emily know about Angela?

Chapter Eleven

October 2003

Angela Hargood and her best friend, Melanie, jumped to their feet along with hundreds of other cheering football fans as Central High School's wide receiver dodged the last defender trying to take him down and raced toward the end zone. The two juniors turned and wrapped one another in a gleeful embrace.

"That was so awesome," Angela said as she pulled away from Melanie and turned to watch Central's team members stream onto the field. The coaches tried to hold players back from the impromptu celebration, but the adrenaline was pumping too much to control any of them. Only after the insistent blowing of the referee's whistle and a whole lot of yelling on the field did the players return to the sidelines. Then all eyes were on the kicker who lined up for the extra point. And made it. After missing two other attempts. And gave Central a one-point lead over Northeast High with just two minutes left on the clock.

"Did you see that?" Melanie shouted, punching Angela's arm.

"Standing right beside you," she laughed. Like everyone

else in the bleachers, on both sides of the field, the girls were too excited to take their seats for the rest of the game. Central was almost always the underdog when playing Northeast High, which had a thousand more students and many more talented athletes. But Central ranked higher academically so it was a fair tradeoff. Still, beating Northeast for the first time in several years would be something to celebrate.

Northeast's final drive sputtered, helped in no small measure by a sack that injured their quarterback's throwing arm, and a pulled hamstring to one of their starting offensive linemen. When the horn sounded and the game ended, Central was the victor. Players, coaches, and students raced onto the field to celebrate and, this time, no one stopped them.

The celebration continued an hour later as Angela, Melanie, and Melanie's boyfriend, Julian, walked up the steps of a modest twin in a neighborhood not far from the high school. Music and laughter drifted out of the first-floor windows.

"Guess the party's already going strong," Julian said, pushing the doorbell. When no one responded, he knocked on the door and it opened easily. The three of them strolled into the foyer. Students hugged the walls in the hallway and jammed into the living room on the left. People moved through the dining room on the right where the food was laid out. Half a dozen pizza boxes, most of them open, covered much of the dining room table alongside some paper plates and napkins. Bottles of wine and plastic cups covered the rest of the table. A cooler of ice sat on the floor, the top slightly open revealing bottles of beer and soda. The table was a cluttered mess. Hungry football players and more than a dozen other teens attacked the food and drinks like they hadn't eaten breakfast or lunch.

Angela wandered around the room and recognized almost

everyone, juniors and seniors from her high school, but there were a few people she didn't know. Like the dark-haired boy who stopped talking to the person next to him as soon as he spotted her from across the room, walked over, and said hello.

"My name's Felipe. Do you want something to drink?"

She looked into the most inviting brown eyes she'd ever seen and mumbled that a diet soda would be great.

Felipe was back at her side a minute later. He covered the top of the plastic bottle with his shirt, twisted the top off, and handed the bottle to her.

"You don't go to Central, do you?" she asked, thanking him and taking the bottle. Her eyes took in his broad shoulders in a maroon shirt he tucked back into tight black jeans. "I would probably know you if you did, but you're wearing our school color."

He smiled, the kindest smile she'd ever seen.

"Yeh, I would have grabbed a different shirt if I'd've thought more about it. I didn't blend in on my side of the field at all."

"You seem to be blending in just fine now," she said, smiling, sipping her drink, her heart floating away.

They barely left each other's side for more than an hour, until Melanie poked Angela in the arm and said it was time to go.

"I'll meet you outside," Melanie said after a quick introduction to Felipe.

"Will you be at the football game next Friday?" Felipe asked, leaning in so close that Angela thought he might kiss her. Hoped he might kiss her.

"I don't know if it's a home game or anything."

"I'll bet you can figure it out," he said. "So can I. I'll find you there." He tilted her head up and lightly kissed her forehead. "If you want me to."

She nodded. "I want you to. And wear the shirt," she said,

nodding at his chest. Her feet barely touched the floor as she crossed the living room, let herself out the front door, and met Melanie on the sidewalk.

"Look who's found a new boyfriend," Melanie teased gently.

"You think?"

"Uh, you two didn't look at anyone else after you met. So yeh. Tell me everything."

"There's not much to tell. He goes to Northeast High and came to the game with a friend. Someone invited him to the party and I'm glad they did," she said.

"Are you going to see him again?"

"What do you think?" Angela said. "I want to see Felipe as much as I can."

Chapter Twelve

Emily was still puzzling over Lacey's comment about Angela the next morning. Seeing her childhood friend stirred up a lot of memories, but Lacey's vague reference about her older sister hinted at something Emily couldn't understand. Well, she could make up all sorts of things if she let herself, but the truth might not be anywhere near what she could imagine. Besides, Emily's current reality was challenging enough. Most of her waking moments were spent thinking about what she was discovering about her past in her therapy sessions with Mandy.

She was eager to read *Getting Past Your Past*, but overnight shipments from Amazon usually came in the afternoon, and she was too restless to sit and wait. She drank her coffee, showered, dressed, then hopped into her SUV and headed west.

Valley Forge National Park was about a half-hour drive from her Mt. Airy home. Sure, there were plenty of beautiful places closer to where she lived where she could walk, but Valley Forge's main trail—connecting monuments and historic structures—was out in the open. Joggers and bikers made steady use of the paved trail. Mothers pushed their strollers along while chatting with friends on their cellphones. Cars passed by regularly. She could enjoy a walk there and let her mind roam without watching her back.

The early October sun gently warmed her face and lifted her spirits. Her gait was strong and determined. She moved at just below a slow jog while working her arms in wide, sweeping motions from front to back. Thirty minutes later, she turned around, paused to catch her breath, and drank in her surroundings. Off in the distance, where grassy fields met the woods, a small herd of deer bowed their heads in search of food. Beyond the deer were green ash, sycamore, and silver maple trees, which populated the park in abundance and were beginning to show hints of color. Fall's full beauty would not be on display for a few more weeks, and she promised herself she'd return for the show.

After one last glance at the deer and one more stretch to keep her leg muscles loose, Emily headed back the way she'd come. She maintained her brisk pace until she broached one hill, which seemed much larger going back up than it did coming down. By the time she reached the peak, she was out of breath. She bent over and closed her eyes, pulling air into her lungs. Her muscles burned. The sweat rolled off her forehead and down her face. She lost herself in deep, steady breathing.

"Coming up behind you."

The man's voice came out of nowhere and jerked her upright, sending her pulse racing even faster than it had been from the fast walk. When he rode by on his bicycle, the bottom of her shirt fluttered. He was way too close. She stepped onto the grass alongside the trail, her hands on her hips, and watched the biker disappear around a bend.

She sighed with relief and closed her eyes. Then her memories kicked in and carried her to the bar. The man stared at her. Next, she was on the sidewalk walking toward her car and worried about what was in the shadows. Why did the red glow of the cigarette cause her such angst? Those memories disappeared, replaced by a flash of black, then a face. She tried to blink it away, but the vision of the face lingered longer than before. She was getting a hint of what he looked like. But she didn't know who he was or why he was determined to force his way into her memories. She stepped back onto the path and hurried to her car, cursing the image that would not leave her alone.

∼

She had just finished showering and dressing when her cellphone chimed.

"I hope I've caught you at a good time," Mandy said.

"You did. What's up?" She fought back panic. Did Mandy call to cancel her appointment? She hoped not; it was hard enough to wait till Tuesday.

"First, how are you doing? We had an intense session last Thursday with some disturbing memories. Have you been bothered by any distressing thoughts?"

"I get a little lost in my thoughts sometimes, but I'm okay." She'd shoved her upsetting memories into the container before starting the car at Valley Forge and was not ready to pull them back out again, especially over the phone.

"As a rule, I don't like to juggle clients' schedules, but I understand your desire to make progress in our work as quickly as possible, and I'd like to accommodate you. I've had some time open up on Monday. We could meet a little longer, for a double session."

"Really? What time on Monday?" She pressed the phone against her ear and wrapped her other arm around her waist for comfort.

"From 12:15 till about 1:45. Would that work for you?"

"Wow, that would be great, Mandy. I'd love to see you then. It'll make the weekend easier."

"My advice is to keep busy. Watch movies, read. Don't dwell on the memories or the work we're doing. Don't try to force yourself to process more. Your memories will make their presence known to you, sometimes when you least expect it. It's best not to force them."

"I saw the face again," she said softly, cracking open the lid of her container and confiding in Mandy. "I was walking at Valley Forge, enjoying the beauty of the park, when the face appeared. Some of his features are starting to take shape. They're still fuzzy, but the image of the face is becoming more real."

"I'm sure it's upsetting to see more details in the image but try to put it in your container and lock it up, Emily. Okay?"

"I'm trying. It just popped out."

"That happens sometimes after we do the work." Mandy's voice was calming, reassuring. Emily let her therapist's words soak in and gently wash over her body. "We'll focus on that image on Monday afternoon. In the meantime, don't hesitate to call or text me over the weekend if your thoughts are overwhelming you."

She tried to take Mandy's advice and watch a movie that afternoon, but she couldn't focus. When the Amazon package landed on her doorstep, she raced to the door, tore open the padded envelope, and thumbed through *Getting Past Your Past* as she walked back to the couch.

By the time she crawled into bed the next evening, she'd forced the face back into her safe container several more times and read through the EMDR book twice, filling it with yellow highlights and pink sticky notes. The face never interrupted her nighttime dreams the way it pushed into her mind when she was awake, but she suspected it wouldn't stay away forever.

Chapter Thirteen

"How was your weekend?" Mandy asked with a warm smile as she opened the door and waved Emily in.

"I almost texted several times, but I didn't want to interrupt your time off, so I managed," she said, walking over and easing herself into the couch. "But that image keeps popping in front of my eyes when I least expect it."

"Did anything else come up?" Mandy picked up the folder with Emily's name on it and pulled out her notes.

"Nothing new. When I was walking at Valley Forge and the memories of the man in the bar and the shadow under the bridge came up, I let them play out. I still got a little anxious, especially when I saw the red glow of his cigarette, but I didn't feel any unmanageable distress."

"When we finished last week," Mandy said, "your level of distress was still about a three or four, so let's work on that memory to get you to at least a one."

After several minutes of holding the tappers and sharing her thoughts with Mandy, she said she felt much better and was ready to move on.

"Then let's target the image of the face that keeps intruding."

"Can I hold the tappers and see what comes up? Maybe figure out who he is and why he's there?" She remembered what Mandy had said in their first session about letting memories reveal themselves slowly, but Emily wanted to push the memory of the face into focus as quickly as she could. Wanted to see who it was.

"We need to structure the process," Mandy said, looking down at the papers on her lap. "Let's begin this way: what does the image of the face represent for you?"

"Evil," she said without hesitating. "First is a flash of black, then the face. I think there's evil."

"So, the image of the face represents evil. What is your negative belief about yourself when you think of the face?"

"I'm scared."

"I understand being scared, but that's not a negative belief. That's an emotion."

She bit her lower lip, lowered her eyes, and thought about the face. He scared her. Why? Because he might hurt her? Anyone would feel threatened by that face, wouldn't they? But what did feeling scared by the dark and the face say about her? What negative belief went along with that?

"Here," Mandy said, handing her a sheet of paper encased in plastic.

Emily read the words at the top of the page out loud. "LIST OF GENERIC NEGATIVE AND POSITIVE COGNITIONS." On the left side of the page were negative cognitions, and on the right were positive cognitions. "This helps. I'm not used to asking myself questions about things like negative beliefs." She looked down the list. "Not that again."

"Not what again?"

Emily shrugged her shoulders in resignation. "I feel

vulnerable, that I can't protect myself. It's the same negative cognition I had when I remembered the night at the bar."

"It's not unusual to have different, upsetting memories with the same negative cognition," Mandy reassured her. "What would you rather believe about yourself? Look at the section with the positive cognitions if that helps."

"I have the same positive cognition just like I did with the other incident, that I can protect myself. But with the man in the bar, the person in the shadows, I knew what I was trying to protect myself from. More or less. I thought the man in the shadows was a threat to my safety. I have no idea what this face means, what I need to protect myself from."

"Let's do some work on that with the tappers and see if you can come up with a little more about what that image means."

"I'm anxious because I don't know what's there. But I know I have to find out."

"Where do you feel that emotion—the anxiety—in your body?"

Emily rolled her shoulders and squeezed a breath out between her lips. "The usual spots: my chest, my arms."

"On a scale of zero to ten, ten being the highest, zero the lowest, how upset are you when you think about the face that keeps popping up out of blackness?"

"It scares me. A lot. I guess it's an eight."

"I'm going to turn on the tappers, and I want you to remember that face and feeling vulnerable. See what comes up."

During the silence that followed, Emily tried to see the face. It was the first time she wanted to see it, but it would not appear. She thought back to the bar and the shadows and hoped the face would come forward with those memories. It didn't. Maybe she was trying too hard, pushing too much. She flexed her shoulders again and turned her head from side to side to work out some of the tension in her neck and shoulders. With her eyes closed, she raised her eyebrows toward her hairline and back down again to maybe give them space to see the face. Instead, she heard someone knocking on a door.

"Em, are you in there?" Cara asks.

"Yep, I'm in bed."

The door opens a crack. Her sister peers in.

"I heard the shower. You don't usually shower at night."

"Some of the boys were smoking at the party, and I wanted to get the smell off me, out of my hair."

"Did you have a good time?"

"It was okay."

"Only okay? You can tell me more about it tomorrow if you want."

"All right. I'm tired. G'night."

She shifted in her seat. The heels of her feet came up off the floor, and she bounced her legs up and down like she was trying to fight off nerves.

The tappers stopped. Mandy's voice broke through her memory. "What's happening, Emily?"

She cleared her throat. "I don't know how what I just remembered fits into any other memories. I didn't see the blackness or the face. I heard my sister knock on my bedroom door and ask if I had a good time at the party. I don't know what party she's talking about. But I'm sure I was in my bedroom where we grew up."

"Do you know how old you were?"

"Not really, but probably a teenager. I was at a party where people smoked, so it makes sense I would be in my teens, maybe late teens." She shrugged her shoulders and threw out her hands. She didn't know.

"Can you think of any upsetting childhood memories beyond the two you mentioned during our first session, the boy on the playground and the girl in math class?"

Emily was quiet for a minute. "Nothing new comes up."

"Then let's turn the tappers on again. I want you to remember the flash of blackness and the image of the man's face. Think about how you feel vulnerable."

She did but, again when her eyes closed, she heard the same conversation after Cara knocked on her door. This time, she heard the click when Cara said goodnight and closed the door. Her vision snapped into black. The face appeared.

"There he is," she said, and a half-second later, "Oh, no, he's gone again."

"Stay with it, Emily."

Her breathing accelerated, and her left arm started twitching. The knock on her bedroom door. Cara's voice. *'You don't usually shower at night.'* Then she was in the shower, scrubbing over and over with the washcloth. She waited for more memories to come. Willed them to come. Almost spoke out loud and asked the face to appear.

"I got a little more this time," she said, slowly opening her eyes. "Right after Cara said I took a shower, I saw myself in the shower, scrubbing with a washcloth. Why would that be a memory?"

"I don't know. Take a deep breath. Keep holding the tappers and think about that image."

She nodded and closed her eyes. The electronic pulses in her palms resumed. The shower. Blackness. The face. Not a man like her father, but a younger man.

"I smell cigarette smoke," she said. "Someone's smoking." Her eyes popped open. She looked around and sniffed. "Do you smell the smoke?"

"No, I don't, and I don't know where it would come from."

"But it's so strong, as if the person smoking is standing right next to me." Her eyes appealed to Mandy to explain what was going on with her senses. With her memories. How could something in the past feel and smell so real in the present? Sitting in Mandy's office.

"Let's get in there and figure it out. Close your eyes again, and think about the smoke, Emily. Think about the face and the smoke you smell."

The image of the face was still blurry, and she squeezed her eyes so tight trying to see his features, her vision filled with flashing white spots. Her arm twitched again, faster now, and she took in hard, deep breaths. The image was weak. What stood out more than the image was the smell of smoke. She waved the nauseating smoke away with her hand. Then she caught a glimpse of his thick dark hair and—

"Damn, he disappeared again, but I got to see more of him, and I keep smelling cigarette smoke. He must have smoked at the party. He must have been high school age or a little older." She stopped abruptly. High school. Party. Shower. Crawling into bed. What was going on? This was like trying to fit together a thousand-piece jigsaw puzzle blind-folded. She blinked rapidly a few times to collect her thoughts.

"I don't understand what's going on, Mandy. These images, flashbacks I guess, keep fading in and out."

"Your memories are coming in snippets," she explained. "Memories rarely emerge in one long, cohesive stream. Pieces of a disturbing event will come to you, sometimes quickly but usually very slowly, revealing them a section at a time. It's a normal part of the process." Mandy took a sip of her tea and suggested Emily drink some water.

"But I want to know what it all means." She stared at Mandy, picked up her bottle of water, and took a long drink.

"The more we continue to work on these pieces of your memory, the more the pieces will connect. I know it's hard to be patient, but with EMDR it's better to let the memory reveal itself a little at a time."

"It feels like a dream, and yet, it feels so real. How do I

know these things really happened, that I didn't make them up?" She took another drink, then put the bottle back on the coffee table.

"Your mind knows. Your body knows," Mandy reassured her. "Remember what I said about how we don't process upsetting memories? The trauma gets trapped inside your body until it comes out. Sometimes when you're ready and sometimes when you aren't."

She sat in silence a while longer, understanding only some of what Mandy was saying. She couldn't remember a time when she'd felt so confused. Her mind tried to force the pieces together. It wasn't working. Her brain raced in so many directions. Yet she also felt frozen, sort of like running in place on a skating rink.

"I could see him a little more clearly this time. It's like the blackness is falling away. From his face. And from what this memory holds."

"That's how it will reveal itself, Emily. Just let go, and it will come to you, I promise. We're almost out of time now, so put all of these memories and images into your container. Then close your eyes and think about your safe space for a few moments."

The tappers vibrated again, this time slower beats from one palm to the other. She shoved the memories into the jewelry box and turned the key in the lock. Double-checked to make sure the lock was secure. Then she pictured her favorite beach. The sun on her face. The sand between her toes. She let out a deep breath to push away the pain, but calmness was a long way off. The tappers stopped. Reluctantly, she opened her eyes.

"We'll learn more on Thursday, Emily. Until then, please try to leave it alone. I want you to think about this instead: remember how brave you are doing this work. You're brave and you're strong. When your anxiety feels overwhelming, think about that. And keep your memories in your container, locked up tight until we get together again, okay?"

"Okay," Emily said so softly that Mandy leaned forward to hear her. She looked at her therapist with tears in her eyes and fear in her heart.

"What if he hurt me?"

Chapter Fourteen

Voices drifted from the lunchroom into the hallway. Cara paused, empty coffee cup dangling from her fingers, and listened.

"Um, I didn't formally complain," Shelley said. "I never went to HR or anything."

"You must've said something to someone," Stan said. "I feel like Cara's watching me all the time now. No one else here has told me they don't like how I interact with them. It had to be you, Shelley."

Cara grabbed the coffee cup with her left hand and grasped it harder when Stan said her name, at hearing the amount of anger in his voice.

"I told you I don't like the way you touch me," the young production assistant said. "I'd rather you didn't."

"I'm a casual, warm-hearted guy who just naturally reaches out to touch other people on the arm or hand when I'm having a conversation with them. You shouldn't read too much into it."

Now Stan sounded defensive, persuasive. And Shelley anxious, scared.

"I don't ... I mean ... I'm not reading into it. I'm ... I'm saying I don't ... like it."

Shelley's voice wavered, and she struggled to get the words out. It was time to stop eavesdropping and interrupt.

"Thanks, Tim," Cara said in a loud voice to the empty hallway. "See you later." She paused, then rounded the doorway and stepped into the lunchroom.

"Hi, you two. I hope you saved some coffee for me." She strode past them to the coffee maker on the far side of the room. Coffee pods were stacked in little rows on a stand beside the machine. She selected a pod, popped it into the machine, placed her cup under the spout, and pressed the start button. Only then did she turn around and look at the two of them.

Shelley was staring at Stan like she didn't know what to say next, but her blotchy, red face and busy hands told Cara all she needed to know. Cara was about to speak when Shelley walked toward the door.

"I gotta go," Shelley said. "See you later. See you, Cara."

The coffee machine hissed; the last drips of brew fell into her cup. She slid the cup out from under the spout, turned back around, and looked at Stan. Looked at him without saying a word, waiting for him.

"Is there something on your mind?" he said. "You look like you want to say something." He set his mug of coffee down on a nearby table and crossed his arms over his chest.

It was a challenge, not an invitation. His voice was friendly enough, but his eyes were not. They were the same cold eyes that looked at her when he turned away from Laura's desk the other day. The same challenging eyes that didn't blink when he realized she had seen him looking Laura and Shelley over like they were dessert.

She took a few steps closer to him, kept her voice low and her look steady. "When someone says they don't want you to touch them, even if you think you're reaching out with a friendly, non-sexual tap on the hand or arm, please make sure you respect their wishes. Just because you think it's innocent doesn't mean the other person finds it appropriate."

"I hear you, Cara."

"But do you hear Shelley?" she shot back. Cara didn't want their conversation to be confrontational, but she struggled to keep her voice even when his body language screamed male aggression.

He paused and held her gaze for too long. "You listened to our conversation?"

"Not intentionally, but yes, I heard the two of you talking a moment before I walked in here. You're making Shelley uncomfortable, and she's asked you to stop touching her. So please stop."

He opened his mouth to respond, but she saw a shift in his eyes. Maybe something clicked, like he just remembered who she was—a member of management at Flagstone Productions. One of his bosses. His arms dropped to his sides. His eyes softened. His lips closed and turned up at the corners. He tilted his head slightly and dropped his chin. When he spoke, his voice was softer.

"No problem, Cara. The last thing I want is for Shelley, or any other woman I work with here, to feel ill at ease. If my actions are not coming across as friendly, I assure you I will pay closer attention."

Cara nodded, then glanced at the doorway as Jessica walked in with a handful of papers.

Jessica greeted them and strolled over to the bulletin board next to the refrigerator, where she tacked up a flyer.

"What's up?" Stan asked.

"We're having a full staff meeting next Wednesday. Seven-thirty in the morning so it doesn't interfere with work assignments," Jessica said. "I know you're new here so you may not know that we have regular sessions, usually once a quarter, about employee concerns or workplace issues." She glanced back and forth between Cara and Stan. "Sometimes the meetings are around financial issues, like planning for retirement or options for health care coverage. At least once a year we have a session about ethics, which is what we'll cover next week."

"And is there a specific topic around ethics that you're going to discuss?" Stan asked.

"Given the MeToo movement and the reported claims against high-powered people in politics, the arts, sports, business, the media, in a lot of places, this upcoming meeting is about sexual harassment and appropriate behavior in the workplace."

"Well, that's certainly important," he said in his most charming voice.

"Yes, it is, and attendance is mandatory," Jessica said.

"Then I'll see you there." He smiled, picked his coffee mug up off the table, and left the lunchroom.

"I get the feeling I interrupted something." Jessica looked at Cara, then taped up another notice, this time on the front of the refrigerator.

Cara went over and, keeping her voice down, told Jessica about overhearing Stan and Shelley and the warning she'd just given him.

"Depending on how you look at it, my timing was either terrific or awful," Jessica said.

"It's fine." Cara glanced over at the empty doorway. "You could say you put the exclamation point on my advice to him to show women more respect."

"Has anything else happened since we discussed this in my office?"

They both lowered their voices so much, they were almost whispering.

"There haven't been any more complaints, and I've been watching Stan. Maybe watching him too closely. The conversation he and I had just now made me uncomfortable, as if I could see another not-so-nice side of him just under the surface."

"It's only the second time I've been in his presence, but I can tell he knows how to turn on the charm," Jessica said.

"Yes, he does." Cara raised her coffee cup to her lips, but her mind couldn't shake her anxiety. "That guy could charm the skin off of a snake. That's what worries me."

Chapter Fifteen

The face invaded Emily's night for the first time. It appeared suddenly and hovered in the black shadow, threatening, dangerous. Threatening what, she wasn't sure, but there were goosebumps on her arms and ripples of tension reverberating in her chest as she lay in bed. The threat was real. It might be from her past, but it felt very much in the present. Both her body and her head were telling her there wasn't a choice. She had to find out who he was and what he did.

After two cups of coffee, her headache began to dissipate, but not the lasting impression of the nightmare, still so vivid it left her fingers icy cold and her legs as wobbly as Jell-O. Rain pounded the roof, pelted the slate patio, and tore fragile leaves off the trees. A quick check with the weather app on her phone indicated the rain wasn't going to let up anytime soon. It didn't matter. She had to move, had to walk and walk and walk, and she couldn't do it at home. Walking would release the energy inside her, and the bilateral stimulation may fill in the rest of the memory that had become more real during her last session with Mandy.

Mandy wouldn't approve of what Emily was about to do,

but she couldn't call her and explain why she could no longer wait to see who was behind the black façade. Her therapist would tell her to lock the memory away into her container, the image still partially shrouded in blackness. She'd tell her to put all her fears in the container until Thursday. But Emily didn't want to do that emotionally. Could not do it mentally, or rationally. Just like she couldn't stop herself from pulling on clothes, donning a raincoat, and stumbling out the door.

Rainwater streamed off her raincoat and soaked the seat when she jumped into the car half a block from her home. The steering wheel was slippery from her wet hands, and she drove carefully, propelled by her mind and body to a nearby school. Her feet lifted her out of the car and onto the synthetic surface of the burnt orange running track. A Phillies baseball cap protected her face from the rain, except when the wind kicked up. Eyes downward, she put one foot in front of the other, pulled the cap lower over her eyes, and wrapped her arms around her chest. One foot in front of the other, one soggy sneaker in front of another, blocking out everything else until she was back in her memory.

"Em, are you in there?" Cara asks.

She's sitting up in bed, hair still wet from the shower, the covers pulled tightly around her chin. Every time she tries to lie down and go to sleep, she bolts upright. She can't calm down. She wants to scream. She doesn't want to stay in her own bed, in her own body. She wants to run. As far and as fast as she can. Away from what's happening to her. From what happened to her.

"I heard the shower. You don't usually shower at night."

Cara's words came back to her again as she walked in the rain. They were as clear as when Emily had heard them in Mandy's office. Her past was intruding on the present and she struggled to think. Snippets of the memory kept returning to her while the rain pounded down, joining the tears now dripping down her cheeks. The tears kept coming and she didn't understand why. Her eyes were puffy and sore. Her nose and sinuses filled, making it hard to breathe, complicating her need to find air between the raindrops. And still, her past found its way in, this time through her own words.

"Some of the boys were smoking at the party, and I wanted to get the smell off me, out of my hair."

Party. Shower. Scrubbing her body raw. Crawling into bed. Pulling the covers up around her. She flinched and heard the snippets of her memory, saw herself curled up in bed. It was like watching a movie while her feet took her round and round the track. Then she saw a flash of black immediately followed by the face. The face had dark hair, not too long, parted on the right. More of the blackness fell away from the image, and she could see he had brown eyes and full lips. His lips. His mouth. Her breath came in quick bursts, her right arm clutched her raincoat, and her left arm twitched with a life of its own. She walked faster and faster, almost jogging, because she couldn't fight the urge to run to something and run away from it at the same time. She was no longer aware of where she was or the squish of her rain-soaked sneakers as she splashed through the puddles and images from her past. She focused on the face and squinted to see it better. It was the face of someone she knew.

His lips on her mouth. Pushing his tongue inside.

She gasped and opened her eyes, looked around, and jerked her head from one side to the other to make sure no one was near, no one could harm her. But someone had harmed her back then, back in high school. Something bad had happened. The face forced itself upon her again. His face too close. His lips full and hard against hers. Then a searing pain.

Her scream sliced through the rain, and she didn't know if she was screaming at that moment or in the memory. It hurt and hurt and hurt. And then it was over.

She fell to her knees and collapsed on the running track, water pooling around her, saturating the rest of her clothes.

Finally, she knew. The haunting dream was replaced with the reality of what had happened to her, what he had done to her. The pain in her body was shockingly real. Now she could see the face of the boy who'd attacked her. She saw enough to remember him, meeting him at the party. He had introduced himself and offered to walk her home. Yes, she remembered. The only missing piece was his name. But he would not remain anonymous for long. She would find out who he was. And then she would track him down.

Chapter Sixteen

E mily's body ached from so many hours when she couldn't stop walking and crying. She hadn't slept well last night and wasn't sure when she'd feel calm enough to sleep again. Every time she closed her eyes, she saw the face and felt the pain. The memory was so devastating, she realized it was a mistake to uncover the source of the flashbacks by herself. Well, she couldn't undo it now, could she? Couldn't push the memory away, couldn't push the face away as if she'd never seen it. She was disappointed that she had no sense of relief in discovering the truth. That was the point of the therapy, wasn't it? Find out what happened. Acknowledge it. Accept it. Let it go and get back to living in the present.

The scotch sat on the coffee table next to her glass. She lifted the bottle, tilted it, then watched the brown liquid cascade over the ice cubes and soften their hard edges. She filled the glass almost to the top, swished it around in the glass, and took a big gulp. The scotch burned the back of her throat and stung all the way to her stomach, but Emily didn't care. She wouldn't feel the path of the scotch after a few more sips, and with any luck, her mind wouldn't dwell on the images that were all too vivid now. She took another drink. This was one way to get some sleep, or at least some relief.

Her cellphone chimed. She had no intention of talking to anyone today, but then she saw it was her sister. They were getting together for lunch soon, weren't they? Was she supposed to have met Cara somewhere for lunch today? She squeezed her eyes and thought. No, they were supposed to meet tomorrow. But there was no way she could go out in public or carry on a conversation. She had to tell her she couldn't do it. Maybe she should text her. She picked up her phone.

"Emily! I'm glad I caught you."

Oops, her finger must have hit the green connection symbol. Emily quietly cleared her throat and said hello.

"I'm checking in about our lunch date tomorrow," Cara said. "Where do you want to go? Should I make a reservation?"

"Oh, Cara, I do want to see you because it's been a while, but I can't get together for lunch tomorrow. I'm sorry."

"What's up? Too much work?"

She paused, trying to figure out what to say. She didn't want to tell Cara what had happened at work, and she couldn't share with her what happened in high school because she was spinning in circles trying to grasp the shock of her memory. Shock. That's what was going on with her. Shock over what had happened and unable to fully grasp it. Learning about the assault was changing her, including the way she thought about her childhood. Was there anything else in her past that was no longer true? Her insides churned too much to think clearly, but she had to say something.

"I'm not at work this week. I took some time off." She put the glass on the table and forced her attention on the conversation. "But, uh, then, I got sick. Whatever it is has hung on for a couple of days. I'm afraid I won't feel well enough to join you for lunch tomorrow. Besides, I don't want to give what-ever I have to you."

"And I don't want it, thanks, not with two young kids in the house. Are you drinking enough water?"

She knew she didn't sound like she had a cold, so she'd better pretend she was ill with some stomach virus. "Water and toast are about all my stomach can tolerate and I have plenty of bread."

"Okay. You do sound kinda dopey, no offense, like I woke you from a nap."

"I wasn't napping but I do feel a little out of it. How's everyone?" She thought it polite to ask but hoped for a short conversation.

"I'm good. Well, mostly. Work's a little strained right now with our new hire—the guy we hired to cohost *Fix It or Ditch It*. I told you about him, right? One of the weekly papers used the headline right off our press release: 'Local Guy Ditches Florida, Comes Home for *Fix It or Ditch It*.'"

Cara's voice radiated with pride and Emily guessed the headline was her creation.

"I must have missed it," she said.

"Must have. It was in all the papers."

"How's he working out?"

"He's great on camera—we knew he would be—but I've got to keep an eye on him. I've had a couple of complaints from women that he's a little too friendly with his hands, if you know what I mean."

Oh, she knew what Cara meant. Hard to find a woman who didn't. She tried to keep her voice steady. "Women are much more sensitive to inappropriate touching these days and more willing to call men out about inappropriate behavior. That's a good thing. And more men are learning the difference between what's okay and what isn't. That's a good thing too."

"Yes, it is. So, HR is hosting a seminar on workplace

behavior next week. Unfortunately, we have plenty of examples of inappropriate behavior from recent events around the country."

"You're having this meeting just because of the new guy?"

"The timing is good because of all the news reports about sexual assault or sexual harassment by men, that whole MeToo movement." Cara stopped speaking abruptly. "But actually, I probably shouldn't be talking so much about this stuff and our new hire. You know, employee privacy. I've said too much already."

"No worries. You can trust me."

"I'll leave it as it is. I know you wouldn't say anything anyway."

"Of course not. So how are Albert and the kids?"

"Everyone is great. Adam took his first grown-up shower with daddy the other day and he thought that was just the best."

Shower. High school. Party. She reached for the glass and took a drink. Her hand shook when she tried to set it down on the table, so she squeezed the phone between her shoulder and ear and grabbed the glass with both hands. Still, there was a loud clunk when the glass hit the coffee table.

"What was that? Em, are you still there?"

"Yep, but I need to go. My stomach is making noises and I think I'm going to be sick." She disconnected the call and dropped the phone onto the couch beside her, then quickly picked it up again. Pressed the button on the side of the phone and slid her finger across the top of it to turn it off. She pressed her hands against her face and pulled her eyes back toward her ears until the pain of her fingers against her temples was the only thing she could feel.

Chapter Seventeen

The face in the darkness that once could not be summoned now refused to go away. It haunted Emily day and night.

Mandy did a quick assessment the moment she stepped into her therapist's office. "Are you okay? You look like you didn't sleep a wink last night."

"I haven't slept much since Monday afternoon," she said, collapsing on the couch. "I would nod off for a few minutes, then jolt awake again, grapple with my memories until I drifted off, then, bam, wake up again. It's been a vicious cycle."

"What's going on? You could've called me." Mandy barely took her eyes off Emily as she walked to her chair, sat, and picked up her clipboard.

"I couldn't call you because I didn't do what you told me to do when my distressing memories took over. You told me to put scary images in the container. And I didn't."

"So, you struggled with the memory, found it difficult to push it out of your mind."

"Worse than that," she admitted, looking down at her

hands, "I invited the face to come out because I wanted to see him. I walked and walked in the rain because I had to look at him and know what he'd done." Then she told Mandy what had happened to her when she was a teen.

"I'm so sorry, Emily."

"You knew there was something bad in there, didn't you?"

"No, I didn't *know*. I suspected."

"Well, now we both know." She reached for a bottle of water on the lower shelf of the coffee table and tore off the cap with a sharp twist of her hand. She took a quick gulp, then set the bottle down on the table without putting the cap back on.

"We need to take some steps back today to work on this memory and ease your distressing thoughts. Let's use the EMDR protocol to process what you stirred up."

"But, Mandy, this was a horrible assault. How could I not remember it until now? How can I be sure a memory like this is real, not something I saw in a movie or on a TV show? Or worse, something my mind made up?" Her voice raced with energy, and her hands refused to sit still on her lap. "How can I, or you, be sure this really happened?"

"Emily, take a deep breath." Mandy's command was firm. "Let's get your anxiety under control before we go any further. Keep your eyes open. Look at me, or the floor, or something in the room. Focus on one spot and concentrate on your breathing. Breathe in for four counts, breathe out for six. I'll do it with you."

Emily stared at the box of tissues on the coffee table for a couple of minutes; the only sounds were Mandy's counting to four, then six, and her own labored breathing. Hard and fast, until her breaths became deeper and longer.

"Okay. I feel more under control."

Mandy peered at her closely as if to make sure it was safe to move on.

"Let's address your question about the reality of your

memory because I understand why you would ask. Your memory is so vivid right now, you wonder why you couldn't recall it for so many years. We've talked about this some, but it's good to go over it again to make sure you understand. Trauma can be trapped in the body until something, or someone triggers a memory. Not talking about a traumatic event keeps it buried inside, keeps the pain inside, and prevents people who have PTSD from getting over the pain. PTSD can contribute to all kinds of behavior issues: obsessive-compulsive disorder or OCD, control issues, loss of normal boundaries, and acting out in ways that are harmful to oneself or others. That's why it is so important to let go of any trauma as much as you can." She paused while Emily grappled with what she'd said. "Does this make sense to you?"

"I think so. Reading *Getting Past Your Past* helped, but I might need to do some more research so I can better understand."

"Before you leave today, I'll write down some other resources for you to investigate, including a couple of books about body trauma."

"That would be good."

Mandy flipped over a page in her notepad. "Now, tell me what your level of upset is when you think about the image of the face and seeing more of his features."

"It's all I can think about, and it haunts me," she said. "It's a ten."

"What picture represents the worst part of the memory?"

"The pain I felt ..." Emily's voice trailed, and she choked back a sob.

"You don't have to tell me every detail," Mandy reassured her. "It seems the worst part of the memory is the horror and pain of the assault, is that correct?"

Emily nodded.

"Can you put a picture to it?"

"His face so close to mine as he pressed me up against a brick wall."

"And what's your negative belief about yourself when you think about that now?"

"I'm weak. I can't protect myself."

"Where do you feel that in your body?"

"My chest. My stomach." She shuddered. "Lower."

Mandy glanced up from taking notes, her eyes full of compassion. "What would you rather believe about yourself?"

"I wasn't strong enough to stop him. He was bigger than me, stronger than me. Then. But I'm a stronger person now."

"Okay, I'm going to turn on the tappers. Focus on the image of when he hurt you and go with whatever comes to mind. If it becomes too intense, tell me, and we'll pause."

The little devices came to life in the palms of her hands. She thought about the face she'd seen in her memories and nightmares the past few days. As she did, more of the memory came into focus. She remembered more about the man who attacked her. Every muscle in her body tensed. Her mind raced back and forth through parts of the memory, trying to see enough of his face.

"He was older than me. I didn't know him well," she said, eyes still closed and hands still grasping the tappers. "He offered to walk me home from a party."

"Go with that. Follow that thought. Try to picture what happened."

Emily was quiet for a while, then she started crying and wrapped her arms around herself, bent over at the waist, resting the upper part of her body on her legs.

"He hurt me," she said. "Then he said he would tell people I wanted him to do what he did."

"But of course, you didn't," Mandy said.

"Oh, God, no."

"I'm going to stop the tappers—"

"No, not yet. Please."

The tappers continued to vibrate, and the details of the assault filled in. There was no stopping the intensity of the memory or the flow of tears. Emily wanted to know it all, and now, finally, she did.

"He told me not to tell anyone or he would hurt me, would hurt my family. I wanted to tell Cara, but I was afraid he would hurt her."

"You kept quiet and suppressed the memory so he wouldn't hurt anyone."

"Yes."

The tapping sensations ceased. She opened her eyes and looked at Mandy.

"This is an intense and distressing memory, Emily. We need to stop for a moment. Take a deep breath."

Emily's body shook as she took the deepest breath she could, which barely went past the back of her throat. She took a few more short breaths, then sat up straighter and sucked air into her lungs. Took a few more cleansing breaths until her body stopped shaking.

"I want to go back to your negative cognition," Mandy said, glancing down at her notes, "that you're weak and should've protected yourself better. Now that you've worked through the memory in more detail, what do you believe about what happened?"

"He was so strong. He had me pinned against a wall. I couldn't move. I couldn't protect myself against him."

"What's your level of distress now?"

"It's still pretty high. Probably a nine. Maybe an eight. Shouldn't it come down more?"

"You're just remembering what happened, feeling it in your body, taking the very first steps to assimilate the assault into your brain. It'll become less distressing, I promise, just not yet. It's a lot to take in."

"I never should've let him walk me home from the party. I should've known better."

"How could you know? He offered to make sure you got there safely—"

"That didn't work out so well, did it?"

"Did you have a reason to distrust him?"

"No."

"Go with that."

The tappers pulsed in her hands. She closed her eyes and drifted back in time. She's a teenager again. At the party. It's in a house she hasn't been in before, and she doesn't know many of the people there. She looks around for the two friends who came with her, but she can't find them. It's getting late. Time to go home. Her eyes sweep the room again.

A boy walks up to her.

"Are you looking for someone?"

"I can't find my friends. We're supposed to walk home together."

"They must've left. I'll walk you home."

"But you don't know where I live."

"You're Cara's sister, right? How old are you now?"

"Eighteen. I just turned eighteen last week."

"Happy Birthday then. Come on. I know who Cara is, and I know where you live."

He puts his arm on her shoulder and waves goodbye to some other boys in the room. Then he walks her out the door, and they make idle conversation until he leads her into the park a few blocks from her home. He pushes her off the path and into a dark place between two trees. Then he shoves her up against a brick wall. She feels the unevenness of the bricks poking her back. And then ...

Sitting on the couch in Mandy's office, her breathing came faster, and her left arm twitched over and over. She kept her eyes closed and forced her breathing to slow down.

"He knew I was Cara's sister and where we lived. I thought that meant it was safe to go with him."

"Follow that thought, Emily."

By the time her session was nearing an end, Emily was exhausted. Her level of upset had at least dropped to a manageable six. She didn't think she had another tear left in her. Mandy made her promise she would call if she struggled to put upsetting thoughts in the container. "Don't hesitate. I mean it. Don't think you can just push through this by yourself. I'm here for you."

"I know what happened now," Emily said, swallowing and feeling the pain in her throat that had grown sore from such ragged crying. "The face looks familiar and I'm sure I'll eventually remember who he is. Is it possible the worst of the memory is over?"

"Neither one of us can say for sure just yet," Mandy said. "But I do think you've uncovered the distressing memory that's been upsetting you, the cause of your flashbacks. We'll keep working on it and keep lowering your level of distress."

Mandy spent a few minutes sending a slower pulse to the tappers, getting Emily to her safe space, then the session was over. She left her therapist's office, carefully taking one step and then another. A gentle breeze caressed her face, and the sun warmed her head and shoulders as she walked on the sunny side of the street for several blocks, eventually circling back to her car. She was always too agitated after a session with Mandy to go directly to her car and drive. That was especially true today. The sensations in her body were similar to the ones she had felt after walking on the track and first recalling the assault. She struggled to hold onto one thought before her mind sped to another.

On the slow and deliberate drive home, she stopped at the grocery store, walked through the automatic doors, and approached the produce section. The apples were bright red and green and inviting. She picked up a large Honeycrisp. Felt it in the palm of her hand. Thought about making a pie. Put it down. Picked it up again and studied it. Put it down again.

"Are you okay?"

She jumped and looked at the woman standing beside her.

"Are you okay?" the woman with white hair asked again, her eyes full of compassion and concern.

Emily didn't know how to answer, wasn't sure whether she could form the words even if she knew which ones she wanted to use, so she nodded once, then spun around and marched out of the store. Fifteen minutes later, she was back in the safety of her home, and five minutes after that, curled up on the couch and snuggled in her dark green blanket, where her exhausted body caved in to sleep.

Chapter Eighteen

Dinner was two pieces of whole wheat toast topped with peanut butter and some strawberry jam she found back in the corner of the refrigerator. She couldn't remember the last time she'd used the jam, but there was nothing green growing inside the jar, so she figured it was safe. Then she returned to her nest on the couch, where she slept and dreamed and cried until the sun came up.

Hot coffee helped clear her head, but the only food her stomach tolerated was toast. She spent the day in a haze of lost thoughts until mid-afternoon when a phone call brought her back to reality. She recognized Chris's number and waited for him to leave a message. Only then did she dare pick up the phone, sure she wouldn't accidentally connect a call she didn't want to take.

"Hi, Emily. I'm looking forward to seeing you back in the office. Let me know if you have any questions; otherwise, I'll see you Monday morning."

Monday morning. Tomorrow was Saturday. Then Sunday. Monday morning was not far away. She could barely function right now—the elderly woman in the grocery store who saw her with the apples could confirm that. No way was she ready to return to work. She composed a brief email to BAM's head of human resources and hit send.

Her phone rang two minutes later. This time the call was from Barb Carter in HR. Emily was tempted to let that call go through to voicemail also, but she wanted to wrap this up as quickly as possible.

"I guess you got my email."

"Yes, and I must say, I was surprised," Barb said. "You've been off for two weeks, on paid vacation, right? And now you want a two-week unpaid leave. What's up?"

"I'm sure Chris filled you in on why he *made* me take vacation time."

"He did."

Emily waited for Barb to say more, and when the silence continued, she realized she was expected to do the talking. How much did she have to tell Barb so she understood Emily's request for additional time off? Barb would tell Chris, of course, and the decision whether to grant it would ultimately be his. She opted for some safe middle ground of the truth.

"I decided to see a therapist after what happened with the guy from Clifton Pharmaceutical, and I've been seeing her twice a week, sometimes for extended sessions." She chose her words carefully. "We're working on some childhood traumas, and I want more uninterrupted time to finish with her as best I can. I can't do that if I come back to BAM next week. Right now, therapy needs to be my priority."

"Is everything okay, Emily?"

The concern in Barb's voice lowered her defenses.

"'Okay' is such a subjective word." Emily paced the living room, down the hallway to the kitchen, and back again, her usual route. She looked down to see if she was wearing a path in the carpeting. "I'm okay as in I'm not dying. But I am *not* okay because I'm in the middle of working through something extremely difficult. Painful. Life-changing. And the middle is not an easy place to be."

"How about a week? Would that be enough time?"

"No, I need two weeks." She might have been an emotional basket case, but she still knew how to fight for herself. "It's not like I haven't earned the right to take time off, Barb."

She listened to the silence. If Barb and Chris denied her request, she'd have no choice but to call in sick for a week at least, maybe two. She didn't want to do that, but she also knew she could no more create a marketing plan for a client in her current state of mind than she could speak Latin.

"I'll talk to Chris and call you back."

"You can just send me an email," she said. "I'm talked out for the day."

An hour later, her phone rang. She let it go to voicemail without looking at the caller ID. When she replayed the message, she was surprised to hear Chris's voice.

"Barb told me about your conversation. I've approved a two-week paid sabbatical. We need you back here, Emily, but only when you're ready and able to contribute. If you say you need two more weeks, I'm not going to push you to come back sooner." He paused, and his voice softened. "Let me know if you need anything."

Two weeks paid leave. That was unexpected. *I guess he's not such a bad guy after all*, she thought, picking up the TV remote control and searching for something to watch that didn't involve sex or violence. She finally settled on the Weather Channel, set her phone on vibrate, and drifted off to sleep watching a line of dangerous thunderstorms pushing east.

When she awoke later that afternoon, she finally felt like her body was connected to her brain again. Only a little bit, but that was a start. What a relief. She heated a can of lentil soup and made a cup of chamomile tea. The warmth of the soup and steamy aroma of the tea calmed and relaxed her.

Martin had texted her after learning she was not coming back to work yet, and she answered as best she could.

I'm doing okay, she responded. Will call u tomorrow

Martin replied before she could put her phone down.

Want company?

Thanks but no. Not yet. More tomorrow. K?

He did not respond, and she was afraid he was offended.

Really, I'm OK. Just need more alone time

K. Call me tomorrow.

 u

On Saturday she had to get out of the house. The couch had a permanent dip where she'd spent hours curled up. TV was boring and so was the light blue wall next to it, where her eyes drifted time and time again. She thought about Martin, but she wasn't ready to see him, or anyone else. Didn't want to be in anyone else's company but her own, and she especially did not want to be with the face in the darkness. She promised herself she would avoid the face, not invite him into her consciousness, and, to be safe, she would steer clear from the memory of that night in the bar. Maybe a drive in the country would be better than a walk. After all, driving required more concentration.

She pointed her SUV west toward Lancaster County, and when images of the memory intruded, she talked out loud to tell herself what she was seeing. Hearing her own voice helped ground her. Not much else did these days. *How long will it take until I don't feel like I'm floating between the past and the present?*

An hour into her drive, she turned off the highway and

stopped at a favorite antique store in Amish Country. The dusty smell of old furniture and lemon polish filled her nose the minute she walked into the two-story barn. She sauntered among a display of art deco floor lamps and was tempted to buy one with a hammered iron base topped with a beautiful soft orange globe. Equally tantalizing was an assortment of old advertising posters for Hershey's Cocoa, especially one with a boy and girl cutting into a chocolate cake. Both children had hungry eyes and glowing smiles. She couldn't resist buying that piece and would give it to Cara and Albert on their anniversary in a few months unless she couldn't bear to part with it.

The huge antique market was jammed with eye-catching displays of old kitchen utensils, older Depression-era glass, and newer Fiesta ware, clocks set into the bodies of eagles, and row after row of Amish-made benches, tables, bedroom chests, and coffee tables. She reached the end of the aisle and rounded a corner, then came face-to-face with a tall bookcase overflowing with books from hardcovers to paperbacks, some almost new, many with folded-down corners and scratched or creased covers.

The second shelf contained at least twenty Nancy Drew books. She had read them when she was in middle school and found refuge in rereading them years later when she was almost the same age as the timeless female sleuth. She pulled one of the books out and blew the dust off. Opened the book to chapter one. And just like that, she was back in high school, spending long hours tucked away in a corner chair in the living room or her bedroom. Except now Emily realized she'd probably disappeared into Nancy Drew books to avoid thinking about what had happened.

Her appetite for poking into the past was gone. Her stomach gurgled as she hurried toward the exit. A peek at the clock over the door confirmed it had been a long time since breakfast, and her body was telling her it needed more than tea and toast. She paid for the poster and drove to a nearby diner known for authentic German food. After settling into the red vinyl booth, she ordered the chicken schnitzel in mushroom gravy, then dug in with abandon as soon as the server set the hot plate in front of her.

Back in her car, Emily dialed Martin's number before pulling out into traffic and was not disappointed to get his voicemail. She'd promised to call him but didn't feel like talking—to anyone. She left a brief message telling him she was fine and on her way back home.

She made a slower drive home on county roads through bucolic farms and quaint small towns along Route 30. The scenery quieted her mind and lifted her spirits. She enjoyed the energy of living and working in the city, but some part of her DNA must have come from the countryside.

After she was home and settled back on the couch, she saw that Martin had called again. She still didn't feel like talking, so she decided to send him an email explaining her current mood. She was about to write Martin when she saw a message from her sister.

The subject read: *Flagstone's new hire from Central High*

Hi Em. I hope you're feeling better. Let me know when you want to reschedule lunch. Do you remember the other day when I mentioned that we'd hired a guy who went to the same high school we did? He graduated a year ahead of me so you might not remember him. I had to send the press release about him to someone else, and since I was emailing it to them, I thought I'd send it to you as well. His name is Stan Hester. Here's a link to Flagstone's website, along with a photo. Talk soon. Love, Cara

Emily clicked on the link and read about Stan Hester. She kept reading, and when she scrolled down and saw his photo, her heart skipped a beat, then raced in double-time. Her heels bounced on the floor. She studied the image with fierce intensity. The eyes and lips were painfully familiar. Could it really be him? Wouldn't that be a weird coincidence?

Her shaking hands guided the mouse to open her internet browser, where she searched for more images. Recent photos appeared at the top of the search window, mostly professional headshots. The further down she scrolled, the younger Stan grew. Then she saw a photo from his senior year in high school. The trembling in her hands spread to the rest of her body until her whole world shook. She tucked her elbows close to her body as she scrolled back to the top of the page and committed the newest photo of Stan Hester to memory, connecting it to a memory she would no longer forget. She recognized the face. Now she had the name. She even knew where he worked.

Chapter Nineteen

E mily was in and out of bed half the night and got up for the last time at three. Perhaps a hot shower would wash away her painful memories, and getting cleaned up might give her energy. She took her robe off the hook on the back of her bedroom door and started down the hallway, but as soon as she stepped into the bathroom, leaned over, and turned on the water, she heard Cara's voice and stopped.

"You don't usually shower at night."

Images flashed in front of her eyes, and she struggled to push them away: Stan shoving her against a brick wall, forcing himself on her, a searing pain.

She dropped her robe on the floor, turned the tap off, and stormed down the stairs. In seconds she was back on the couch and wrapped in a blanket, which is where she was when Martin rang the doorbell hours later. The chimes shattered her quiet and startled her, but she made no attempt to respond.

Martin rang again, then a minute later knocked with what must have been his fist because the door rattled against the frame. "Em, your car is right out front, so you must be home. Let me in. Please."

Her eyes filled with tears. Of course, Martin would show up on her doorstep to check on her because they hadn't spoken on the phone yesterday after she'd promised they would. It wasn't her fault they kept getting each other's voice-mail, although it was true that she hadn't picked up the last time he called. She was bone-weary and struggling to form complete sentences. Martin wouldn't care. He had shown up unannounced to make sure she was okay, knowing she probably wasn't.

She trudged to the hallway, dragging the blanket behind her, turned off the house alarm, and opened the door.

"Ramón insisted I bring you leftovers from last night's dinner."

She squinted into the bright sunlight behind him and tried to guess what time it was. After ten? Before four? It was difficult to know how long she'd been lost in her head this time. "I haven't showered. I can't remember when I last brushed my teeth. And I'm not very good company."

He dropped his chin and looked at her with eyes like a kind uncle's. Or a best friend. "You don't need to shower for me, sweetie, but you can run upstairs and clean up a little, maybe brush your teeth, while I take this into the kitchen and warm it up."

He turned her around by her shoulders and gently nudged her toward the stairs. By the time she'd brushed her teeth and hair, washed her face, and put on clean clothes, he'd heated the food in the microwave and placed a glass of water on the table. Then he set the plate next to the napkin, fork, and knife, and sat down across from her.

"Don't tell me you can't eat," he said, smiling. "I haven't met anyone who could turn down Ramón's chicken marsala dinner. You look a little worse for wear. I'm guessing a hot meal will do you good."

She picked up the fork and poked a piece of chicken, lifted

it, and used it to scoop up some mashed potatoes, then put it in her mouth.

"Yum," she said, smiling at him while she chewed.

They said little while she ate, then they returned to the living room, where she curled up on the couch in her blanket again. He gave her all the time she needed to decide what to say.

"Remember when you were in therapy and you said things came up, conversations between you and Sara that you had forgotten?" Emily asked.

Martin rubbed her blanket-covered feet and nodded once.

She swallowed hard. "I've worked with Mandy on some upsetting childhood memories, like when a boy pushed me on the playground and broke my wrist. Recalling some disturbing but not terrible incidents unlocked a truly awful memory from when I was a teenager and a boy from my high school assaulted me. He told me to never tell anyone or he would hurt me, so I shoved that memory so deep in my subconscious mind, I didn't remember until EMDR drew it out of me. Then there it was—the memory of the boy who assaulted me. Sexually." She pushed the words out fast, knowing that was the only way to tell him. Tears welled in her eyes, and she looked down. "Assaulted isn't strong enough. Raped. He raped me." She wiped the tears away with the back of her hand. "I'm trying to get used to using the words 'rape' and 'me' in the same sentence."

"Oh my God, Emily. I'm so sorry."

He reached out to hug her, but she put up her hand. She couldn't handle a hug yet. Martin stopped rubbing her feet, probably unsure whether any touch was welcome.

"I'm trying to understand how I could bury such a major trauma so deep inside of me that I couldn't remember it until EMDR brought it into my awareness."

"What did Mandy say?"

"The guy who raped me threatened to hurt me, my sister, and other people in my family if I told anyone what he did. I think he scared me into silence. Mandy said it's not unusual to bury such a painful trauma, and because he threatened to hurt me and others, I kept my mouth shut. To almost deny that it had happened." She paused and glanced at the book on the table next to the couch. "I also read that the brain can completely cut off a traumatic childhood event. Just doesn't even store the memory because the brain can't process it." She released a block of air that had been stuck in her lungs. "I'm struggling with this on so many levels."

"The body remembers what the mind forgets," Martin said. "I don't know where I heard or read that." He tentatively touched her feet again. "Is it okay if I rub your feet?"

She pressed her lips together and gave a quick nod.

"Do you remember who it was, the boy who hurt you?"

"Yes," she whispered, "I know who he is, and I know where he works."

"And what're you going to do with that information?"

"You mean, am I going to buy a gun and shoot him between the eyes? Or lower? Or run him down with my car?" A series of questions flew through her mind. *How do you buy a gun anyway? And where? Should I check out a place where people shoot their guns in the city? What do they call them anyway? Shooting shops? Gun shops?* She shook her head again.

"Em—"

"Relax, Martin," she said, coming back to the moment and patting the hands that were rubbing her toes. "I want to kill the guy, no question, strangle him with my bare hands and watch him suffer. Point a gun at him and hear him beg for mercy. Those are good images for me to channel my anger right now. But I'm not going to do anything stupid."

"What about going to the cops and reporting the assault, especially since you know who did it?"

She shook her head.

"Well, what about talking with an attorney then? Your brother-in-law's an attorney. Why don't you talk to him?"

"Talking to an attorney feels like an even bigger step than going to the cops. And I couldn't tell Albert. I'm not ready to talk with Cara about this, and I can't talk to Albert without telling her. The only two people I can talk with right now are you and Mandy."

"I understand, but at some point, you may want to talk to the police or a lawyer."

"Maybe, but look, I just figured this out. I can't see a way forward yet because I'm still in the middle of sorting out the past. There's a lot to deal with, including understanding how so much anger built up inside me that I slapped the new sales guy from Clifton." *And why*, she thought, *was that the incident that triggered me? What made Shelby's assault different from other times I've been offended by men's actions or comments? Was it the way he groped me? The smirk on his face? The way he denied touching me? Well, probably yes, yes, and yes.*

"Are you working with Mandy on what Shelby did?"

"Not yet. But while I buried the memory of the rape itself, the anger and rage of what happened to me and stories about how so many women are abused, assaulted, and harassed, have taken a firm hold of me, sometimes bubbling up close to the surface." She sighed, grabbed a tissue from the box on the coffee table, and dabbed the tears from her eyes. "I have a lot of work to do with Mandy. I haven't begun to address the anger of being raped, or the frustration of being pushed around or aside by men in my personal life and career."

"Is that why you asked for more time off?"

She raised her eyebrows and laughed. "Look at me. Do I look like I'm ready to go back to work? I can't even brush my teeth or put on clean clothes without prodding. Can you imagine me trying to conduct civil conversations with my colleagues or handle the smallest annoyance?"

He didn't speak but kept rubbing her feet in quiet acknowledgment.

"Work will have to wait, because this can't."

Chapter Twenty

"Thanks for calling the Women Organized Against Rape hotline. How can I help you?"

Emily had rehearsed what to say, but as soon as the woman answered the phone, her tongue froze. Her mind emptied. Apparently, the woman on the other end of the line was used to this sort of thing, because after a short pause, she gently asked again if she could help her.

"Um, I'm calling for some advice about a sexual assault."

"Are you in danger right now?" The voice was warm and soothing, yet assertive.

"No, I'm not."

"Let me transfer you to one of our sexual assault counselors who can help you. One moment please."

She barely had time to swallow her nerves when another woman came on the line.

"This is the WOAR hotline. Erika speaking. How can I help you?"

"I want to talk with someone. I was sexually assaulted, and I need some help."

"Do you want to give me your name and phone number in case we get cut off?"

She gave Erika her information.

"First, Emily, I'm here to help you in any way I can, to offer you our support. Have you looked at our website, read about our groups and the other services we provide? We have many ways to help people who've been assaulted."

"Yes, I did check out your website. I'm not much of a group person, but my therapist suggested I might find it helpful to talk to others who've had a similar experience."

"Let me tell you more about the groups than you may have read on the website. Our core group is an open group. It meets every Monday. It's for any adult survivor of any gender. The counselor goes over different topics. One week it might be about coping skills, and the next they might talk about anger and forgiveness. The important thing to know is this is not a group where you discuss your own experience."

"What if I want to talk about my experience?" She didn't need more tips. She needed to hear from others who'd also been assaulted.

"We have those kinds of therapy-type groups also. We have a women's group, an LGBTQ group, a men's group, one for younger children, and one for teens. These groups meet for ten weeks, and people who want to participate go through an intake process to make sure the group is right for them."

Erika's voice was calming, and Emily suppressed the tense energy that told her body to get up and pace. Instead, she concentrated on Erika's voice and thought about how WOAR's programs might help her.

"That's probably the kind of group my therapist was thinking about. I'm still trying to wrap my head around the thought of being in a room full of strangers and talking about such a traumatic experience."

"I understand. However, sharing your experience with

others can be very validating, help you know you're not alone, that you are supported by others. In this kind of group, you can set some goals and work on healing."

"I'm definitely interested in healing, so I'll think about that group." Emily looked at the notes she'd written on the paper in front of her—questions she wanted to ask WOAR. Some personal. Some legal. "What if I need to talk with someone about legal issues?"

"We have a sexual assault court support group for adult survivors of sexual violence. This group is for those who need help dealing with the criminal justice system, to know what will happen during a court hearing and even a trial. Those types of legal questions."

"Like I said, the assault happened several years ago. I don't know whether I should go to the police, whether I can at this point."

"I can explain the basics about the statute of limitations around rape and sexual assault crimes. We don't have attorneys on staff, but I can refer you to other agencies that can provide legal advice. Tell me more about what happened and when."

Emily paused, preparing herself to tell her story again. It wasn't getting any easier. Not yet anyway.

"Take your time," Erika said.

After another moment, Emily began. "The assault took place when I was eighteen years old, and it happened in my senior year in high school, so that was..." She tried to do the math in her head. "About twelve years ago."

"There could be an issue with the statute of limitations," Erika said slowly. "But you should speak with an attorney to be sure. I can give you the name of two agencies we refer people to for legal questions."

The phone line went quiet except for the soft sound of Erika typing on her keyboard.

"One agency is Women's Law Project, and they are based

here in Philadelphia. The other is P-CAR, the Pennsylvania Coalition Against Rape. Their office is in Harrisburg, but they have contacts all over the state. I have an 800 number for them."

Emily wrote down the numbers Erika dictated and thanked her.

"If you have any problems contacting someone at these agencies, don't hesitate to call back. We're here to help support you in any way we can. And please consider coming to one of our groups."

"I'll think about it, and thanks again for all your help." She hung up and stared at the names of the agencies she had written down. Before she made another call, she looked up the two agencies on their websites and learned more about their services. Then she picked up the phone.

After telling the woman who answered at PCAR that she was not in a crisis situation, she asked to speak with an attorney. She was given a name and extension number, then connected to the legal department, but was disappointed when she heard a voicemail recording. She left her name and number. Fingers crossed, she called the number for Women's Law Project and let out an exasperated sigh when she had to leave a message there as well.

"Where the hell is everybody?" she hollered to the empty room. "It's Monday morning. Aren't people supposed to be at work now?" She crossed the living room to her music system, thought about streaming some music, but decided to play a CD instead. She pulled out Pink's CD but stopped when she saw the title: *Hurts 2B Human*. She thought, *Nope, I don't need a reminder about that.* Then she came across an old Wyndham Hill CD called *Sanctuary* that might help calm her down. The first track had just finished when her cellphone rang.

"This is Celia Hunter from the Pennsylvania Coalition

Against Rape," the woman said. "I understand WOAR gave you my number and you're looking for some legal advice around a sexual assault. Why don't you tell me what's going on?"

Emily recounted her conversation with the woman on the WOAR hotline.

"Did you go to the police at the time of the assault?"

"No, I didn't because he threatened me. And I didn't recall the assault until I recently began working with a therapist. Is it too late to go to the police now?"

"How long ago did the assault take place? Was it in Philadelphia?"

"Yes, it was in Philly," she said, then explained the circumstances and how she'd come to remember what had happened and the name of the boy.

"How old was he at the time?"

"Probably about twenty or so. He graduated from the same high school I went to, but he was a few years ahead of me. I'm not exactly sure, but I think the assault took place over Thanksgiving break when I was a senior in high school, because he and my sister, Cara, would've both been home from college."

"And how old were you then?"

"Eighteen"

"How old are you now?"

"Thirty."

"When did you turn thirty?"

"Last November. I'll be thirty-one next month, on November 14."

The line went quiet for a moment. Emily waited and hoped.

"There probably isn't any evidence, correct? Since you didn't recall the attack until recently, you probably didn't keep the clothes you wore that night so there would be none of his DNA on those clothes."

Emily mumbled no and felt her pulse begin to quicken again.

"I'm sorry, Emily, but you can't have him arrested for a rape that happened almost thirteen years ago. The statute of limitations for filing charges for rape or sexual assault in Pennsylvania is twelve years when the victim is an adult."

She let that sink in. "I missed the limit by, like eleven months?"

"I'm afraid so. If you had been a minor—under the age of eighteen—at the time of the assault, you would have had much more time, decades, to file charges. Some states have lifted the statute of limitations around most sexual offenses, including rape and sexual assault, largely because of the scandal involving priests and boys and the Catholic Church, but Pennsylvania is not one of them. There's been a lot of pressure on the Pennsylvania legislature to eliminate the statute of limitations, and there's proposed legislation to that effect, but hearings probably won't be held until next year, so that wouldn't help you."

"That's so unfair," she whispered.

"I know it is. I wish I had better news for you. And the harder part, Emily, as I said, is you have no evidence. So even if you had legal standing, as it would technically be called, your case would be impossible to prove. You would be defined as an unreliable witness because the assault happened so long ago, and there wouldn't be enough proof beyond a reasonable doubt."

"So that's it. I can't have this guy arrested, and I can't take him to court." The energy drained from her body.

"I'm afraid so. I'm sorry I don't have better news. I'm sure this is disappointing."

"Disappointing doesn't begin to say it," she said in a whisper tinged with anger.

"Emily, you aren't the only person this has happened to. I encourage you to look into WOAR's groups. They may help you get some closure you can't get legally."

She thanked the attorney for her time, walked over to the sound system, and punched the button to eject the CD, her desire for soothing music gone. Seriously? She'd missed the deadline by less than a year? How unfair was that? She fell onto the couch and clutched a pillow to her chest. Now what? There had to be something she could do. Her mind churned with ideas, her eyes blinking rapidly as she tried to keep up with her thoughts.

Maybe I can't have him arrested, but I don't have to hide the truth of what he did to me any longer.

Emily sat up abruptly.

Or what he could do to someone else. I don't know a lot about sexual assault, but I do know some guys are repeat offenders. Not only can I speak the truth about what Stan Hester did to me, I can use my voice to help protect other women. Now, how am I going to do that?

Chapter Twenty-One

It wasn't easy to find an empty spot in the parking lot at Flagstone Productions, but Emily drove down one row after another until she saw an opening in the second to the last row. Then she scrunched down behind the steering wheel, low enough not to be obvious, but not too low to create suspicion. At least that was her hope. She held a newspaper up around her chin and peered over it, watching the front doors. Now she had to wait. Several minutes later, she tapped her phone to double-check the time. It was 4:52. People should be leaving soon.

A few minutes later, the man she recognized from his publicity photos as Stan Hester strode out the door, crossed the parking lot to her left, and hopped into a black sports car. The engine revved so loudly a small flock of birds in the bushes on the edge of the lot shot into the air. Her body tensed. She was so close to him. She slid up higher in the driver's seat, pressed the ignition button, and prepared to follow him.

She was so busy watching Stan's car that, at first, she

didn't see Cara walk out and glance around the parking lot as if to refresh her memory about where she'd parked. Emily held her breath and willed herself to disappear. Stan's car started to move, and she wanted to get behind him as quickly as possible, but Cara would surely see her if she pulled out right now. Just then, Cara dropped her head and studied her phone, slowing her pace but still walking toward her car. Cara took more steps deeper into the parking lot and farther away from Emily. Stan pulled out. Emily waited half a beat, then followed him.

Please don't let Cara see me. Please don't let Cara see me. She prayed until Stan left the parking lot and turned onto Columbus Boulevard. Emily fell in behind him. Her fingers drummed on the steering wheel, sometimes matching the rapid beating of her heart. She wanted to control her adrenaline, to stay calm, but that was impossible. Anger and energy raced together through every muscle in her body. She couldn't believe she was about to come face-to-face with her assaulter. She was eager to confront him. And scared.

Several turns and ten minutes later, Stan pulled into a small parking lot near Sixth and Lombard Street. She turned the wheel and pulled into a spot across the street, blocking a fire hydrant, but she didn't care. There wasn't time to find a legal parking spot, and she probably wouldn't be there long. She jumped out of the car and glanced over her shoulder to make sure no cars were coming. Then she dashed across the street.

Stan reached for something on the passenger front seat, then stood, closing the car door. He must have heard her footsteps because he turned in her direction and looked at her with curiosity. Emily forced a smile, as much as she could muster under the circumstances. All the words she'd practiced when she began planning to confront him jammed in her throat. With every step closer to him, the anger bubbled up a little more and begged to be heard. She tried to slow her breath and talk normally so she wouldn't scare him away.

"Hey there. I don't mean to interrupt, but aren't you Stan Hester from *Fix It or Ditch It*? I read about you in the papers. We went to the same high school. Central."

He visibly relaxed, apparently relieved by the connection.

"I don't remember the face," he said, breaking into a wide smile, "but it's been a while since high school, you know. There were a couple of thousand students at Central back then. Were we in the same class?"

"No, I was a few years behind you," she said, straining to keep the nervousness out of her voice. "I'm Emily Archer."

Did he just flinch at the mention of her name?

"Nice to meet you, Emily, but sorry, the face and name aren't familiar." His smile faded and he was on the verge of dismissing her. Dismissing everything he'd done to her.

Her knees buckled as if she'd just been pushed, and she struggled to maintain her balance. Was it worse he didn't remember her, what he'd done? Or was he lying? Pretending she wasn't worth remembering.

Emily didn't know, but all the anger she'd been suppressing like a hiccup she was trying to control shot into her arms and legs. She wanted to pummel him in the chest or kick him in his crotch to inflict pain on him as he had on her. She settled for a sharp jab toward his chest.

He deflected her punch and stepped back. His smile disappeared. A hard look that she'd seen many years ago glared back at her. She wrapped her arms across her chest and rubbed her arms rapidly.

"Are you crazy?" Stan asked.

"No, I'm not," she said through clenched teeth. "And stop pretending you don't remember me. You raped me when you walked me home from a party one night. I trusted you to see me home safely. And you raped me."

He looked around to see if anyone was watching. "I don't know who you are. I didn't do anything to you. You're making this up. And if you don't leave right now, I'm calling the cops." He reached into the back pocket of his khaki slacks and pulled out his cellphone. Then he spun around and walked toward his front door.

"You can't get rid of me that easily," she called out after him. "I saw the recognition in your eyes. You know exactly who I am and what you did to me. I'll make sure you regret assaulting me." Never mind the lawyer said the statute of limitations had expired. Never mind the lawyer told her she had no credible or admissible evidence, that she wouldn't have a case even if time had not legally run out. Never mind all that, she would find a way to make him pay.

Her feet wouldn't move. Her brain was stuck in place as well, back in that moment when he'd attacked her. Emily stared at the door long after Stan had gone inside. She was tempted to walk up the front steps and pound on the door, but he might make good on his threat to call the police. Emily stood in the middle of the entrance to Stan's small parking lot, trying to figure out what to do next.

A horn beeped. She jumped and spun around. The driver of a small sedan, maybe one of the other condo residents, honked again and motioned her to move aside. She gave a quick wave of apology, hurried out of his way, and ran back across the street. Emily climbed into her car, but she was shaking too much to hold onto the steering wheel, so she squeezed her hands together until she calmed down. Stan's face and voice were no longer flashes of a bad memory. They were as real as the car she was sitting in, as real as the ring on her finger.

She took a few more minutes to compose herself. Then the familiar roads and her inner compass led her home, her thoughts distracted from her confrontation with Stan Hester.

She'd stood right in front of him, and told him she knew what he'd done, but instead of feeling better, she was even more frustrated. He'd lied and said he didn't do it. That wasn't good enough. And it wouldn't be the end of it.

Chapter Twenty-Two

"You did what?" Mandy asked, her voice filled with astonishment and disbelief after Emily blurted out how she'd confronted Stan.

"I found out who he was and where he worked. I followed him home. I had to."

It was Mandy's turn to take a deep breath and let it out slowly. "Did you think about how he might react? How he could turn on you? You clearly planned this out ahead of time, but I don't think you considered the possible consequences. Dangerous consequences."

"I needed to look him in the eyes and tell him I knew what he did to me. I wanted to see his reaction."

"I can understand why you would want to do that," Mandy said. "But you put yourself in grave danger." Mandy paused and put her hand on her chest, just below her throat. "It's frightening to think how he could've lashed out at you. What did you hope to accomplish?"

Emily tried to take a step back and consider how her actions looked to Mandy. She was so caught up in her emotions, it was difficult to think clearly. How could she explain the sense of relief she'd been feeling from processing her distressing memories and learning what was behind them? Rape was a horrific attack, but now that she knew that was what had happened to her, she understood the anger that had been growing, festering inside of her for so long. All the triggers about sexual assaults in the news—sexist comments in the conference room, unnerving stares in the bar, or shadows on the street—her reactions to them were all in the range of normal when she framed them around the assault. Slapping Shelby for grabbing her ass was easier to understand now.

But simply knowing what terrible thing had happened to her wasn't enough. She had been driven to find Stan Hester. She'd had enough of looking back. She wanted every step now to move her forward.

"What were you feeling when you crossed the street and met him face-to-face?"

"I was scared and angry in the moment. I think I was shaking so hard I could barely stand up. Then my emotions took over, and I tried to hit him."

Mandy's eyes shot wide open.

Emily shrugged. "That wasn't part of my plan. But I couldn't help it. I wasn't fast enough though, and he blocked my arm and pushed it away."

Mandy covered her mouth with her hand. "He could've hurt you, Emily. You have no way of knowing what he's like, if he's attacked other women. And if you had actually struck him, he could have you arrested."

Emily stroked the top of her legs to comfort herself and warm her suddenly cold hands. "I thought I could control myself. I had no idea how angry I'd get at the sight of him. At standing right in front of him."

"How old did you feel when you confronted him?"

"How old was I in that moment?" she asked. "Well, I was driving so I guess I was an adult."

"Think back to when you called out to him and told him you went to the same high school. How old did you feel then?"

"Like me, an adult. Talking to another adult." She shrugged again, not understanding what Mandy was getting at.

"And when you reached out to strike him, then told him he raped you, how old did you feel then?"

She tried to remember her thoughts and feelings at Stan's condo, but it had happened so fast and was so different from what she had planned. Her eyes darted back to Mandy's, and she shook her head. "I don't know how to answer your questions."

"Let's see if the tappers help."

Emily took the tappers from Mandy and held one of the plastic pods in each hand.

"How high is your level of upset, on a scale of zero to ten, when you think of your confrontation with Stan?"

"It's a ten," she said without hesitation. "It's as high as it was when I remembered so vividly what he did to me."

"When you visualize meeting up with him, what is the negative belief you have about yourself?"

"About me? I don't know. I'm not thinking about me. It's all about him, how he hurt me."

"What emotion are you feeling right now, Emily?"

"Anger. A boatload of anger."

"Let's start there. I'm going to turn the tappers on, and I want you to think about you and Stan in his parking lot and how angry you felt."

Emily took a deep breath, and the vibrations began. She visualized getting out of her car and racing toward Stan. She heard the forced friendliness in her voice as she said hello. Then she saw his face and remembered how he had assaulted her. What he'd done. How he'd hurt her. She was shaking. Was she in the memory still?

"Emily, tell me what's going on."

She heard a voice she didn't recognize and didn't know what to say. She was thinking about the boy who offered to walk her home from the party. He seemed so nice and said he knew her sister. She had just turned eighteen. She'd trusted him, never imagining that someone who seemed so nice could hurt her. Her stomach churned. Her eyes felt like they were blinking really fast, but they hadn't actually opened; she couldn't see anything. Emily heard the voice again and this time she recognized it. Mandy's voice. She was in her therapy session.

"Emily, I'm turning off the tappers. Take a deep breath and tell me what's happening."

She sucked air into her lungs, in and out several times until her racing pulse slowed. "I don't know when I stopped being the adult me yesterday, but I was eighteen when I screamed at him," she said, opening her eyes and bringing Mandy into focus. "I told him I was just a girl and he had hurt me. All I wanted to do was tell him what he did so I could see his reaction, but my younger self was in so much pain, she took over and yelled at him."

"What was his reaction?"

"He said he didn't remember me and had never touched me, but the moment I saw his face, I knew it was him." She practically spit the words out. "And I think he knew. He flinched when I told him he'd raped me, and in that moment, all my doubts washed away."

"How do you feel now that you've confronted him?"

"I don't know. I guess I wasn't thinking as straight as I thought I was or could. When I saw him ..." Her voice trembled, and her eyes filled with tears, tears that streamed down her cheeks. She dropped the tappers on the couch beside her, tugged some tissues out of the box, and covered her face. Blew her nose. Tried to breathe. Just when she thought she had herself under control, her eyes filled again. She sobbed so hard her stomach hurt, and she doubled over in agony trying to push the pain out of her body.

"Emily, talk to me." Mandy's voice drifted to her like a gentle wave washing ashore.

She opened her eyes and looked at the tan-carpeted floor, at her navy shoes, at her knees inches from her face. Using all the energy she could summon, she straightened up but kept her arms wrapped around her body, holding herself, protecting herself.

"I hate him," she whispered. "I hate him for what he did."

"I know," Mandy said softly. "I hate him, too."

"I felt so much hate when I saw him, I wanted to kill him," she said, her voice growing stronger. "I never thought I would ever say I could kill someone. But given the opportunity, I believe I could kill Stan Hester and not feel one ounce of remorse."

Chapter Twenty-Three

Thanksgiving Day 2003

Angela sauntered up the sidewalk, paused at the bottom of the steps in front of her family's home, and pulled the house key out of her pocketbook. A contented smile turned up the corners of her mouth as she walked up the steps, taking her time as if trying to delay moving beyond what had happened a little over an hour ago. She unlocked the door and walked into the enticing aromas of turkey, mashed potatoes, dressing, glazed carrots, and pumpkin pie. Her nose registered the familiar smells, and she remembered it was Thanksgiving, but that was about all that clicked in her foggy brain. She was lost somewhere between walking on clouds and dragging her feet through fast-moving waters, seesawing between happiness and regret. It was too soon to sort out.

"Angela, is that you?" Her mother shouted from the kitchen. "You should've been home a half-hour ago. It's almost time to eat. Help Lacey with the table."

Angela grabbed a quick breath and tried to sound normal. "Be there in a sec. I need to run up to my room." She strode past the living room where her father was stretched out on the recliner watching football and climbed the stairs to the second floor. At the top of the stairs, she veered into the bathroom where she turned on the faucet and splashed cold water on her face. The sudden blast of cold sent shivers through her body, then she straightened up and studied her face in the mirror to see whether she looked any different, to see whether it showed. When they'd parted, Felipe said she looked more beautiful than ever, and he kissed her gently, told her how much he loved her, how happy he was that he was her first.

Her first. She didn't know how she felt about that. She hadn't planned what happened, wasn't sure she was ready for that next step in their relationship. They'd been dating for several weeks, but she'd felt so comfortable with Felipe from the moment they'd met, it seemed like they'd been together longer. And earlier today, at the post-game party, Felipe had been insistent.

"Come on," he had said, leading her into a bedroom on the second floor. They'd been in the same room a couple of weeks ago, but they never did more than kiss a lot and touch a little. Felipe had slid his hand under her blouse that day, lifted her bra, and gently stroked her breast. But she stopped him when he reached down between her legs. He didn't push. Not then. Today was different. Today, he'd been more forceful. He said he wanted to show her how much he loved her.

Angela loved him too, maybe not as much as she thought she might that first day when she met him, maybe not as much as she wanted to in a forever after kind of way. She was seventeen, and while being showered with Felipe's kisses made her feel wanted, loved, she had plans. She wanted to go to college and become a math teacher, then do some traveling before settling down and raising a family. She'd paid attention in health class and knew unprotected sex could lead to pregnancy, but Felipe had a rubber—he'd showed it to her.

Angela looked in the mirror and touched her lips. They looked puffier than usual. Must have been all the kissing.

Felipe was such a good kisser. Her mind drifted off again. She loved the feel of his lips on hers, his body pressing down on hers. Most times she didn't want him to stop, even when she asked him to. Today, when she pushed his hand away from pulling down the zipper on her jeans, he kissed her ear and mumbled about how special it was going to be for them. She tried to tug his hand away again, but he was so much stronger. He forced her hand aside and his fingers reached in. Then she was lost in his kisses. And then ...

"Angela, where are you?"

"Coming," she managed to say, her voice barely loud enough to carry to the first floor.

She splashed more cold water on her face and quickly dried it with a hand towel. She ran into her bedroom, changed her underwear, put on a clean pair of jeans and a sweater, and raced downstairs.

Chapter Twenty-Four

The day after an EMDR session often left Emily tired and confused, her mind shifting between past and present, trying to absorb the latest information her brain had told her about the trauma she'd endured. Her emotions swirled, unable to settle in one place, like a tornado bouncing along the landscape. She was in the middle of sorting through what had happened, what it meant about who she was, who she had become, how this devastating event had shaped her present and, undoubtedly, her future.

She'd always been reluctant to trust other people, and now she had a better understanding of why. She had trusted Stan Hester to walk her home safely, and he hadn't. Not only had he failed to protect her, he'd taken advantage of her. Hurt her. Badly. Except for her parents, her sister Cara, Albert, and Martin, how could she trust anyone else? She wondered if she should work on the trust issue with Mandy but pushed the thought out of her mind just as quickly as it had come up. She was dealing with enough already.

How else had that childhood trauma influenced her character, her emotions, and her development as a young woman?

She sat on the couch, sipping coffee and thinking about her life, growing up, going to college, embarking on her career, and interacting with colleagues. Relationships never came as easily to her as they did to Cara. She'd always envied her sister's ability to interact equally well with familiar colleagues or people she'd just met. Cara was quick to let people in; Emily, not so much. Cara had several female friends she kept in close contact with, juggling time with them along with work and the needs of her family. Emily worked too much to have the time and the emotional capacity for more than a couple of friends and she was fine with that. Years ago, Martin had told her she was harder on her male colleagues than she was on the women. Guess that made sense now, didn't it?

Thinking about her female colleagues at BAM brought a smile to her face. They always looked out for each other and supported one another, especially when issues of discrimination or harassment came up, sometimes at BAM, and other times dealing with clients. Sure, the women were driven to succeed—marketing and advertising was a very competitive field—but when it mattered most, the women came together.

And then she thought about Lacey. What would have happened if Lacey had still been at Central in their senior year when Stan had raped Emily? Stan had threatened to hurt her family, maybe anyone she knew. Would he have hurt Lacey if he'd found out Emily had confided in her? Would Emily have dared put her friend in a precarious position? Probably not, no matter how much she needed to talk with someone. But they did have secrets, Emily and Lacey, didn't they? The biggest one was when Lacey disappeared.

It was just so weird. Somebody must have known what was going on with Lacey's family. What about her mother? Her mother and Mrs. Hargood knew each other pretty well considering they had daughters so close in age and lived nearby. They must have seen each other at school events and in the community. *I wonder what Mom would tell me now about why Lacey's family moved away so suddenly.* Without thinking more about it, she connected to her mother's cellphone. After exchanging a few pleasantries, Emily asked about the Hargood family.

"Remember when I mentioned that I ran into Lacey Hargood at Central High's career day over a week ago?" Emily asked. "She and I didn't get a chance to catch up very much, but I keep wondering why her family left so quickly. Why Lacey never got in touch with me. Do you know?"

Her mother hesitated. "It wasn't an easy time for the Hargoods. Especially for Angela. And her father. Her mother asked me to keep it to myself, but I knew there'd come a time when you'd want to know what had happened. It was too complicated to explain at the time. You were only sixteen. But you deserve to know."

Emily leaned back, closed her eyes, and was pulled into the past by the sound of her mother's voice.

"I guess Angela was just a year or so older than you and Lacey. I remember Mrs. Hargood telling me how difficult it was to have two toddlers so close together in age. I think Lacey and Angela were fourteen months apart. Over a year, but not by much. Anyway, about halfway through her junior year, Angela got pregnant. She tried to hide it, but, you know, you can only hide a pregnancy for so long."

Her mother paused, and it sounded like she took a sip of water or tea. Then she continued.

"Her parents were upset, as you might imagine, but especially Mr. Hargood. Mrs. Hargood was in tears when we ran into each other in the grocery store one day, and she confided in me about her husband's reaction to Angela's pregnancy. He told Angela she'd brought shame on herself and on the family and asked how she expected her parents and her sister to hold their heads up in their community after she'd gotten into such a terrible situation. An embarrassing situation was how Mr. Hargood put it."

Her mother paused again, likely combing her memory for the details about the conversation with Mrs. Hargood.

"That was the last time I saw Mrs. Hargood. Just before we parted at the grocery store, she asked me—begged me—not to tell you and Cara about Angela's pregnancy. The following weekend, a large moving van blocked off part of the street, half a dozen men got out of the vehicles and packed up the house. It took from early in the morning until evening, as I recall, and I never saw any of the family there during that time, or ever again. A few days later, a For Sale sign was posted in the little front yard. And that was the end of the Hargoods in our neighborhood."

Chapter Twenty-Five

Cara surveyed the lunchroom, the chairs scattered around the tables and pushed up against the walls, the counter filled with empty coffee mugs, and the small trash can almost overflowing with used coffee pods. The air in the room was as stuffy as you might expect after ninety minutes of sometimes tense discussion among almost seventy-five employees.

"I thought that went well, don't you?" Cara said quietly as she and Jessica gathered extra copies of the handouts they'd shared during the sexual harassment seminar. She and Cara had the room to themselves. As expected, almost every employee had shown up, and the seriousness of the issue was apparent on their faces.

"I agree. People seemed genuinely interested in the presentation, and I thought the questions were appropriate, sometimes a little too specific, but overall, it went well." Jessica put the documents into a file folder and tapped it lightly on the table to straighten the papers. "If you hadn't told me of the complaints about Stan, I would've tagged him as someone who understands the issues and is respectful of how he treats women."

"Yeah, me, too." Cara winced. "No reference to the current movement intended. When he said he grew up in a family that was generous with giving hugs and where people were used to putting their hands on each other's shoulders or arms when they talked, I had to stop myself from countering that he wasn't working with his family, that he doesn't even know most of the people here yet. But I noticed some of the women nodded like they understood what he'd said."

"Perhaps they did."

"Perhaps." Cara was beginning to wonder if Stan was a bit of a chameleon, adapting his attitude to whatever he thought the current circumstances warranted. "I still sense tension between him and Shelley, sometimes between him and Laura, as well."

"All I can say is keep an eye on them." Jessica walked over to the recycling bin and tossed in her empty water bottle. "It was a smart idea to have this seminar now, not only because we may have an issue within our own walls, but also since there are new allegations about sexual harassment in the workplace almost every week. Media outlets. Law firms. Sports organizations. Hollywood. Well, women have always complained about 'the casting couch' in the film industry, but more women are telling their stories and implicating some of the biggest names in the industry."

"I know. I can't believe some of the things that have been reported." She looked at Jessica and lowered her voice even more. "Have you ever had to deal with such egregious behavior? Has a supervisor or boss ever suggested you accept his sexual overtures or find another job?"

"No, thank goodness. And I don't think I could be in the same room with someone who's been accused of those things." Jessica tucked the file folder under her arm and picked up the last of the pens.

"The MeToo movement has brought to light all kinds of abhorrent behavior and shown how so many women have to deal with those issues."

"Isn't that the truth," Jessica said as the two of them walked into the hallway. "Let me know if you need anything. I think we sent a clear message to our employees and have reduced the likelihood of a problem here."

"Let's hope so."

Cara spent the rest of the afternoon at her desk, working on tedious administrative tasks: approving vacation requests, signing off on expense reports, and viewing video from the latest on-site taping by the *Fix It or Ditch It* crew. By five o'clock she was about to pack up her stuff when she spotted Stan and Laura walking into Laura's cubicle. Cara lowered her chin, returned her gaze to some papers on her desk, and watched them out of the corner of her eye.

A couple of minutes later, Stan had his hand on the small of Laura's back, guiding her away from her desk. Laura's handbag was slung over her shoulder. *They must be leaving together*, Cara thought as the two of them walked out of her sight. She sat still, thinking about them, but especially about him, unable to ignore a nagging feeling in her gut that Stan was not as nice a guy as he pretended to be.

She shook off the uneasy feeling and strolled toward the restroom before heading out. As she walked down the hallway, she glanced out the window and saw Stan and Laura chatting by her car. He was motioning with his hands—directions perhaps—then Laura got into her car. Stan's black sports car passed by hers, and Laura immediately pulled out behind him.

Were they going out for an after-work drink perhaps, maybe dinner? When Stan first started working at Flagstone, Cara encouraged Suzie and Laura to get to know him outside of the office to help them build a comfortable rapport. The sooner everyone on the team felt comfortable, especially the two cohosts, the more smoothly the production sessions were likely to go. It sounded so easy, and it was true—the better everyone got along, the better the on-air result. If it wasn't for Shelley's complaint, and Stan's questionable past dealing with women, Cara wouldn't think twice about him and Laura leaving work together. But a bad feeling nagged at her while watching them.

What I wouldn't give to know where those two are headed. Cara gazed out the window for another moment, lost in thought and worry, then finished her business in the restroom and left work.

Chapter Twenty-Six

The windshield wipers barely kept up with the pouring rain during Cara's drive to work the next morning. Blustery winds blew the rain against her windows with such force, it looked like she was going through a car wash. She was relieved when she reached Flagstone's offices and parked as close to the building as she could. Unlocking her seatbelt, she reached for the umbrella wedged between the door and the driver's seat but couldn't find it. With no other choice, she wriggled out of her raincoat, clasped her bag close to her chest, pulled her raincoat over her head, and stepped out into a big puddle. Great. Wet shoes. Not a good way to begin the workday.

A blast of wind nearly ripped the raincoat from Cara's hands. She ran to the main entrance and tugged on the handle, fighting the wind for control. All the while rain, with a hint of hail, pelted her body. Her raincoat flapped in the wind, failing to provide even an inch of coverage. Great. Wet shoes *and* wet clothes. She pulled the door open, and the wind propelled her into the lobby, where she stopped to catch her breath and shake off the water.

"Nice day for ducks, isn't it?" The receptionist gave her a bright smile.

"I don't think ducks like this kind of weather either," Cara said, shaking her raincoat one more time. She punched the code into the keypad next to the employee entrance, grateful to be inside. Her shoes squished all the way to her office. She hung her coat on the back of the door and fussed with her hair in front of the wall mirror. Not much she could do with her wet hair now. She sat at her desk, kicked off her shoes, and spotted the blinking light on her phone console. As she waited for the first message to play, she glanced out her window into the room of cubicles and was surprised to see that Laura, usually among the earliest to arrive at work, was not in yet. She learned why in the third message.

"I'm not going to make it into work today. I'm sick. I'll spare you the details. I'll check my email when I can. Just so you know, there's nothing urgent on the *Fix It* calendar today."

Laura must really be ill, she thought. *I can't even remember the last time she called in sick.*

After listening to the rest of her messages, Cara booted up her computer and was working on an email to the *Fix It* staff, alerting them that Laura would not be in, when Stan hurried by without so much as a glance toward Laura's desk or Cara's office. She thought about the two of them leaving work together the day before, and her mind shifted into overdrive. It's not that she would begrudge Laura a day off if she'd had a late night; Laura regularly worked long hours and never complained. But she couldn't get the image of Laura and Stan chatting at her car, then Laura following Stan's sports car out of the parking lot. *I'm not nosy*, she thought, *just curious. And protective*. Cara stood and left her office.

"Good morning, Stan." She issued her greeting through the narrow opening of his door, then knocked, pushed it wider, and said hello again. His head spun in her direction, then he quickly looked away, set his briefcase on the shelf behind his desk, took some papers out, and snapped it shut.

She walked in and sat in a chair across from his desk.

"I was about to send an email to the crew, but I spotted you coming in just now and wanted to let you know Laura won't be in today." She waited for his reaction.

"Okay," he said, glancing at her over his shoulder. "I was going to spend most of the day reviewing video and working on some scripts. We don't have tapings the next couple of days, so we have a light schedule."

"So she said."

"You spoke with her?" His head jerked toward her, but his eyes didn't quite meet hers.

She didn't want to jump to conclusions, but Stan was jittery, like he'd had too much coffee, or maybe not enough sleep. "No, she left me a voicemail this morning."

"Oh." Stan turned around and sat down. That's when Cara saw red scratches on the left side of his face.

"Ouch. That looks a little painful. Where'd you get those scratches?"

His fingers stroked his cheek. "I was jogging on one of the wooded trails in Fairmount Park and didn't see a branch until it caught me in the face."

"Lousy morning for a jog."

"I went yesterday after work." His tone was curt. His eyes glanced at his computer, probably hinting he had better things to do.

"I guess it's a good thing you don't need to be on camera today, although a good foundation might conceal those. At the very least, makeup would minimize them." She stared at the red streaks on his cheek for a little longer, then met his gaze as he took his eyes off the screen and glanced over at her. There was another moment of uncomfortable silence.

"Thanks for letting me know about Laura," Stan said. "Is there anything else you need from me?"

Well, yes there was. She wanted Stan to tell her what happened in Jacksonville and Tampa. Wanted to know if the women at Flagstone were in any danger. But that information was not within her grasp at the moment.

"No, nothing else. For now." She left without another word and thought about how unlikely it would have been for Stan to go jogging after drinks or dinner with Laura. A dozen questions darted through her mind as she walked back to her office, two of them crying out for answers: Did a tree branch cause Stan's scratches? And is Laura really sick?

Chapter Twenty-Seven

Cara was even more surprised and a little concerned when Laura called in sick again on Friday. Her immediate reaction was to call the producer, but she waited to see if Laura checked in with her during the day. After lunch, when she still hadn't heard anything, she picked up the phone.

"I'm not checking up on you, Laura," she said when Laura answered. "I wanted to see how you're doing today. Must be some kind of virus that's still got you under the weather."

"It sure is. I still don't have much of an appetite."

"Would you like me to bring you some chicken soup from Stein's Deli? It's practically guaranteed to cure whatever ails you."

"Oh, no, don't," Laura said, a little too quickly. "Don't trouble yourself."

"Can I get you anything else then?"

"No, thanks."

Laura sounded defensive, abrupt, which was unlike her. Then again, someone who had been sick for a couple of days was bound to sound different. Cara had to remind herself not to read too much into anything or try so hard to find problems. If any existed, they'd turn up.

"If you're sure then ..."

"Really, I am. I'm better than yesterday, but since it's Friday and it was going to be an easy day at work, I stayed home again so I could get over this. Whatever it is."

Cara wished her well and hung up. She couldn't shake the feeling that something wasn't right, but she didn't know how to figure it out. She sat at her desk, lost in thought when Stan tapped on the door.

"I'm heading home a little early this afternoon if you don't mind."

Stan clasped his briefcase in one hand and jingled his car keys in the other, obviously on his way out whether or not she approved.

"Okay. Thanks for letting me know." Her eyes drifted to the scratches on his cheek. "Have a good weekend and try to avoid branches on your next run." She held her smile until he walked away, then the muscles in her face tensed.

She wanted to talk with someone about her nagging feeling that things weren't right with Stan and Laura. She'd seen the two of them leave work, in separate cars, but apparently headed somewhere together. The next day, Laura called in sick; Stan had scratches on his face. Laura called in sick a second day; Stan was skittish. Albert would tell her those weren't enough facts to build a case and wouldn't hold up in court. But he was a lawyer. What would Jessica in HR say? Cara and Jessica had already talked about the importance of protecting the women who work at Flagstone. Did what was going on—what might have gone on between Laura and Stan —rise to the level of alerting Jessica?

Thank goodness it was the end of the workweek. Weekend video shoots were rare, and there weren't any on *Fix It*'s video production calendar. She could bounce ideas off Albert and come up with a plan, then meet with Jessica first thing Monday. She didn't have enough information to do more. That didn't mean she could put it out of her mind. Cara was still stewing about the possible Laura—Stan situation a few minutes later when her cellphone pinged.

Hi! We still on for dinner tomorrow?

At least Emily was healthy again. Maybe she and Laura had the same stomach virus. Her sister never rescheduled their lunch date, so they hadn't seen each other in weeks. It had been even longer since Emily visited with the children.

Yep. Drinks at 5:30?

Sounds great. What can I bring?

Bottle of white wine?

Can do. Plus I have a couple of things for the kids

You spoil them

That's what aunts are for 😊 See you tomorrow

Cara leaned back in her chair and thought about their lack of contact over the past several weeks. She had no idea what was going on in Emily's life except for what she said about taking a long-overdue break from work. But that was more than two weeks ago, wasn't it? Emily must be back at work now. She was the type who got antsy on a one-week vacation, never mind two, and Cara couldn't imagine Emily taking off more time than that. She'd find out what her sister had been up to soon enough.

She watched a few other people carrying handbags and computer bags head for the exit and decided she could take an early Friday as well. It would be nice to get a head start on traffic and the weekend. The parking lot was emptying fast. She slid into the driver's seat and joined the others heading out of the lot. As soon as she turned right onto Columbus Boulevard, a red light appeared on the dashboard, along with the gas pump icon. Uh oh. She had meant to stop for gas on the way to work, but it had slipped her mind. While she didn't live far, she hated to leave the tank empty in case of an emergency, like taking one of the kids to urgent care in the middle of the night. Any other time, Cara might have gone to the Wawa gas station a block from work, but it was on the other side of the busy roadway, and making back-to-back U-turns during rush hour was difficult and dangerous.

She continued north toward Spring Garden for a couple of miles, took a left then a quick right, and pulled into a gas station she rarely used because it had the most expensive gas around. *Beggars can't be choosers*, she thought. *I'll take any gas right now.*

About half of the pumps were taken, so she quickly aimed her car at an available pump. She pulled up alongside, dug her wallet out of her handbag, and slid the credit card out of its slot. When she glanced up, she saw a familiar car two pumps over. The person got out and turned in her direction. She forgot about gas for the moment, left her car, and approached her.

"Laura?" She tilted her head to see better.

Laura dropped her wallet as she spun around. "Cara. Oh, hi. I needed some, um, food, and stuff." She bent down, retrieved her wallet, and brushed the leather clean. "I thought I might as well gas up at the same time."

Laura half-turned away from Cara as she stood, but not before Cara saw the swelling around the producer's right eye and the bruise on her cheekbone.

"Laura, what happened? Where did those bruises come from?"

"Oh, these?" She touched her cheek. "I got up from the couch too quickly and lost my balance yesterday, probably because I was dehydrated. I fell against the coffee table."

She wanted to get a closer look, but Laura maneuvered to keep some distance between them.

"Did you have a doctor look at it?"

"No, it's not that bad. I'm fine."

But Laura wasn't fine. A single tear fell onto her cheek, and it was all Cara could do to curb her mother's instinct to reach out. Something was wrong. She took another step toward her. Laura took another step back.

Then Laura swiped her credit card again. "Damn, it won't take my card. I need to go inside and pay cash."

Cara grabbed Laura's arm. "Laura, talk to me. Tell me what really happened."

Laura's eyes pleaded with her. "I'm fine. Please. Let it go."

"I don't want to pull the boss card on you, but you give me no choice," Cara said. "You and Stan both work on *Fix It*. I'm the executive producer. I can't ignore what I see, and I need to know if there's a problem."

"Things aren't always what they seem, Cara. I told you, I fell. Now, please let it be." Laura turned and rushed into the store.

Cara would have bet a month's salary those bruises were not caused by a fall. She walked back to her car and finished filling the tank, her mind spinning with the implications of those bruises on Laura's face. When she pulled away from the pumps, Laura still hadn't returned to her vehicle.

The short drive home didn't give her nearly enough time to sort out her thoughts. Bruises on Laura's face and neck, and scratches on Stan's face added up to a conclusion she couldn't ignore. If it had been rough sex, would Laura be hiding from Cara, and would she be so upset? It was no longer a matter of Cara butting into someone else's business. It was her duty as a member of senior management at Flagstone to find out what had happened between two people who worked for her.

Chapter Twenty-Eight

"Aunt Emily!" Four-year-old Adam threw his body into hers as she closed the front door. Luckily, she'd been fast enough to set the bag with the wine and gifts on the hallway table the minute she'd stepped into the foyer. Her arms were free to pick him up and she kissed his forehead before he could object.

"Hey, little guy. How's my favorite nephew?"

"Mommy says you're having dinner with us."

"Yes, I am." She kissed him again and set him down, then turned to hug her sister.

"Gosh, it's so good to see you. It's been ages."

"Yes, it has." Cara kissed her cheek and smothered her in a hug. "Come on into the kitchen. Albert is feeding Kelsey an early dinner."

The toddler squealed and spit out the teaspoon of squash Albert had just put into her mouth. She sprayed a few more pieces of food on her father's face and pumped her little arms in happiness, like a golfer who'd just shot a hole-in-one.

"Can I take over feeding Kelsey for you?" Emily asked as Albert wiped his face.

"You sure can." He gave her a quick kiss and handed her the dish of squash and peas, along with a pink plastic spoon.

The three of them chatted while Emily cooed and fed the baby. Cara and Albert finished preparing dinner, and they all moved into the dining room, including Kelsey, who was given a secure cup of apple juice while the adults and Adam ate dinner.

Their conversation was light and mostly about the children. After dinner, Adam and Kelsey tore open the packages Emily had brought. Adam pushed his new train around the dining room floor while saying, "toot, toot," and Kelsey flipped through the pages of her new book and pointed at the pictures. Then Cara put both children to bed, and the adults went into the living room.

"I'm going to let you two have some long-overdue time for sister-talk and besides, I'm due in court tomorrow on a complicated antitrust case, and I need to review my motion. Good to see you, Emily," Albert said, blowing a kiss to the two of them as he left the room.

Emily thought about lawyers and motions and things she wanted to do in court but couldn't. Then she thought about what she wanted to tell Cara and mentally crossed her fingers. She dropped onto one end of the couch. Cara sat at the other.

"It's unusual for you to take so much time away from work," Cara said. "Were you off on some great adventure you didn't tell us about?"

"I've been having an adventure of some kind, that's for sure." Emily sipped her wine and steadied her nerves.

First, she told Cara about slapping the vice president of sales for Clifton Pharmaceuticals and how Chris had forced her to take a couple of weeks off.

Cara's eyes grew wide, and she opened her mouth to speak, but Emily cut her off.

"I need to tell you a few more things," Emily continued.

"After that, you can ask all the questions you want." She explained how Martin convinced her to see his therapist to deal with what had happened, and how this person was an expert in helping people with trauma. Then she got to the hard stuff. "I'm going to need more wine for this," she said, picking up the bottle on the coffee table. "Can I top off your glass?"

"I'm fine," Cara said. "You're scaring me, Em. What's going on?"

Emily took a healthy gulp of wine, followed by a deep breath. "This EMDR therapy I've told you about is especially helpful for people dealing with PTSD, from big physical or psychological traumas like those suffered by our war vets, to what EMDR therapists call little traumas that happen more frequently but can lead to issues like neurosis. EMDR can clear out the painful memories of the trauma. Because the process enables people to tap into their memories, it sometimes uncovers trauma a person has suppressed or doesn't remember."

"Like when people don't remember what happened during a car accident?" Cara asked, her eyebrows scrunched together. "They don't black out, but their brain sort of blocks that memory from their consciousness. Isn't that right? Is it something like that?"

"Close enough," Emily said, nodding. "You might start working on one trauma with EMDR that's disturbing but not a big deal, then suddenly a memory comes up you weren't aware of before, and it turns out that one *was* a big deal. At least it was for me."

"That sounds weird. A memory, but you don't actually remember it?" Cara leaned toward her and rested her hand on the couch between them. "What's this about?"

The look on Cara's face told Emily she was stringing this out too long. Cara was scared and anxious, like Emily would have been if their roles had been reversed. The air had gone out of the room, and she had to tell Cara what had happened so they both could breathe again.

"There's no easy way to say this," Emily whispered, eyes downcast. "I was raped when I was eighteen."

Cara gasped and almost dropped her glass. Her eyes never left Emily's face.

She gave Cara time to absorb the news.

"Emily, no. Why didn't you tell me?" Cara asked after she'd found her voice.

"I couldn't tell you at the time, not after he threatened me to keep quiet or he'd hurt you. I couldn't let him hurt you, too, so I kept my mouth shut and pushed the memory as far away as I could. So far away, I buried it deep in my subconscious and my brain didn't let me remember it." Her eyes filled with tears as she watched the pain in Cara's eyes spread to the rest of her face.

"When did this happen? You said you were eighteen? I must have been away at college."

"Actually, you were home for Thanksgiving break. I was coming home from a party. The boy who walked me home assaulted me. Then when it was over, he lit a cigarette and walked me the rest of the way home like it was nothing unusual. Well, maybe it wasn't for him, but it sure was for me." She brushed her tears away with the cuff of her blouse.

"Oh, my God. I'm so sorry. I never even suspected something so bad had happened to you." Cara set her glass on the table, got up, and pulled Emily to her feet. "I wish I could've helped you."

The two of them clutched each other tight and cried until they were drained of tears. After another minute huddled together, Cara took Emily's face in her hands and stroked her hair. Then came the question Emily knew Cara would get around to at some point. Her answer would be the second bombshell of the evening, and she wasn't looking forward to what that information would mean for her sister.

"Who was the boy who raped you? Who did this to you? Did I know him?"

Emily's eyes filled with fresh tears, and she nodded at Cara. "He also graduated from Central. A year ahead of you." She paused, but there was no way to soften this news either. "It was Stan Hester."

"Are you serious?" Cara froze, her words and movements brought to a standstill. She stared at Emily. "Are you positive? I mean, how can you be so sure if you buried the memory so deep for so long?"

"I see his face in my nightmares," she whispered. "I know it was him."

"Of course. I'm sorry. I don't mean to doubt you, it's just, it's a lot to take in." Cara dropped her hands and stroked Emily's shoulders. "Stan Hester. And what a coincidence he's the guy I hired recently."

"Yep, it's eerily weird. But you know what some people say: there are no real coincidences in life. Things happen for a reason. Flagstone brought Stan Hester back to Philadelphia and seeing his publicity photo in the press release, then finding his high school photo, confirmed that he's the guy who raped me."

"Jeez, and I'm the one who brought this awful memory back to you, brought this monster back to our city. We'll have him arrested for rape."

"Oh, I wish we could, but we can't." Emily slumped back onto the couch. "I talked to an attorney at the Pennsylvania Coalition Against Rape, and she told me the statute of limitations has expired. Plus, I have no physical proof it was Stan who raped me. Or, as the lawyer put it, insufficient proof. The police would never arrest him. They wouldn't have enough evidence for a jury to convict him." Emily waved her hand in the air. "It's that same old problem: He said, she said. There's nothing I can do."

"Oh, there's something we can do," Cara said, dropping onto the couch next to Emily and taking her hand. "I'm not sure what that is yet since we can't legally go after him for raping you, but we are going to make the bastard pay. He'll rue the day he got on the wrong side of the Archer sisters. I promise you that."

Chapter Twenty-Nine

Emily lifted the gun off of the counter, felt the weight of it in her hands, and the power of the weapon in her heart. She turned it over a few times, her fingers gliding over the cold gray barrel, then the textured plastic of the grip.

"It's heavier than I thought it would be," she told the man behind the U-shaped counter. Henry, according to the rectangular name tag on his navy polo shirt.

"Yep, a lot of women say that. It's heavy but very balanced. And you want balance because you don't want to tire your muscles if you have to keep lifting it up."

"I can't imagine holding this up for a long time, but I guess I shouldn't need to."

"The Glock 19 is about the biggest concealable pistol made. I can show you some revolvers that are smaller, but you'd probably have to order online if you want one of those cute little pistols."

"I'm not looking for cute," she said, her eyes never drifting from the gun in her hands. "I want a gun that looks like a threat, not something Dolly Parton might twirl on her finger in a bar scene in some music video or movie."

"You said you want protection. This here Glock 19 is an excellent choice. It's like the Glock 17, which is very popular, only smaller. Here, let me show you how to fit it in your hand."

Henry positioned the gun in her palm. "Take hold of it with your right hand. It should fit nice and tight, like this." He gently folded her fingers over the grip, then let go but continued his instructions. "Slide your hand up all the way. When you bring it up, this thumb is parallel to the slide. Now bring up your other hand."

She kept her eyes on her hands and followed his instructions closely. "Like this?"

"That's right. This thumb goes on top of that thumb, and you're going to wrap these fingers around there. Now, you're going to push forward with this hand." He motioned to her right hand. "Pull back with your left hand, and that basically locks the firearm into your hand. So it's a nice solid grip, and it should feel and move as one item."

"Like an extension of my arm," she said.

Henry nodded. "How does it feel?"

"It's a good fit," she said. The gun settled into her hand like a glove.

"When you look down the barrel, you should see a red dot. That dot is dead on where the bullet will hit the target."

She pointed the gun toward the back wall. Her finger rubbed the trigger, her mind thinking about Stan Hester. What would it be like to point this at him and pull the trigger? An awareness of power strengthened her arms and her sense of purpose.

"I'm sorry," she said, turning her attention back to Henry, aware that he'd just spoken. "What did you say? I was focused on keeping my arms straight and looking at the red dot."

"I said, if you do buy a gun, you should take a class on gun safety and maintenance, and you also need to spend time practicing at the range. We have a small range for people to test-fire a gun before they buy it, but you'd need to go to one of the bigger ranges for practice and classes, like the one a lot of law enforcement people and others use right off of Spring Garden Street downtown."

She nodded, already on to her next question. "How many bullets does the Glock 19 hold?"

"The magazine holds fifteen bullets, plus one in the chamber. Just keep in mind, while Glocks incorporate three safety mechanisms, there's no standard switch. There's a tab on the trigger to prevent accidental discharge, but it can be easily disabled. So the weapon should be kept in a holster until you're ready to fire a round."

Emily fought the urge to put the gun back down on the counter even though she knew there was no bullet in the chamber. It suddenly felt more dangerous than she had imagined it would be. And how would she carry it? Would she keep a gun in her messenger bag? Would she put it in a holster in her bag? Wouldn't that be cumbersome, make it difficult to grab it in a hurry? It's not like she planned on needing a gun in a hurry.

"How much does this one cost?"

"The Glock alone costs about $500 or more. One with sights will cost ya close to a grand. But it's better to buy it that way than buy the sights separately because sights aren't cheap. You get a break buying them together."

"I think I'd lean toward the package deal. But I'm not ready to buy yet. You talked about .38 revolvers a little bit ago. Do you have any of those I can look at?"

"Sure." Henry took the Glock out of her hand, put it into the glass case, and locked it. Then he walked over to the other side of the counter and pointed at another group of handguns. "The Glock is a nine-millimeter. Revolvers don't come in nines. They have different sizes, from the .38s to the .44s. and

.357, with others in between, many of them less common. But for your purposes, all you need to think about is the .38."

Her brain tried to grasp what all the numbers meant as Henry unlocked the case and pulled out one of the guns. "This here's a Smith & Wesson .38 Special called the Lady Smith."

"It's much lighter than the Glock," she said, turning it over in her hands, wrapping her fingers around the grip, and sliding her index finger onto the trigger, the way he'd showed her with the Glock. "The barrel is shorter too, isn't it?"

"Yep, this one's got a two-and-a-half-inch barrel. The Glock has a three-and-a-half-inch. The longer the barrel, the farther the distance and the more accurate you are. Another big difference is the number of rounds it holds. He spun the empty cylinder. "These revolvers hold six bullets."

"Wow, six compared to fifteen."

"But for personal safety, six bullets oughta be enough."

"I would hope," Emily said, remembering she had told Henry she was shopping for a gun to protect herself. "Does this have a safety feature?"

"The .38 Special would be loaded all the time, but it's not going to go off because you have to pull the trigger. You can lock it, but if you don't carry that key to unlock it, you've just created a paperweight. And one other thing to think about ..." He took the revolver from her. "See here. This has a lacquered wooden grip. Feel it." He handed it back to her and watched.

"It feels so smooth," she said, looking at him and raising her eyebrows. "Maybe a little too smooth?"

"Exactly. If somebody's at your door, and you're nervous, what do your hands do? They sweat. So, you have lacquered wood and sweaty hands. They don't mix. Now, you can get all different kinds of grips, sandpaper grips, composite grips. You can get different colors, like this one in light green. You can make it as pretty or scary as you want."

"Scary is good."

"This one also runs about five hundred bucks, and Smith & Wesson makes other small revolvers so you can find exactly what you want." He looked up from the glass case. "Now, what else can I tell you about these guns?"

"You've given me a lot of good information," she said. "I really appreciate it. You said you have a small range. Can I try shooting each of the guns?"

Henry glanced around. It was a quiet Monday morning. He locked the Lady Smith back in the case. "I'll be right back." He walked over to a man sitting behind a desk on the other side of the shop and pointed at Emily. The other man nodded, then Henry disappeared through a door back in the corner she hadn't noticed before.

A few minutes later, Henry walked back through the door and stopped to take the Glock 19 out of the cabinet. He put it in a black leather box and closed it. Next, he took the Lady Smith out of the cabinet and put that in another black leather case. He came around to the other side of the counter and led her to a door with the words, FIRING RANGE. Another key opened the door to stairs leading to a lower level.

Emily caught her breath. This was something she never imagined herself doing. But then again, she was a different person now than she'd been just a couple of weeks ago. A lot had changed. Her past had changed. So had she.

Henry set up a target about six feet from where Emily stood in a small, partitioned space. There were a couple other booths, but no other targets hanging from the ceiling, and she didn't hear any gunfire, so she suspected it was just the two of them.

Henry returned to her side, retrieved the Glock, and loaded the magazine. "Remember how I told you to hold it? Keep it pointed at the floor until you're ready to aim at the target."

She swallowed the lump in her throat and nodded, then wordlessly put on the headphones he handed to her. There was hardly room for a stick of gum between them as he monitored her every move. She raised the gun, adjusted her grip, and looked at the black-on-white target, the shape of a man's body from his head to about his waist. Taking a deep breath to steady herself, she aimed at the target and pulled the trigger. Henry had warned her about the kickback, but it still caught her by surprise, her arms rising in the air after the first shot, and her body tottering back a step or two. Even with the headphones on, the noise shocked her. Then she drew in another deep breath, planted her feet, steadied her grip, and pulled the trigger, better able to control the recoil. She pulled the trigger again and again. When she had emptied the magazine, she laid the Glock down on its side and stepped back.

She stared at the holes in the target while Henry returned the Glock to its box, pulled out the Lady Smith, and loaded six rounds into the cylinder.

"Ready?" he asked. When she gave a curt nod, he placed the Lady Smith on the counter on its side and motioned for her to pick it up.

It was so much smaller and lighter it almost didn't feel like a real gun after firing the Glock. She wrapped her fingers around the revolver, lifted it up, and took aim at the target. Bang. Bang. Bang. Bang. Bang. Bang. She'd taken archery while in college and was an excellent shot, but the placement of the holes in the target still surprised her. Many of them had struck the chest close to where she'd wanted the bullets to go; a couple put a hole in the head. She felt proud. Then scared. Then nauseous. A few minutes later she hurried out of the gun shop, knowing all she needed to know about what kind of gun to buy and how to accurately shoot it. Shooting targets was easy. The question still lingering in her mind was whether she could point the gun at Stan Hester and pull the trigger.

Chapter Thirty

M onday mornings were never easy for Cara, leaving her kids at the neighborhood childcare center and going to work, but this Monday was especially daunting.

She picked up the lip gloss and aimed for her mouth, but she couldn't see her lips clearly because her eyes weren't focusing. Her reflection was distorted in a wavy pattern, like she was looking at herself through one of the special effect filters the video editors used. How on earth was she was going to look Stan in the face and hide the hatred she felt toward him for what he did to Emily? People often told her she wasn't good at hiding her feelings, but she'd better figure out how to do that quickly because there was a lot at stake. And it wasn't just knowing how Stan had assaulted Emily. She'd be in the same room with him and Laura, and the two of them would be together for the first time since their—what should she call it —their evening together? Given what she suspected, it was going to be awkward. How was she going to see Laura and her bruises without pressuring her again to tell her what had happened?

Cara grabbed the tube of lip gloss again and leaned on the

counter to steady herself. She'd figure it out; she had to. She finished applying her makeup, drove to work, and settled into her usual chair in the conference room.

A few minutes later, Laura walked into the production meeting with a purposeful stride and her head held high. Instead of her blonde, shoulder-length hair swept back from her face or pulled into a high ponytail as it often was, it was parted on the side and fell across her face.

"I like what you did with your hair today," Cara said. "It's very flattering."

"Thanks," Laura said. "I was ready for a change."

Laura took the chair beside her at the long conference table, and other members of the *Fix It* team wandered in. Stan was the last to enter, barely glancing at her or Laura, hurrying in and taking the seat farthest away from them.

"I don't have any high-level comments from management about *Fix It* or any other Flagstone news to share with you this morning," Cara said. "Laura, why don't you get right to the updates on the taping and editing schedules."

Laura briefed the team without looking up and making eye contact with anyone. She lost her train of thought a couple of times, which was unusual for her. Stan feigned interest and doodled on his notepad as Laura's flat voice droned on. Someone's ceramic coffee mug hit the table with a loud clunk and Laura jumped. Stan stopped scribbling and grasped his pen tightly between his thumb and forefinger, his eyes on Laura.

"Did everyone sleep okay last night or were you all partying over the weekend?" one of the camera operators asked, breaking another uncomfortable silence. "This is the least energetic meeting we've ever had."

"I get your point, Randy," Cara said, looking around the table. "If no one has anything else to discuss, let's wrap up."

No one needed further encouragement.

"Laura," Cara said as the producer stood to leave. "Got a minute?"

Laura sat back down reluctantly but didn't look at her. Cara closed the door after the last person hurried out.

Cara swiveled her chair to face the producer directly. "Something is obviously wrong. I'm your supervisor, and I can't ignore it, so I need to know what happened with you and Stan."

"I appreciate your concern, and you're right, something did happen, but please don't make this worse than it already is. I just want to forget it and move on."

"I can do that more easily if I was sure what happened wasn't inappropriate, that Stan didn't cause your bruises."

The only sound in the room was a low buzz from the overhead fluorescent lights. It was one of Flagstone's smallest conference rooms in the middle of the building with no windows and few opportunities for distractions. Laura tried to wait her out and swallowed hard a few times. When she began speaking, she could not meet Cara's eyes.

"Stan and I went out for drinks last Wednesday after work. After the second drink, I told him I was ready to go home. I said I needed to eat, so he asked if I wanted to go out to dinner, but I told him I was exhausted and just wanted to go home and make some pasta." Laura closed her eyes. "I should've been firmer with him, but he said he'd taken cooking classes and practically begged me to let him make dinner. It sounded good. I mean, how often does a man make dinner for you?"

The air of confidence Laura had displayed when she walked into the room was gone; she slumped in her chair, talking to the table or her hands, anywhere but to Cara.

"We had most of a bottle of wine with dinner, and I guess my defenses were down. He began kissing me. I immediately pushed him away. He laughed and said I was just playing hard to get." Laura leaned forward, placed her hands on the table, and spread her fingers, then made sweeping motions with her hands on the tabletop.

"He's so strong. He had my blouse off before I knew it, even though I struggled and told him it wasn't what I wanted. He had this steely and faraway look in his eyes. I wondered if he could even hear me, like maybe he was in a world of his own." And then the tears came, just a trickle at first until Laura was weeping and cupping her head in her hands.

Cara bit her lip and tried to brush aside her own emotions, but it was impossible to sit next to Laura and not feel her pain. A few tears slipped from her eyes and down her cheeks.

"I'm angry for putting myself in that position, for not using good judgment. I keep beating myself over the head for not being firmer with him earlier in the evening. I should've gone home alone, and I'm smart enough to know that. So why didn't I?"

"Do *not* blame yourself," Cara said. "If you told him you didn't want to have sex, he should've respected your wishes."

"But did I lead him on?"

"By inviting him into your home and letting him make dinner? No, you absolutely did not. Men and women have dinner together all the time, even dinner dates, which I know this wasn't, and they don't end in sex. Especially forced sex."

"It wasn't even a date. I just saw it as two colleagues going out for drinks, then having dinner because we were hungry."

"And he saw it as something different. Very different. An opportunity to get something he wanted. That doesn't mean you led him on. Do you hear me?" Cara leaned closer and tilted her head down so the producer could meet her eyes.

Laura nodded, but her tears didn't stop. Cara grabbed a handful of tissues from the box on the table and handed them to Laura.

"Do you want to talk with HR?"

"Absolutely not. I don't want anyone else to know what happened."

"But you have to work with him every day. How is that going to go? If today's meeting is any indication, there's a lot of tension between you two."

"It's just seeing him for the first time since that night." Laura sniffed and wiped her eyes, finally looking at Cara.

"He called last Thursday after I didn't come to work and left a message. His voice was soft and tender, asking me if I was okay. Thanking me for dinner," Laura said, shaking her head back and forth. "Then he said he hoped I enjoyed our time together. I listened to the message and thought, 'Is this guy for real?'" Laura's voice went up a few octaves, and she shuddered. "Did he think that was a date? I couldn't delete the message fast enough."

Cara shook her head in disbelief. "Listen, I could have someone else oversee *Fix It*'s production for a week or so," she said. "Perhaps it would help to have a buffer between the two of you."

"No, Cara. It's my show." Laura sat up straighter in her chair. Her voice was stronger. "I'm not going to let what happened interfere with my job. I'll be fine. I've always been good at compartmentalizing whatever's going on in my life. I can handle working with him."

They sat in silence for a moment longer.

Cara pressed her hands together and tried not to think about what Stan did to Emily more than a decade ago. She was furious over what Stan had done to her sister and angry at him for assaulting Laura. If Laura didn't want to talk to HR, she probably wouldn't go to the police. Was Cara wrong to pressure her to report what had happened? She set aside her personal feelings and stepped into her management role.

"I hear you, Laura, and now you need to hear me. What Stan did wasn't just wrong, it was a sexual assault. Rape.

That's a crime. I know it won't be easy to report this to HR or the police, but you must. If you don't, he could hurt someone else."

Laura tensed. Her lips were pressed together and clamped down between her teeth. The tears were gone, and the look in her eyes was firm and resolute.

"I'm going to give you time today to think about your next steps," Cara said. "But understand this: you're not making a decision just about you. You're making a decision that could affect every woman in this building. I have a decision to make, as well. Whether or not you want to go to HR, I have to."

Later that afternoon, Laura and Stan walked past her office, deep in conversation. Their voices were low. Laura clutched her clipboard to her chest and clenched her jaw. It didn't look to Cara like Laura was successfully compartmentalizing now. A few minutes later, Stan rushed past in the other direction, briefcase in hand. *Now what?*

Cara found Laura in the women's restroom, standing in front of a sink, rubbing off splotches of black mascara below her puffy red eyes.

"What's going on?" Cara asked.

Laura looked at her in the mirror. "Can you believe the guy? He said he knew you and I talked this morning after the meeting, and he asked if everything was okay. I mean, really, he asked if everything was okay. I told him no, it wasn't, that he needed to back off." She sniffed and wiped away another tear. "He got angry when I told him to leave me alone. '*Don't you go stirring up any trouble,*' he said. He got this hard look in his eyes, and it scared me."

The tears started flowing again and Laura threw the tissue

she'd been using into the trash can. "Look at me," Laura challenged her. "I'm a mess."

"Don't worry about how you look or feel ashamed because you're crying. You've had a horrific experience. You're the victim of an assault, a violent crime."

Laura grabbed another paper towel and blew her nose. "I'm not a big crier, you know. Stoic Laura. Stiff upper lip. That's me."

Laura didn't acknowledge her comment about being a victim of a crime. Cara wasn't sure why, but she decided not to push it. "That's you facing a production problem with the video crew in the field; that's you when a lightning strike blows out the power and shuts down the edit system, destroying hours of work. This is not one of those situations. You need to cry. You have to let it out."

"You sound like someone who knows about these things."

Cara hesitated. "Between you and me, in total confidence?"

Laura faced her and nodded, eyes wide with curiosity.

"You've met my sister, Emily, right?"

"Yes, I have. She's in advertising or something, right?"

Cara nodded. "Emily was assaulted once, and she and I recently talked about it, so I have a sense of what you're going through. Emily told me she struggled with some of the same emotions you're having, including feeling like she did something wrong, that somehow the assault was her fault."

She held Laura's eyes and weighed her next words carefully, knowing she was about to step into precarious territory. "Maybe it would help to talk to someone else who's been through the same thing. I mean, you could go to a support group for victims of sexual assault, and maybe that would help, but perhaps, for a first step, you might want to talk with someone you know. Even a little. Like Emily."

Laura let out a deep sigh. "Do you think she would talk to me?"

"If she thought she could help you, she absolutely would."

A wave of relief crossed Laura's face as she considered the idea. "Okay, would you ask Emily to call me?" Laura wadded up another paper towel and tossed it away.

Cara promised, then guided Laura toward the door. Emily would talk to Laura and explain how the three of them had to work together. Stan could not be allowed to keep preying on women.

Chapter Thirty-One

"We have a problem," Cara said to Jessica as she closed the door and collapsed into the chair across from Jessica's desk. She fidgeted like she'd stepped in a nest of fire ants and was trying to shake them off her legs.

"What's up?" Jessica set her pen down and gave Cara her full attention.

"I can't give you names or be more specific at this time, but I need to tell you one of our female employees was sexually assaulted by one of our male employees."

Jessica's eyes shot up. She blew out a breath through taught lips, then looked back at Cara. "Oh, damn. Was the male Stan?"

"I'm treading very carefully here, because the woman did not, does not, want me to come to you, although I told her I had no choice. She's embarrassed and just wants to move on."

"What happened? Was she raped?"

"That's why the woman's hesitant. She says she told him no, but he kept groping and kissing her, and she struggled with him. She has bruises on her face. Alcohol was involved. The woman feels some responsibility, although I told her forced sex is not her fault, is never the woman's fault. Still, she didn't want to alert HR when I suggested it."

"Then tell me why you're here. What can we do if she doesn't want to take action against him?"

"Plain and simple, I'm worried about the women on our staff, and we need to protect them. We need to protect Flagstone. This is similar to what happened at the one station in Florida where the woman declined to press charges. There's a pattern here and—"

"So it was Stan." Jessica's voice was as firm as her look. She flexed her fingers open and closed in rapid succession.

"Well, yes, it was. But I'm still not at liberty to disclose the woman's name. It would be a breach of confidence."

They stared at each other for a moment. Cara had sought Albert's advice about how to handle the situation with Stan and Laura, but it was up to HR to take the lead and determine next steps. Cara had participated in several training sessions about sexual harassment—or worse—in the workplace, but she'd never had to deal with any issues. If she remembered correctly from their previous conversations, neither had Jessica. But as head of HR, Jessica knew the rules and protocols that needed to be followed better than Cara did.

"Let me see if Jim or Aaron is available." Jessica picked up the phone and punched a few numbers on the console. The conversation didn't last long. "We'll be right there."

Neither woman said a word, their eyes glued to the carpeting in front of their feet as they walked around the corner.

"It doesn't sound like you have enough information to take any action," Jim said after Cara explained the situation. "Aaron and I agree we have to go slow here. Perhaps we should ask Stan what happened. You say the woman won't file a formal complaint?"

"She's badly shaken, hesitant about what to do next, and

just trying to cope with what happened."

"As you know," Jessica said, joining the conversation, "we need to protect all the women on staff if there's a predator—"

"Whoa, hold on. Predator is a strong label to slap on someone," Aaron said, bending forward toward the two women.

Cara and Jessica leaned back almost as one, away from the anger in Aaron's face and the almost physical threat as he intruded on their personal space.

"I'm not slapping a label on anyone," Jessica said. "But I repeat, *if* there is a predator on staff, the women who work here deserve to be protected. Not only that, it is our *duty* to protect them."

"And how do you suggest we do that?" Aaron asked.

"The first step is this meeting." Jessica glanced from Aaron to Jim. "Management needs to be aware of what's going on. You need to talk with Stan, and, as head of HR, I need to be there. Then we'll begin a paper trail to document people's actions. Cara and I will keep an eye on our staff for signs of any further problems."

"Stan hasn't had any of these kinds of issues in his past, right?" Jim said. "We would've heard about them when we checked his references and looked into his background prior to hiring him."

Jessica turned to Cara. "Well, yes, but no." She looked back at the two men. "This information was relayed to me in strictest confidence, and I cannot stress enough that you must not let it leave this room." Jessica then told them what she learned about Stan's days in Florida.

"So, it's another case of the woman claiming something happened but not filing charges with police or even making a complaint to HR," Aaron said. "You know, he's a good-looking guy. I'm sure he has no trouble getting what he wants without, you know, taking advantage of someone."

Aaron's smug smile infuriated Cara, and she bit her lower

lip so hard she tasted blood. *What a stupid thing to say*, she thought, wanting to say it out loud. Instead, she chose her next words carefully and struggled to keep from shouting. "I can't believe you just said that. Rape is not about the sex, Aaron. Rape is a crime, a *violent* crime."

Jim jumped in to defuse the tension.

"I appreciate that you brought this to our attention," Jim said, "and I promise our full support. Nobody wants any member of our staff to act inappropriately or create problems. And we don't want anyone uncomfortable with working here. *Philadelphia* magazine has identified Flagstone as one of the Delaware Valley's best places to work. Let's keep it that way."

The meeting ended on that note.

"Thank goodness at least Jim understands how serious this is," Jessica said after she and Cara were far enough away from his office. She looked around to make sure no one was close by and lowered her voice even more. "Aaron made my blood boil talking about how Stan didn't need to force sex on a woman. He doesn't get it. Doesn't understand the severity of this situation. Then, when he leaned in toward us, I almost jumped out of my chair."

Cara nodded and ran her tongue over her lower lip. "I'm still tasting blood from biting my lip so hard to keep from reacting to Aaron. To be honest, I've always suspected he doesn't have a lot of respect for women, but I was alarmed at how quickly he took Stan's side."

"Please start your paper trail as soon as you get back to your office," Jessica said. "If you need to refer to Stan's victim as 'Female One' or something like that, do it. But be very thorough in what you've seen, what's been reported to you. I can't stress enough the importance of documenting all of this." Jessica thanked Cara and told her to let her know immediately if anything changed.

Cara stewed over Aaron's comments all the way back to

her office. She walked toward her desk and turned to sit down but stopped when she spotted the photos on her bookshelf. Family photos. Albert and her with the kids. Emily and her at a Phillies game. The two of them in the Poconos with their parents. Anyone sitting in the chair across from her could see those photos. Sometimes people would come over to get a closer look and comment on what a nice-looking family she had.

During his interview visit, Stan had spent a couple of days at Flagstone. She thought about the conversations they'd had, with Jim and Aaron, with Laura and a couple of other people on *Fix It*'s crew. She was sure she had mentioned to Stan that both she and he attended Central High, but she didn't remember any response or reaction from him. He didn't ask her if they were in the same grade, whether they had any classes together, or give any indication he remembered her. She was using her married name now, but high school was about a decade ago. Didn't they all still look familiar enough to recognize a fellow classmate? Or maybe he had good reason not to open up about his past.

She tried to think about how much Stan had been in her office. Not that often, she decided. They met more in the conference room or at Laura's desk. He never indicated any interest in her photos, but now that her sister had stood face-to-face with him and accused him of rape, Stan might recognize Emily. Cara wouldn't take any chances. She removed all the photos with Emily in them, opened the bottom drawer of her desk, and placed them safely inside.

Thinking about Emily reminded Cara she hadn't told her sister that she'd suggested Laura talk to her for support. And she needed to tell Emily it was Stan who'd raped Laura. She second-guessed herself and hoped she wasn't making a mistake, connecting the two of them. Things couldn't get any more complicated. Could they?

Chapter Thirty-Two

Early April 2004

Angela's fingers were bitterly cold. She rubbed her thumbs repeatedly over her fingers inside of her mittens, then reached up and wiped her frigid nose. She was sure her nose was in danger of freezing into a chunk of ice and falling off. She wrapped her scarf tighter around her face, slid her hands out of her mittens, and rubbed them together to give them a better shot of warmth. The plastic bag with the carton of milk, two onions, a head of broccoli, and some bananas hung from her elbow. She hadn't realized how cold it was when she'd offered to walk to the neighborhood store for her mother, willing to do anything to escape the tension in the house. Some days she could barely look her parents and sister in the eyes she was so sure they hated her for what she'd done to upend their lives. She put her mittens back on and let the bag of groceries slide down her arm to her hand.

A screeching howl echoed between the houses, then a sharp wind came up behind her and almost knocked her over. Angela pulled her collar up tighter around her neck and picked up her pace. Even home wouldn't feel this bad, no matter how distant her family was to her.

Flurries filled the skies, flying sideways as if they wanted to avoid touching the ground. Angela's breath came in short bursts through her scarf and disappeared into the air. She hated winter in this place. It wouldn't end. April was supposed to mean spring temperatures and bright flowers. But it didn't here in western New York State. It was ten degrees above zero and four inches of snow was forecast by nightfall. But she didn't have the right to complain. It was her fault they were here in the cold and snow instead of enjoying the bright yellow daffodils and purple crocuses exploding in neighborhoods all over Philadelphia. Her fault that her father insisted the family move to someplace near Buffalo, of all places. Her fault she had gotten pregnant and, as her father had told her, her fault that she had shamed the family so much they needed to start a new life in a new city.

The past ten days had been filled with nonstop activity. Angela had finally confided in her sister that she was pregnant. It was almost impossible to hide now. Lacey had asked her a few times if she was gaining weight, why her body was looking different. Angela shrugged her shoulders each time Lacey brought it up, but Lacey was smart and figured it out. It was actually a relief to finally share the truth with someone else. Someone other than Felipe, who'd stopped seeing her a couple of months earlier because she didn't want to have sex every time he did, every time they were together. He'd been so loving and gentle in the beginning of their relationship. Until he'd gotten what he wanted. She guessed he'd found someone else because he stopped calling. Stopped texting. By then, she knew she was pregnant. She didn't love him anymore, especially the way he dropped her so quickly, so she decided her pregnancy was none of his business.

Angela couldn't imagine having an abortion, but that's as far as she got. She didn't know how to tell her parents, so she kept her secret as long as she could. Until the day Lacey told her she knew Angela was pregnant. Until the day her mother guessed the reason for her occasional sickness and finicky appetite. Until her mother said she had to tell her father.

"You're pregnant?" He looked her up and down, studying her body that was filling out in ways no one could deny. He looked away, but not before she spotted the grimace on his face. She thought he might yell, but when he spoke next, his voice was low and calm.

"Who is the boy?"

"He goes to another school, not Central."

"That's not what I asked."

She glanced over at her mother sitting on the couch, her hands worrying themselves, her eyes unable to look into the face of her older daughter. Angela knew she couldn't dodge the question for long. "His name is Felipe," she said quietly.

Her father flinched. "Does he know?"

She shook her head. "We stopped seeing each other a couple of months ago."

"Who else knows? Your friends?"

"I haven't told anyone else. Just Lacey. Mom." She looked at her mother again, hoping to find strength there, but apparently, her mother found it as difficult to look at her as her father did in this life-changing moment. Well, the life-changing moment for Angela was a few months ago, but the ramifications for her family were just beginning.

"Felipe. A Hispanic boy?" Her father's voice was still low. It would almost be better if he yelled at her, but her father didn't often yell.

It wasn't actually a question and Angela knew better than to respond. She knew her father would be disappointed that she was pregnant. She had no idea how he would react to the identity, the nationality, of the baby's father.

"Decisions will have to be made, and soon," her father

said. "You'll have the baby and then we'll determine how to find a proper home for it—"

"Dad, no. I don't want to give my baby away." Angela pleaded with him. "Please."

"It's not your decision, not as long as you're living in my house."

Angela's eyes filled with tears. She crossed her arms over her chest and tried to keep the tears from falling down her cheeks.

"Your mother and I have things to discuss," he said. "You should go to your room."

Angela turned and left the living room without a word and without looking back, but she didn't go far. She paused at the bottom of the stairs where she could still hear their voices.

"Do you know this boy?" her father asked her mother.

"No. She never brought him home. She was going to a lot of football games last fall and the after-game parties, but I had no idea she was seriously involved with any boy."

"We'll have to decide what to do, especially since she's not seeing the boy anymore. A teenage boy can't provide for a baby anyway," Mr. Hargood said.

Silence filled the living room and Angela was afraid to move, almost afraid to breathe. It was so quiet on the first floor of the house that her parents would hear her, no matter how quietly she crept up the stairs. She thought about what her father said about finding a home for the baby. She couldn't give up the baby any more than she could have an abortion. Her parents were devout Catholics and the Hargood family regularly attended Mass at the nearby Catholic church. Even if she'd told them sooner about being pregnant, an abortion would have been out of the question.

Angela couldn't see many ways out of the mess she'd gotten them into, and her shoulders slouched in sadness, remembering the disappointment in her father's eyes. She'd let him down, let both of her parents down.

Voices drifted out of the living room, softer, quieter. Her parents were talking again. She took advantage of the moment and tip-toed up the stairs, not knowing this would be one of the last nights she would sleep in their house.

Chapter Thirty-Three

"Timothy, I'd like to speak with Ms. Archer alone for a few minutes," Lacey said. "Would you please find another table and do your homework?" She smiled and patted him on the shoulder. "Or play video games, but not for too long, okay?"

Timothy nodded, sauntered over to a table in the corner, dropped his knapsack on the bench next to him, and locked his eyes on his phone.

"Thanks for finding time to meet with me, Em, especially on a weekday afternoon." Lacey set her bag on the chair next to her and pulled out her wallet. "I'm going to grab a cup of coffee. Can I get you anything?"

"I'm good," Emily said, tapping the plastic top of her coffee. Lacey walked to the front of the café and placed her order while Emily thought about her phone call that morning. In a shaky voice, Lacey asked if they could meet. Emily wasn't venturing out much these days, but Lacey said she'd put off talking to Emily long enough and could she please see her. So here she was, sipping coffee and waiting to find out what was going on with her former friend.

"I know you have a lot of questions about what happened to my family," Lacey began as soon as she sat. "The short version is Angela got pregnant, and Father was so mortified he made us leave Philly. An abortion was out of the question. Angela didn't want one anyway. I know you didn't spend much time in the company of my dad, but he was a generation, almost two behind in his attitudes, very old-fashioned, with a strong moral compass driven by his Catholic faith." Lacey took a deep breath and a quick sip of coffee before continuing. "It was bad enough Angela got pregnant, and when she told him the name of the baby's father was Felipe ..." Lacey's voice faded away, and she gathered her thoughts while Emily sat quietly and tried to imagine what was coming next.

"But I need to back up for a minute. Father wanted her to give the baby away. Angela resisted and the two of them were adamant in their positions, even though she was still seventeen and a minor. She threatened to run away and Father didn't want that. Instead, he said our whole family would leave the area and go where people didn't know us. He said Angela had brought shame upon our family, not just that she had gotten pregnant, but that, as Father said, 'she had contaminated the family gene pool' because the father was not white."

"Ouch, that's pretty strong," Emily said, shaking her shoulders as if a shiver had swept over every inch of her. "Interracial marriages and children are more common now, especially in cities like Philadelphia. Maybe they weren't as accepted more than a decade ago, but still." Emily shook her head slowly. "Still, that's such a harsh comment."

"I agree, although I never knew he expressed it that way until many years later when my mom told me." Lacey glanced at Timothy. "Angela was determined to have the baby and raise him with my mother's help. In one day, father had arranged a company transfer to their district office in the Buffalo area, and a day or two later—I can't exactly remember—we were driving west. Father asked us to say goodbye to Philadelphia, to our friends. To everything here."

"Seriously? Just like that?" Emily's voice jumped an octave. "But couldn't you have called? Or sent a text or an email? Something. And where did you go to school?" She had so many questions begging to be answered. Information was coming at her too fast to understand.

"I'll take the last question first. I missed part of my sophomore year but was allowed to make it up over the summer and finished my last two years at a good high school. I did try to call you from a friend's cellphone once, but you didn't answer, and I couldn't find the words to explain what was going on, without sharing the family secret that was so embarrassing to my father. And there was no way you could safely call me back, so I hung up. We didn't have internet at first and father didn't want us to use email except when we needed to for school. One time, Father asked if I had tried to reach out to you. The guilt must have shown on my face because he said how it would be best if we all let go of the past. I cried and told him much I missed you. I was surprised to see Father's eyes tear up and I realized how difficult this had been for him." Lacey pulled a napkin out of the aluminum canister on the table and dabbed her eyes. "But he was adamant."

"But you must've gone away to college at some point—"

"Yes, of course." Lacey's words were brisk, a little defensive. "It's difficult to explain, Em. I was young, impressionable, and my dad was so deflated. You remember how quiet he was whenever you came to our house. He was reserved, dignified. And he felt Angela had taken that away from him. I wanted him to be happy again, so I stopped pushing him. Then college essentially took over my life. I made some friends and focused on my education. Honestly, Emily, it's not that I didn't want to reach out to you, I did. It was easier to let go of the past than to hurt him any more than he'd already been hurt. Then after a while, the past faded away."

Lacey looked over at Timothy again, the love evident in her eyes and smile.

Whatever difficult times Lacey had gone through, Emily thought, *she seemed to accept her past for what it was, how what happened with Angela drove events over which Lacey had no control. Emily thought if she'd been in Lacey's position, she surely would have reached out. But it slowly dawned on her that she couldn't really know what she would have done if her own father had been like Lacey's dad.*

Emily took a long sip of her cooling coffee and tried to understand. It wasn't going to happen in half an hour. She needed more time to absorb this. Angela getting pregnant. Mr. Hargood insisting the family move. That's why Emily lost one of her best friends. Lacey had this whole other past Emily knew nothing about. And never reached out to her—until now. Emily tried again to imagine being Lacey back then, but her mind simply couldn't grasp it.

This was a lot to take in when Emily's emotions were already overwhelmed trying to understand a past she never knew she herself had, a past that sometimes felt like someone else's until she remembered that what had happened—the awful attack—had happened to her. Now she was learning Lacey had a past with Angela and Timothy that Emily knew nothing about. So much of what she once thought was real wasn't anymore. Her head was spinning, trying to find a safe piece of her past to grasp onto. Was she in some alternate reality? Was someone going to jump out behind the counter and yell, "Surprise," like this was all a setup, a joke, a big trick of some kind? Because so much was not making sense.

She'd had five EMDR sessions with Mandy, well, four, since they didn't do any actual EMDR in the first session while Mandy took a history and figured out how to proceed.

Sometimes it felt like her past was moving too quickly, which was an odd thought. How could the past move any faster than what it had been? But some days, and this was one of them, Emily asked herself how much more was she going to learn that would alter her perception of her past. And would it affect her ability to hold on to who she thought she was?

Chapter Thirty-Four

Emily's life was a roller coaster of new information and overwhelming emotions. There were times over the weekend when her thoughts had bounced back and forth between thinking about Lacey, Angela, and Timothy and what had happened in their lives over the years and trying to absorb what it meant for her to have been sexually assaulted as a teen. Sometimes she tried to escape from it all by putting on soft music, stretching out on the couch, and focusing on taking deep breaths; other times she took a long, hot bath with lavender oil; and sometimes she fell into a deep sleep and let go of as much as she could.

Cara had called several times, in part to see how Emily was doing, but also because *she* needed to talk about what had happened to Emily. Their past had always seemed, maybe not quite idyllic, but at least free from disasters or major traumas. Not anymore. Both of them struggled to grasp their new reality.

During their last phone call, Cara told Emily that Stan had sexually assaulted Laura. Her news was met with another round of stunned silence, then Emily exploded.

"This guy is unbelievable. We've got to stop him. We can't let him keep getting away with this." She jumped up from the couch and began pacing the familiar path between the living room and the kitchen.

"I agree, and maybe Laura will help by going to the police, but she's not willing to, at least not yet. I did suggest you could talk to her, give her some support about what she's going through."

"Did you tell her Stan assaulted me?"

"I think you should be the one to tell her. I hope it's okay that I suggested you could talk to her. I think she really needs someone who understands."

Emily added this latest bit of news about Stan and Laura to her overcrowded, overflowing, emotional bucket. "I'm willing to help her out any way I can."

"Thanks. I knew you would. She's upset, and I am so angry at Stan right now," Cara said.

"Laura's probably still in shock," Emily told her sister. "I know that was my first reaction when I realized what had happened to me. I don't think I fully understood what it meant to be in shock until then. It's debilitating. Give her some time."

So with all of this going on, it was a relief when Emily walked into the safe space of Mandy's office Tuesday morning. As soon as Emily and Mandy took their seats, she told her therapist about how she had confided in Cara about how Stan had assaulted her.

"Are you relieved to have told her?" Mandy asked.

"Absolutely. My sister and I have never had secrets, except for this one. A big weight was lifted from my shoulders. And of course, she was so wonderful and supportive and said she wanted to help me in any way she could."

"Good. What's your level of upset now when you think about the rape?"

"It's still up around a six."

"Then let's work on getting it a little lower."

After almost half an hour and several more sets of EMDR, Emily told Mandy she was now at a fairly comfortable upset level of four.

"But I'm still struggling with some feelings we've touched upon but haven't talked about in depth yet, and they're weighing on me." She looked down, picked up the small pillow on the chair next to her, and hugged it close to her chest. "I can't figure out whether what I feel is guilt or shame, or both."

"Ah, that's a difficult and very important part of dealing with many traumas, but especially when the issue is sexual assault," Mandy said, her voice soothing. "First, let's define the two. Simply put, guilt is remorse for having done something wrong, whereas shame is a feeling of humiliation, embarrassment, or disgrace." Mandy gave her a moment to consider what she'd said. "Do you understand the difference?"

"Yeah, I've got that much."

"You have no reason to feel guilty. You did nothing wrong. Your attacker is the person who's in the wrong. He's the guilty one. I repeat, you did not do anything wrong. Now, the shame part of this is more difficult because, of course, you feel humiliated or disgraced by what Stan did. But you did nothing to deserve that."

Emily nodded. She understood—intellectually—the difference between guilt and shame, but her heart, her self-confidence, her self-worth, were on a different level. Her eyes drifted from the floor to the soft yellow wall behind Mandy to a framed print—a field of bright red poppies with a mountain rising in the distance. She squeezed her eyes closed once and shook her head.

"The red poppies in that print on the wall behind you remind me about a weird dream I had last night." Emily's voice was low and distant. "I was in a roomful of people, a big, comfortable living room, with chairs, a couple of couches, some bookcases, and side tables. The lighting was soft, from table lamps and wall sconces. There were open doorways to other rooms on either end of the living room. One doorway led into the dining room where food was laid out on a long table. I could barely see into the other room, but I got enough of a look to notice it was a den with lots of bookshelves. And a big lighted world globe sitting on a side table." She closed her eyes and squeezed the pillow tighter.

"I don't know who the people were, but they had drinks in their hands, and they were laughing. It's like I was floating above everyone and watching the party, you know, like a drone hovering overhead. Then I saw myself, standing in a corner. Alone. And I kept pulling my hair over my face. Watching from above, I wondered why I'd pull my hair over my face. Then I saw." She stopped abruptly, her eyes sliding back and forth, left to right, as she remembered the dream, searching for words to describe it. "One side of my face was all red, the part I tried to cover up. Not just red, but a big angry welt with blisters. It looked awful. I turned away from everyone, and even with my back to the roomful of people, I tried frantically to hide my face so no one could see how hideous it looked—how *I* looked."

Emily paused and tilted her head. A police siren wailed in the distance; angry voices of people arguing drifted in from behind Mandy's office windows. Their voices sounded fuzzy, garbled, like Emily was underwater, or those people were.

"What are you feeling when you think about that dream?"

"Ashamed. Embarrassed. Shocked. I feel like everyone knows what had happened to me, and they're laughing at me."

"What picture represents the worst part of that memory?"

"My red, blistered face. People laughing at me."

"And what's your negative belief about yourself when you think about that?"

"That I'm ugly, an embarrassment. No one wants to look at me."

"Where do you feel that in your body?"

Emily was prepared now for the series of questions Mandy posed at the beginning of each EMDR sequence. But instead of immediately answering that she felt the pain in her chest and arms like she usually did, she took time to scan her body. She put the pillow on the couch beside her and rubbed her arms, then her stomach.

"I feel it in so many places now. I can feel it in my legs, as well as my arms. I still feel it in my chest, but there's also this big knot in my stomach."

"One more question. What's your level of upset between zero and ten?"

"It's an eight."

"Here, hold the tappers, Emily." Mandy leaned forward, separated the left disc from the right, and gave her the tappers. "Think about the image of you at the party, feeling ashamed, that you're an embarrassment. Now, what would you rather think?"

"That I didn't do anything to be ashamed of. It wasn't my fault. I was just a kid."

"Go with that. Follow your thoughts."

Her palms vibrated. The police siren disappeared. The angry voices out back faded away. The dream held all of her senses. She smelled one man's cologne and stale cigarettes on another man's breath. A woman laughed too loudly. Another woman looked on in detached amusement. From her perch above the room, Emily stared at the ugly blisters and knew they told the world what had happened to her.

"I don't know how to get beyond this feeling of shame," she said. "I feel like everyone knows."

"How could they know?"

"By the red blisters on my face. They can all see my embarrassment, my shame."

"Can you imagine your face without the blisters?"

"No, they're so ugly. And huge."

"Try."

She grasped the tappers and struggled with short sips of breath that weren't enough. Her throbbing pulse echoed inside her eardrums. *They call them eardrums for a reason,* she thought. *It sounds like someone is banging on a drum inside my head.* She took a deep breath. *Please, God, help the blisters go away. Please help me look normal like everyone else.* The tappers kept a steady beat while she trained her shuttered eyes on the redness on her face, prayed, and willed the blisters to get smaller. A minute later, fewer blisters and red blotches covered her face, and she didn't try so hard to hide behind her hair. Soon, that part of her face looked like she had nothing worse than a bad sunburn.

"My face is still red, but the blisters are almost gone."

"What's your level of upset about this dream now?"

She sighed. "Maybe a four."

"That's good, Emily. Good work. Take a deep breath and open your eyes."

The vibrations stopped, and she looked up at Mandy. "What do I do if the dream comes back?"

"Keep a picture in your mind of your face without blisters, of you with nothing to be ashamed of, no reason to feel embarrassed. Think of that image if you start having feelings of shame again."

"Wow, that was intense. I saw so much more of the dream with the tappers. It's like the whole dream kind of, I guess I would say it came alive. It sounds weird, but that's what happened."

"The dream revealed more to you because you opened

your mind to it, and then you were able to let go of the worst parts of it. It's like the positive reinforcement steps we've done before. You can get yourself to a better place. If you feel comfortable enough later today, try writing down your thoughts, reinforce your positive ones, then you can read them over again if you experience any distressing emotions."

"I just wanted someone there to give me a hug and tell me it's going to be all right."

"If that dream comes back," Mandy said, "choose someone in the room you might be able to trust. Try to encourage that person to come over to you. A hug would probably be too physical for you, but another friendly gesture like a smile, maybe a handshake, could ease your feelings of isolation from others in the room."

"Okay, I'll try that."

"We're getting near the end of our session, and there's not enough time to do any more EMDR. I know we've talked about Women Organized Against Rape and you've called them, but I'd like you to think more about going to one of their group sessions and talking with other women about what happened to you. Discussing your attack with others could be very comforting and give you another level of healing."

"The first counselor I spoke with when I called WOAR mentioned the support groups, and I've considered going to one. I'm actually thinking of going with Laura."

"Who's Laura?"

Oops. She hadn't meant to mention Laura to Mandy yet, not until after the two of them got together. The bigger question was when or how to tell Mandy that Stan had also attacked Laura. As much as she wanted to share everything with Mandy, her therapist probably wouldn't approve of her getting in the middle of Laura's situation. She told Mandy what had happened to Laura and how Cara suggested Emily talk with her.

The room grew very quiet, the only sound the soft ticking of the clock next to the couch. She studied Mandy's face and tried to interpret her expression.

"Emily, you're still in a somewhat fragile state." Mandy chose her words carefully. "I know you're a strong person, but have you considered how difficult it might be for you to talk about what happened to Laura? It's different if you're in a group session at WOAR. A professional therapist controls the discussion and is prepared to help anyone who feels over-whelmed. I'm not sure it's a good idea for you and Laura to share your experiences without having a professional with you."

"I don't plan to tell Laura graphic details of what happened to me, and I can ask her not to share too much as well. I'm thinking of suggesting she visit WOAR. Maybe we'd go together. I'm going to give her your name, too, because you've been so helpful to me."

"Your heart is in the right place, Emily, but please go slowly. I would hate to see you take a step back in your healing."

"I'll be very careful. But I have to help her if I can."

She called Laura as soon as she got home.

"Thanks for reaching out. I told Cara it was fine for you to call and talk about—" Laura's voice cracked, and she sniffled.

Emily gripped the phone and dropped into a chair at the kitchen table. "It's okay. I know what you're going through, and it might help to talk to someone who's had the same kind of experience. Not exactly, but, you know."

"Yeah, I do. Not about what happened to you, of course.

But I do think talking might help. I can't tell you how much I appreciate your offer."

"How'd you like to meet Wednesday after work? Or whatever time's good for you." Emily stood, lifted the whistling kettle off the burner, and poured boiling water into a large mug with a bag of Earl Grey resting on the bottom. "We could also meet for coffee, which might be the smarter thing to do, but I don't mind admitting it's easier to talk about this over a glass of wine."

They settled on a time and a quiet bar near the Art Museum about halfway between their homes.

She emailed Cara a quick update, then thought about what she could say to convince Laura to go to the police and file a complaint against Stan. Maybe when she told Laura what Stan did to her all those years ago, Laura would understand what a lecherous predator he was and agree that he had to be put behind bars before he hurt anyone else.

Chapter Thirty-Five

E mily spotted Laura the minute the producer walked in. Morgan's Pub was a cozy place in the city's Fairmount Park neighborhood, a stone's throw from the majestic Philadelphia Museum of Art. The oval wooden bar was an island in the middle of the room with small tables and booths along the right wall. The restaurant had nicer booths, softer lighting and music, and bigger tables on the left side.

"I'm so glad you could meet me." Laura had a warm smile and a firm handshake.

"Are you sure this is a comfortable place to talk?" Emily asked as Laura sat down opposite her. "It's a bigger crowd than I thought would be here in the middle of the week. Maybe you'd rather go someplace a little quieter. Or get a booth on the other side?"

"Actually, this is fine. It's loud enough that no one can overhear our conversation."

A waitress came over and took Laura's order for a glass of white wine. She returned quickly and dropped a couple of menus on their table. "Just in case you want a bite to eat," she told them. "Our burgers are great, fish and chips, too. After that, you're on your own."

The two of them laughed with the waitress.

Emily tilted her wine glass toward Laura. She paused, wasn't quite sure whether a toast was appropriate, and laughed at Laura's quizzical look. "What the hell," she said. "Here's to us."

"I'll drink to that." Laura smiled and took a drink of her pinot grigio. "I hope you don't mind if we skip the small talk. I'm not very good at making idle chitchat in the best of times let alone right now."

"That works for me. Would you like me to go first?"

"Do you mind?"

"Not at all, and on the advice of my therapist, who I love dearly, I'm not going to give graphic or specific details." Emily twirled her glass on the tabletop but did not pick it up. "I was raped when I was younger, by someone I trusted to walk me home. And then I never told anyone because he threatened to hurt me or my sister. I'm working with Mandy—she's my therapist—to come to terms with what happened and to heal from the trauma of the attack."

"So, it was someone you knew?"

"I didn't really know him. But he indicated he knew my family and where we lived, so I thought I could trust him."

"I thought I could trust my coworker, too."

Laura was quiet for so long, Emily thought she had changed her mind and found it too difficult to talk about what had happened. Emily looked at her wine glass, picked it up, and took a sip.

"I'm struggling with how I could've been so wrong to trust him." Laura spoke softly, and her eyes never looked up.

Emily leaned forward to catch Laura's words.

"I've encountered guys in bars who were too aggressive, and I knew how to get them to back off. I've met men who just gave me the creeps, and I knew better than to go anywhere near them, much less accept a ride or invite them into my home." Laura licked her lips and swallowed. "I knew my coworker was probably a player, but I thought I could handle him."

"How can you possibly work with him now?"

"We haven't had much interaction lately, and I'm avoiding him when I can. Cara offered to give me a break from *Fix It or Ditch It*, but I told her no. I was on the ground floor when the show was created, I launched it, and I'm not giving it up, not even for a little while. Not because of him." Laura's eyes finally met Emily's and her voice was strong. "I'm confident it'll get better. I will get through this."

"I'm sure you will. It takes a while before what happened stops haunting you, a fair amount of talking with others, especially a therapist, and accepting that it wasn't your fault."

"That's a tall order. You've done all that?"

"Don't I wish." Emily laughed. "No, I'm in therapy, but I've researched information at rape crisis centers and looked into support groups. I've learned about the stigma of rape and other kinds of sexual assault, and ways women can cope with what happened. I've done a lot of reading, so I understand the process of recovery. It helps me to see the light at the end of the tunnel."

"What I wouldn't give to see that light right now."

"It'll come in time," she assured Laura. "It's still so new with you, isn't it? Your memories of what happened must still be pretty vivid."

Laura opened her mouth to respond, but she hesitated as the waitress approached.

"You two doing okay?" She passed their table with a tray of empty beer mugs.

"Do you want another round?" Emily asked Laura as she assessed what was left in their glasses. "If you do, I think I'll order the fish and chips, because it's been a long time since lunch."

"I'm hungry too." Laura stole a look at the menu. "I'll have a mushroom burger, medium well. I'm not ready for another wine yet."

"You want fries with the burger?"

"Sure," Laura said. "What's a burger without fries?"

"A very sad burger, that's what." The waitress laughed. "I'll be right back."

They smiled at the retreating waitress, then looked at each other, Emily thinking about where to pick up their interrupted conversation, and when to tell Laura about Stan.

Laura cleared her throat. "I've never been in therapy. I guess I'm a little intimidated at the idea of telling my innermost thoughts and intimate details to a stranger."

"I'd never been in therapy either until now, and I'm learning how much of my anger is connected to being raped." She stopped speaking as their waitress came by, planted a glass of wine on the table in front of Emily, and snatched up her empty glass before resuming her path back to the bar.

"A few weeks ago, at a major client event," Emily explained, "someone grabbed my butt on the dance floor." Then she told Laura the rest of what happened at the party, taking time off from work, and about her closest friend suggesting she needed therapy.

"I think I would've slapped the guy who assaulted me, too."

"But why then and not the other times when guys have been inappropriate? My therapist and I talked about how the anger built up inside of me over the years. Then I began having frightening flashbacks. Until finally, my anger exploded. With a slap."

"I have plenty of anger right now." Laura struggled to hold

back the tears. "Anger at myself for letting it happen, and anger at Stan for forcing himself on me."

Emily's right hand jerked so hard, she almost knocked over her wine. Cara told her Stan had raped Laura, but hearing Laura say his name hit her like sharp blow to her head. She grabbed the glass with both hands and held on tight.

"Are you okay? Did I say something wrong?"

She swallowed hard. "No, you didn't say anything wrong. I'm the one who'll be in the wrong if I don't say something soon. If I don't tell you something you need to know. About the person who attacked me."

Laura set her wine glass down and clasped her hands on the table.

Emily took a deep breath, then let it out. Raised her eyes to meet Laura's. "You may know that Stan went to the same high school as Cara and me. He was older. He said he knew who Cara was and where we lived. I had never met him until he offered to walk me home from a party."

Laura listened in stunned silence.

"Stan raped me, too. More than a decade ago. I was eighteen." Emily then took a big drink of her wine and felt the smooth liquid move through her body, loosening the muscles that had been so tense as she struggled with how to tell Laura everything. She knew keeping that information from Laura wouldn't be fair.

"That's why Cara suggested I talk with you, isn't it?" Laura asked.

"I think she wanted you to be able to confide in someone who'd also been assaulted, someone who could understand your emotions, your pain. She also told me you're struggling with the shame and guilt that trouble most sexual assault victims, and she thought it would help you to talk with someone who's also faced those issues."

"It wasn't just a matter of *someone* assaulting me. Cara

should've told me Stan also raped you," Laura said tersely. "She should've trusted me enough to tell me before I agreed to meet with you."

"Please don't be angry with Cara. She and I agreed it's my story to share. Besides, I wanted you to be able to tell me what happened to you without the complication of knowing Stan was also the person who attacked me. It just felt like the right thing to do. I'm sorry."

Laura shook her head and dropped her eyes. "I don't even know what to say. Telling me Stan also assaulted you is the last thing I expected." She was about to say something more, but the waitress appeared with their food.

"Fish and chips here. Burger and fries here." She set the plates down in front of them along with bottles of ketchup and malt vinegar. "You two let me know if you need anything else."

Neither one moved to pick up their napkin. They stared at their food.

"Let's eat while it's still hot, okay?" Emily said.

Laura picked up a french fry. She blew on it to cool it off and nibbled on it. Then she squeezed ketchup on the rest of the fries and her burger.

After a few minutes, Emily put down her fork. She'd eaten about half of the beer-battered cod, but she didn't have much of an appetite. "It's not like someone's written a book on how to do this," she whispered. "I want to be here for you, to help you if I can. Forgive me if I've handled this poorly."

Laura nodded, then set her half-eaten burger on her plate, and pushed it toward the center of the table. "I remember so many details from that night. It's a movie that keeps playing in my head. I can be in the middle of a deep sleep and wake up, my body covered in sweat from a vivid flashback. It's like it keeps happening."

"I have flashbacks, too. It's one of the most difficult,

lingering parts of the assault. Therapy can help with that." She pulled a business card from her pocket and handed it to Laura. "I brought one of Mandy's cards in case you want to call her."

Laura took the card without comment.

"Have you considered going to the police to file a complaint against Stan?"

"I did briefly think about that, but he warned me about taking any action against him, insisting he's done nothing wrong. I'm not even sure the cops would talk to him if I filed a complaint, and, you know, it's my word against his." Laura sipped her wine and raised her eyes. "Did you report your attack to the police?"

"I didn't at the time because I was so scared. I was just trying to understand what had happened. Plus, he threatened to hurt me and Cara and said he would tell people I asked for it. Then, after I recalled the attack during my EMDR sessions with Mandy, I contacted an attorney, and she told me the statute of limitations had run out in my case."

Laura grimaced. "That must've been upsetting. Knowing you didn't even have a choice if you wanted to go to the police. Still, I don't think I could report this."

"He assaulted me more than ten years ago, and he recently assaulted you. Who knows how many other women he's assaulted? Going to the police might be the only way to stop him. I would go with you for support."

"Oh, I couldn't ask you to do that."

"You didn't. I offered, because you shouldn't have to go alone. It wouldn't be easy but having someone with you would help."

"Thanks, I'll keep that in mind, but mostly I just want to forget about what happened."

"Wouldn't that be nice," Emily said, nodding. "If only it were that easy."

Chapter Thirty-Six

"At first, Laura was angry you hadn't said anything to her about Stan raping me," Emily told Cara as she cradled the phone between her shoulder and ear, then wiped the counter, and put the last dish in the dishwasher. "But I explained we both felt I should be the one to tell her, and she understood. She still doesn't want to go to the police, but I think maybe, maybe, she could be persuaded."

"What makes you say that?"

"She was pretty upset when I told her I was only in high school when Stan raped me. I even asked her how she would feel if she knew there were more victims."

"Wow, how did she react to that?"

"She shuddered. And didn't look at me for a minute. I stressed what a violent guy he is, and guys like that, well, they're likely to attack again. I told her it's bad enough when someone rapes you. You wonder if you did something wrong, and hopefully, you eventually try to push it aside and move on with your life. But when you find out your attacker has raped other women—"

"Especially a teenager," Cara cut in.

"Yes, especially a teenager, then it's no longer just him and you. It's him and another woman, and then it becomes a dangerous pattern of sexual assaults. If Laura thinks about that long enough, she may decide to report what happened."

"I'll check in with her tomorrow. I'll also reinforce that I'm sorry I didn't tell her about you and Stan, that we weren't trying to deceive her; we just didn't want to complicate matters."

A baby cooed and Cara murmured something, words Emily couldn't quite catch. "Oh, you've got Kelsey with you. I hear that little girl. Isn't it past her bedtime?"

"She was sleeping but woke up about half an hour ago. I've been trying to put her back down ever since."

"Then I should let you go."

"No, it's fine. She's hearing our voices because I have you on speaker and she's calming down. I'll put her back in her crib in a minute. Tell me what you've been up to."

Emily turned on the dishwasher and sat on a kitchen stool.

"For starters, I had an intense session with my therapist about guilt and shame. I'm still mulling over what she and I discussed, trying to stop blaming myself for what happened. And I shopped for a gun."

"You what?" Cara's shout undid all the good of calming her sleeping child. Kelsey let out a cry. "Shhhh, baby, it's okay. Mommy didn't mean to wake you. Shhhh." A moment later, with Kelsey cooing softly again, Cara returned to their conversation. "What were you doing, shopping for a gun?" Her voice was quieter but insistent.

"Um, checking out the kinds of guns that are best for women. Holding one. Feeling it in my hand so I would know what it was like."

"Where did you go?"

"After I did some basic research on the internet about different types of guns, especially the best kinds for women, I found a gun shop over in Roxborough and talked to the owner. He gave me a lesson in handguns, revolvers, bullet size, and how to find my target."

"Listen to yourself. All this gun lingo coming out of your mouth like these are words you use every day," Cara said a little too loudly. Kelsey began to stir. Cara lowered her voice again. "Did you shoot the gun? God, I can't believe I'm asking you this question."

"Well, yes. They have a range where you can try out the gun before you buy it, to make sure it's the right weapon for you."

Even Kelsey must have been stunned into silence.

"Emily, please tell me you didn't buy a gun."

She sighed. "It's a strange feeling, holding a gun in your hand and pointing it at a target. Staring at a bull's eye with a dot in the center. Or the kind of target with a figure, head and shoulders and torso. Thinking of someone you hate, seeing that person instead of the black and white target, and pulling the trigger. Seeing the bullet hole right where you aimed. It was incredibly empowering."

"And?"

The only sound on the other end of the line was the gentle breathing of a baby. *Cara must be holding her breath waiting for an answer*, Emily thought.

"And no, Cara. I did not buy a gun. I filled out the application and made a deposit on my credit card. The next day I called the guy back and told him I wasn't ready to buy yet."

"Thank goodness. I don't know what I would've done if you'd actually gone through with it."

"I don't deny that, at first, it was exhilarating, imagining Stan in front of me and firing a gun. But then I looked down at the weapon in my hand and started shaking." She paused, drawn back into the memory and reliving her moment of clarification. "We are not gun people, Cara. I am not a gun person. While it felt good in the moment to take out my hurt and anger on a paper figure six feet away that could've been Stan, I realized that no matter how much anger I have toward him, I could never shoot anyone. Not even him."

"I'm so relieved to hear you say that."

"I had a dream later that night that was so upsetting, I jumped up in bed. I was shooting the full fifteen rounds a Glock 19 can hold, all of them flying into Stan. I think I actually traumatized myself."

"Maybe you should bring it up with Mandy the next time you see her."

"Oh, yeah, she's going to love the idea that I thought about buying a gun and fired one with Stan's image as the target. It'll probably take a couple of therapy sessions to work on that image, and Mandy may need to hold the tappers herself for a while thinking about what I did."

"I'm sure she hears all kinds of upsetting things from her clients without reacting to them. You did say shooting the gun helped release your anger."

"Yes, but maybe not in a good way. Unless you do it, Cara, and I'm not suggesting you do, you probably cannot understand how upsetting it is to see that side of yourself. To even think that side of you exists."

It was a stunning admission, and they were both silent for a moment thinking about it. Thinking about how Stan attacking Emily could tap into a darker side of themselves they never knew existed. And maybe wish they hadn't discovered. But there was no turning back on the past. They were learning that over and over again.

"Sometimes trauma doesn't bring out the best in a person," Cara said. "That's all it is, Em, the trauma of Stan raping you brought out the worst of you at that moment. Don't judge yourself."

"I don't want the memory of his assault to pull me into an

abyss I never knew existed. I feel dirtied by the assault, then I felt dirty because I considered responding with violence. I want to make Stan pay for what he did to me, what he did to Laura, but I can't destroy my soul at the same time. That would be like having him attack me all over again."

Chapter Thirty-Seven

M andy's voice sounded like an old vinyl record that had been played too many times.

"I'm sorry I'm too ill to see you today, Emily, but I'm glad you're able to join me for a phone session. I know you're returning to work on Monday, and I expect you may be a little stressed about it, so I wanted to make sure we could at least talk."

"You're right about that," she laughed. "I'm sure once I walk through the doors, I'll be fine, but right now the idea of seeing my colleagues after so many weeks away gives me a bad case of nerves. I know people are going to ask me about what happened with the sales director from Clifton, and Martin told me some people are upset that Chris didn't support me more." It wasn't just the reactions that Martin told her about; she'd received emails from coworkers, especially women, complaining about how unfairly she'd been treated.

"I'm also thinking about how difficult it might be for you to focus on work while you continue to process your distressing memories around the attack." Mandy coughed. "Sorry, hang on for a minute."

Mandy covered the mouthpiece, but her sustained cough was loud and deep, and Emily winced at how sick her therapist sounded.

"You probably shouldn't even be working today," Emily said. "Even if it is from home and only a phone call."

"Don't worry about me," Mandy managed to say. "I had a brief call with another client earlier, and you're the only other person dealing with a sensitive situation I need to check in with." Mandy cleared her voice one more time. "So tell me, what do you think about when you see yourself walking through the doors at work on Monday morning? Close your eyes and tell me what you see. If you want, begin with driving into the parking lot."

"Pulling into the lot and getting out of my car is a good place to start," she said, closing her eyes and visualizing the scene. "I feel a little anxious just thinking about that."

"Where do you feel it?"

"In my chest."

"Take a deep breath and let it out slowly. Remember, breathe in for four beats, out for six. Good. Now do it again. Remember this Monday. Take deep breaths to calm your nerves."

After almost a minute of controlled breathing, Emily spoke again.

"Okay, I'm breathing more normally now. I'm getting out of my car, and there aren't too many people at work yet because I'm going in early." She opened her eyes but kept her gaze low on the floor. "I enter through the front doors and walk down the hallway to my office. The door is closed. I open it and ..." Her voice jumped with excitement. "There's a bouquet of flowers on my desk!"

Mandy laughed and started coughing again. "That's good, Emily, really good. Keep thinking positive thoughts. And don't hesitate if you need to step back at any point during the day and take a break."

"Imagining flowers on my desk, from Martin of course, helps a lot."

"You have Martin to lean on, and that's a gift, so let him know you need his support on Monday."

"I won't hesitate to reach out to him. He's been the best friend a girl could have." Her voice cracked and her eyes filled, thinking about the many ways Martin had supported her over the past weeks. He'd been her sounding board, her cheering section, her only reassuring supporter besides her therapist until she'd let Cara in.

"It sounds like you're really going to be fine at work. You'll have the jitters—it's only natural—but you have Martin and the women at work who are in your corner and will be there for you. Just remember to keep breathing."

"I will. Talking with you about it and preparing to return to work has already eased my nervousness. Thanks."

"Then take a few minutes to tell me about your conversation with Laura. How did that go?"

Emily recounted her evening with Laura and how they shared their stories.

"And did you tell her Stan is the person who also assaulted you?"

"I almost knocked over my glass when she mentioned his name, so then I told her what Stan did to me."

"You found it upsetting, of course, to hear about Stan's assault on her. Did that trigger disturbing thoughts for you? I imagine it must have."

"Yes," Emily admitted.

"We can't do EMDR over the phone, but we can talk about your distressing thoughts and how to get them under control until we meet next Tuesday. Now tell me what your level of upset is when you think about that night with Stan."

Emily rolled her shoulders, then inhaled deeply and let it out through her mouth. "It's about a five. I feel tightness in the upper part of my body, my chest, shoulders, neck." She looked down at her legs. "Oh, and my knees are bouncing pretty good, so there's tension in my legs."

"We're not going to dwell on any images about the attack, so when you see any of them, I want you to put them into your container, okay?"

She put the phone on the table in speaker mode and used both hands to push her knees to the floor. She applied pressure until she could take her hands away and her legs were no longer bouncing up and down. Then she mentally opened the top to her jewelry box and willed all the remaining tension in her body—along with the images of Stan attacking her—into the container. And she took all the images she conjured up when Laura had told her what happened to her and put them in the container. She slammed the top shut and locked it. Tucked the key into a pocket and blew out a breath.

"Was that a good breath?"

"Yes, it was. I'm not going to touch that key until I see you again."

"Remember what I said last session about writing down your thoughts if you can't keep them in the container. If you want, bring in your notes and we can go over them in our next session to see if anything else comes up for you."

Emily told Mandy that sounded like journaling, which she'd never done much of, but she promised to write things down if she couldn't control her emotions.

"I know we can't have sessions twice a week anymore because of your work, but don't hesitate to call or text me if you need to talk. And keep busy over the weekend. Do you have any plans?"

"Cara and Albert invited me to spend some time with them and the kids on Saturday," she said. "I think they're trying to keep a close watch on me, especially since I told Cara I shopped for a gun. Even though I told her I wasn't going to buy one, I'm sure she's still worried I might."

Mandy swallowed hard enough for Emily to almost feel it.

"You shopped for a gun?" Mandy finally asked. "To use for protection because you fear for your safety, or because you want to retaliate?"

"I didn't buy one. I held it and thought about Stan while I pulled the trigger. I still considered buying a gun, and yeah, not because I wanted it for protection. But in the end, I didn't."

"Promise me you won't have second thoughts and buy one."

She had heard concern in Mandy's voice many times over the past several weeks, but this was on a different level. She hadn't considered how it would sound to her sister and her therapist when she told them about the gun. They probably thought she was out of control; she hadn't thought enough about how much her actions might alarm them.

"I promise, Mandy. After that experience, I have no intention of ever picking up a gun again. I saw a side of myself I didn't know existed, and it scared me."

"Sometimes it's good to be scared. You are full of surprises, Emily. Please be careful. I worry about what you might do next."

Chapter Thirty-Eight

E mily replayed Mandy's words over and over in her head during her drive into the city. After a quick stop for organic foods at Essene, she headed north toward Cara's. This one was of her favorite areas of the city. Blocks of historic homes connected to Headhouse Square and artistic and trendy South Street.

She took another turn and realized she was a block from where Stan lived. She tried to resist the urge to drive by his condo, but her willpower wasn't that strong. No cars were behind her, so she slowed down and peered into his condo building's parking lot.

Stan was standing near his car. He took something out of his vehicle and put it in a trash bag. He looked over his shoulder at the condos as if to see whether anyone was watching, then tossed the bag into the small dumpster in the corner of the lot.

What was that about? she thought as she watched him through the black wrought iron fence.

When he started to turn toward the street, she stepped on the gas, afraid he'd spot her. She turned down the first available street and circled back. Her heart thumped, her throat too constricted to swallow. She passed by his condo again but didn't see him or anyone else. A car sped up behind her, preventing her from lingering. She drove a couple more blocks, turned, and slammed on the brakes to avoid rear-ending the car ahead of her. Flashing red and blue lights announced the police presence up ahead. Yellow police tape blocked cars from turning onto narrow Delancey Street but didn't prevent people from slowing down to see what was going on. Emily was as curious as the next person.

A police officer with a silver whistle between his teeth startled her with a sharp blast. He gestured his arms to urge drivers to move along. Suddenly he pointed straight at her, blew his whistle once, and swung his arm to the left.

She obeyed his directions, then turned down another side street as soon as she could. She managed to fit the SUV into a tight parking spot and walked back to the taped-off area.

"What's going on?" she asked an officer standing on the corner, one hand on his hip and the other hand resting on the end of his gun.

He barely looked at her. "I'm not at liberty to say. Unless you live down that street, please keep moving."

Two young men walked in her direction, ducked under the police tape, and continued on.

She walked fast to catch up with them. "Excuse me. Do you know why police have blocked off Delancey Street?"

The two men looked her over. "You don't look familiar. Do you live around here?"

"Well, over on Sixth near Pine," she fibbed. "Sometimes my exercise walk brings me into this neighborhood, and I couldn't help but notice the cops."

The men looked at each other, then one nodded to the other and returned his gaze to her. "A man walking his dog early this morning found a woman," he said, thrusting his hands into the pockets of his neatly ironed jeans. "She was unconscious. She'd apparently been attacked. That's what our neighbors said."

Shivers raced up her spine, and goose bumps popped up along the tops of her arms. She shook as if the temperature was ten degrees, not sixty with a full sun in the mid-morning sky. She thanked the men and retraced her steps to her car, then drove back around to Stan's condo. His car was gone and the gate to the parking lot was open.

Without thinking much about what she was doing, she parked in front of the fire hydrant and ran over to the dumpster. When she lifted the heavy black lid, the smell of rotting garbage overwhelmed her. She dropped the lid and stepped back, fighting the urge to throw up. Trash day must be soon because the dumpster smelled full. Was she really thinking about grabbing Stan's trash out of the dumpster? Was she crazy?

Emily held her breath and opened the top of the dumpster again. Several white plastic bags sat at the end of the big container where Stan had tossed his bag a short while ago. Many of them were larger kitchen-size trash bags, but there were several smaller ones like those from a drug store or the minimarket. She looked around to see if anyone was watching, reached in, grabbed several of the bags, and ran back to her car. She tossed the bags into the back seat and sped away.

"You did what?" Cara shrieked. They'd barely said hello when Emily told her sister she had trash bags from Stan's dumpster in her car.

"Let me wash my hands and I'll tell you everything." She stepped into the kitchen and turned on the hot water.

Cara sat on one of the stools in the kitchen's center island and drummed her fingers along the granite surface.

Emily pulled out the stool next to her sister and sat. "I stopped by Essene on my way here, then I realized I was close to Stan's condo." She filled Cara in on seeing him toss a white plastic bag into the dumpster, then explained what happened when she drove by the cops on Delancey Street. "I had goosebumps thinking the two might be connected, so I drove back to Stan's and grabbed some trash bags out of his dumpster."

Cara shook her head. "You're making a big assumption trying to connect the two, and by the way, dumpster diving does not become you."

"You wouldn't say that if whatever Stan pulled out of his car and tossed into the trash was connected to the woman who was found. What if I'm right? What if he has attacked another woman?"

"Who attacked another woman?" Albert asked as he stepped into the kitchen.

Cara told Albert what had happened while Emily watched his face.

"And because you got spooked, you think Stan is responsible?" Albert placed his empty mug on the counter and poured a fresh cup of coffee. "That's quite a leap."

"He looked, I don't know, suspicious," Emily said. "He glanced at the condos like he was trying to hide something and hoped no one was watching. If you'd been there, you would know what I mean."

"So you decided to play amateur sleuth and take matters into your own hands?" Albert said with a heavy sigh. "And the bags are still in your car?"

"Yes. I hoped you two would go through them with me."

"I've got to tell you, Emily, any good attorney—and I count myself as one of them—would tell you that you are grasping at straws. And if there is any evidence in one of the plastic bags, and I emphasize *if*, you have contaminated it by interrupting what law enforcement and lawyers call the chain of custody. Meaning it would not be admissible in court. If there was a case. Which there probably isn't." He sipped his coffee and set it down on the counter. His voice dropped and his eyes softened. "Look, Cara told me about what happened to you in high school, and I'm really sorry you were assaulted, but you shouldn't go around trying to make connections that probably don't exist. A woman was assaulted. Stan took something out of his car and tossed it into the dumpster. That's it."

"Don't you want to see what's in the bags?"

Cara looked at her husband.

"Not particularly," he said. "I doubt there's anything there the least bit interesting other than a bunch of trash."

"If you don't think there's anything in them, there's no harm in looking." Emily smiled and stood. "Come on, it won't take long."

Cara followed her out the front door. Albert trudged along behind them, stopping to grab his keys off the table so he could open the garage door.

"How many did you take," he asked, spotting the white bags in the back seat.

"I didn't count. I just snatched as many as I could feel and got out of there."

They pulled the bags out of her car and set them on the short driveway. Albert pressed the garage door opener and they brought the bags inside.

"Six bags," he said. "Two of them are kitchen-size bags with not much in them. The rest are smaller. Still, that's quite a haul."

"Yeh, well, I just grabbed what I could without checking to see how big the bags were. I knew I needed to get out of there quickly."

"I'll get a lawn and leaf bag so we can dump stuff into it."

She set aside the larger bags, undid the knot in the first small bag, and opened it. "Ick, that smells really bad," Emily said. "Like urine."

Cara held her nose and leaned over to peek inside. "And it

looks like kitty litter in there. Yep, I see the clumps of litter and some empty packages of cat food. You can toss that one aside."

The second bag contained household trash, including wadded-up tissues, rotten lettuce, and remnants of a rotisserie chicken dinner.

"If the next one has diapers, I am outta here," Cara said.

It didn't have diapers, but it was also filled with everyday trash.

"Last one," Albert said to Emily.

She felt her pulse quicken as she opened the bag. She pulled the plastic apart and looked. And gagged. "This one has diapers," she said, quickly closing the bag up again.

"All right. That's enough," Albert said. "Let's put all these in the other bag and I'll put it out with our trash next week."

"I'm telling you, Stan acted guilty. I didn't think it was a coincidence." Tears stung Emily's eyes. "I thought I grabbed all the bags that were similar to the one he tossed in. Maybe I didn't get the right one."

"Maybe, maybe not." Cara put her arm around her. "I know he hurt you a lot, but Albert's right. Perhaps your imagination went into overdrive because you worried Stan might be responsible for that woman's attack. And you wanted to find the evidence to prove it. I get it, Em, really I do."

Emily let herself be led into the house, but she couldn't let it go, couldn't brush away the nagging feeling that Stan was involved in the Delancey Street woman's attack. Chances are she didn't grab the bag he had tossed into the dumpster. But she wasn't done looking for a connection between Stan and the poor woman. Not by a long shot.

Chapter Thirty-Nine

Emily woke up with an unusual hangover. Every cell in her body was swollen with pain and disappointment. She swallowed two aspirin with a big glass of water, went back to bed, and waited for the pills to kick in. A half-hour later, she came downstairs. While the coffee brewed, she fired up her iPad and tapped on the stately Gothic I, the icon for *The Philadelphia Inquirer*. She poured her coffee, then grasped the mug like she'd never let it go. She scrolled through the news, not finding much of interest, then froze. The headline hit her like a hammer slamming her finger instead of the nail.

"Woman Assaulted in Society Hill, Suspect Sought"

She massaged her temples and continued to read. The article reiterated what the two men in the neighborhood had told her. Police were asking the public for help finding the person who'd assaulted the woman.

Suddenly everything moved in slow motion: she picked up her mug and took a gulp of heat and caffeine and reread the story of how the woman's friends said they'd been drinking at a bar on Friday night, and the woman had accepted a ride home from a man who said he lived in her neighborhood.

Every aching pore in her body told her Stan was involved. Cara and Albert might think she was irrational, but she was thinking very clearly. And she knew what she had to do.

Rising from the kitchen table, she put her almost full cup of coffee in the sink, went upstairs, and showered. She dressed and was out the door in fifteen minutes.

The birds sang with enthusiasm, filling the air with their sweet songs; a dog two houses over barked and whined, probably left outside alone for too long. Most people weren't up yet, and that worked in her favor. She sped into the city and parked in her favorite illegal spot in front of the fire hydrant on Lombard just before Sixth.

A young couple out for a walk approached. She tapped her fingers on her leg, impatient for them to pass, then jumped out of her car. She rushed through the gate and over to the dumpster, lifted the lid, and peeked inside. Not much had been tossed into it since she'd looked yesterday. More white trash bags sat inside the dumpster where she'd removed the others, including one that was much smaller. She grabbed it and a few more small bags nearby, eased the heavy lid back down, then hurried to her car.

The discovery of the smallest bag was exciting. From what she could see from her vantage point across the street the previous day, the white bag Stan dropped into the dumpster wasn't very full. She should have realized that yesterday when she grabbed the two larger kitchen trash bags. Then again, she'd been in a hurry. She willed her hands to stop shaking as she steered toward the highway and the fastest route home.

She took the bags out to the slate patio in her little backyard. The bushes and trees gave her a lot of privacy. She picked up the smallest bag. It was light. Not much inside. She paused for a moment, wondering whether she should call Albert and Cara, but she didn't want to go through the whole routine with them again. But she did remember at least some of what

Albert said about contaminating evidence, so she went inside and found a plastic baggie and her gardening gloves. The bulky gloves made opening the small knot on the bag a challenge. After a couple of frustrating minutes, she finally pried the plastic bag open and peered inside.

She squinted at some papers and lifted them out. They were menus from restaurants, but she didn't recognize any of them. A closer inspection told her why. The menus were from Florida. The Tampa area. A shiver ran down her spine. She peered back into the bag and pulled out more papers, some crumpled up, and looked through them. An empty takeout container and other small trash lay in the bottom of the bag. She couldn't see anything connecting Stan to the injured woman.

Frustrated, she collapsed on the wrought iron chair and stared at the menus and other papers in her hands. She dropped her hands to her lap and heard a metallic sound, like a metal paperclip falling onto a desk. The slate beneath her feet was mostly in shadows, but a glint of sunshine broke through, highlighting a piece of silver like a beacon in the night. Something was attached to the silver. She looked closer. It was a stone or piece of bluish-green glass.

She put the menus and other stuff on the table and bent over, picked up the silver piece, and brought it close to her face. A hook held three silver teardrop loops, connected at the base of the hook with a piece of turquoise. The turquoise wasn't perfectly round. It jutted out in the center like a slight bulge. The blue-green color shimmered in the morning sun. It was a beautiful earring.

Was it hers—the woman from Delancey Street? Or had it been on the floor of Stan's car since he'd lived in Florida? Should she take it to the police? And do what? Tell them she dug it out of the dumpster of a guy who'd raped her more than a dozen years ago—a guy she suspected assaulted the poor woman found unconscious in his neighborhood? It sounded like the right thing to do until she said it out loud and realized how it might sound to the cops. They'd probably think she was grasping at straws just like Albert and Cara did. How could she go to the police now? Well, she couldn't. She needed more evidence to prove Stan was involved, then she could show them what she'd found.

She left the other trash bags sitting on her patio, collected the menus and other stuff from the table, and put them back in the bag. Then she secured the bag with a tight knot and took it into the kitchen. She opened one of the lower drawers and dropped the bag inside. How could she connect Stan, the earring, and the woman? Did the police find the earring's partner at the site where the woman had been attacked? Had she been wearing the other earring when she was taken to the hospital?

She picked up the newspaper and reread the article. At last report, the woman was still unconscious. The cops didn't give her name, of course, because she'd been sexually assaulted. They didn't identify her friends either. But the women had been drinking at a bar on Delaware Avenue. Could she find them? Would her friends know if the victim had been wearing the earring Emily held in her hands on the night she was attacked? Her mind raced with so many questions she had trouble focusing on what to do next. But one thing was clear. She had to go back. She placed the earring in a small baggy and left it on the kitchen counter.

Traffic slowed when she turned the corner and came upon a cop standing guard; yellow police tape still prevented everyone except residents from walking down Delancey. Wasn't that unusual? It seemed like a long time to block off a crime scene. What was going on? Finding a parking spot was difficult on a Sunday; most people were home, enjoying a lazy morning. After circling the area for fifteen minutes, she realized it was probably futile to approach the cops again.

Emily swore under her breath and turned back toward home. It was time to take her mind off Stan and think about tomorrow. Work, for the first time in four weeks. On one hand, she was mentally ready to go back, but on the other, her mind never drifted far from what had happened to the Delancey Street woman, to Laura, and to her. The sexual assaults weighed her down. Albert had criticized her for, what did he say, being an amateur sleuth? Yeah, that was it. Well, if she could come up with evidence, police might be able to put Stan behind bars. She couldn't sit around and do nothing.

Chapter Forty

The *Fix It or Ditch It* theme music played in the background. Stan and Suzie stood in front of the big green screen in the Flagstone studio and put on their best smiles. Scenes from the house renovation project in Villanova filled the screen for several seconds, then the camera cut to the cohosts while the video continued to play on the big monitor behind them.

Cara stood near the studio door, almost behind the black curtains covering the studio walls. Even if Stan and Suzie looked her way, they probably couldn't see her because of the bright studio lights. She was conducting another behind-the-scenes investigation into how Stan interacted with the women on the show.

"Next on *Fix It or Ditch It*," Suzie said, "we'll peek behind the stucco and poke under the cedar siding to find out how much work is needed on this once-elegant house in Villanova." She finished her part of the script and turned to Stan.

"Should the owner invest in repairs before putting it on the market or sell it 'As Is' and save himself tons of money and aggravation?" Stan said. "Join us for our newest episode of *Fix It* ..."

"...*or Ditch It*," Suzie added.

Both held their smiles until the director's voice came over the studio speakers. "Cut. Nice job. Let's do it again."

"Hang on," Laura said, walking toward Stan and Suzie with Shelley trailing behind. "That was a good take but, Stan, I think it works better if you're looking at Suzie when she delivers her lines on the two-shot, then you turn to the camera as you begin speaking. It seems more natural for you to be watching her. Does that make sense?"

"Sure, I can do that." Stan nodded.

"And what's with the air quotes around 'As Is'?"

"People put air quotes around things like that," he said, shrugging. "It was spontaneous, but I like it. I think it works."

"I'm not so sure it does," Laura said. "Let's go again and leave out the air quotes this time. We can look at both options once we have two good versions in the can."

Laura returned to her position next to the camera in the middle of the studio. She turned to say something to Shelley and saw Cara back in the corner. While the makeup person touched up Stan and Suzie's powder, she quietly walked over to her.

"Have you been watching long enough to see the last take?" Laura asked under her breath. "What do you think about the air quotes?"

"I have to say, I'm not a fan," she told Laura. "They're okay in conversations but not so much on camera. I can tell Stan wants to keep them in, and you're right to tape a version without them. How did the air quotes hand motion look in the monitor?"

Laura winced. "Unnatural is how I would describe it."

The director called for silence in the studio, and the taping resumed with Stan following Laura's directions.

"Okay," Laura said, walking back to where Stan and Suzie could see her. "That's one good one. Let's get another good one and wrap up."

"And one more with the air quotes?" Stan asked, cocking his head to one side and smiling at Laura.

Laura shuddered and averted her eyes, looked at Suzie instead of him. She turned and walked away. "And one more with air quotes," she said, handing her clipboard to Shelley. She whispered a few words in Shelley's ear and returned to Cara's side.

"You okay?" she asked Laura.

"Yeah, mostly I'm fine," she said, leaning toward Cara and speaking softly. "I just can't take it when he pushes me to get his way, then gives me what he thinks is some cute or coy smile. I have to swallow the urge to throw up. I'll watch the rest of the tapings here with you."

After a few more successful takes, the promo session was over. The bright studio lights dimmed, and the crew shut down the cameras. Stan called Shelley over as he took off his microphone and handed it to one of the sound technicians.

Laura tensed as Shelley reluctantly walked toward Stan. He said something to the young production assistant and laughed, then playfully bumped his shoulder up against hers. Cara couldn't see Shelley's face; what she did see was how quickly Shelley tried to back up from Stan.

Laura grabbed Cara's arm and squeezed hard. The producer's eyes were moist with pain and wide with fear.

"Shelley's so young, so vulnerable," Laura said. "What if ...?" Her voice trailed, and she was unable to finish her thought, but she didn't need to.

Cara was also watching and worrying. Was it time for her to step in, to issue another warning to Stan? He didn't think he was doing anything that could be described as overt sexual harassment, except that Shelley had already said she didn't like it when he touched her. Bumping her shoulder was likely an unwelcome touch. Maybe she should tell Jessica and let her determine the next steps.

Then Laura spoke again and changed everything.

"It's not just about me. I can't let him hurt her, or anyone else. I'd hate myself forever if I didn't do something to stop him." Laura turned away and rushed out of the studio.

Chapter Forty-One

Four weeks away from work felt like an eternity. Being immersed in her life and traumas only intensified Emily's sense of distance. She pulled herself out of the driver's seat and leaned against her SUV, then took a moment to settle her racing pulse and prepare her trembling legs to walk normally. Breathe, she reminded herself. She took several deep breaths, closed the driver's door, and strode toward the main entrance.

The moment she passed through the front door, she was greeted with a friendly smile and hello from the receptionist, then pulled into a warm hug by Martin. Martin, who knew from their conversation the night before that this would be difficult, had offered to drive her to work. He also understood why she needed to walk in on her own, but his presence inside BAM's front doors reminded her she didn't have to do this all by herself.

"Oh, it is so good to see you here," Emily whispered after kissing Martin's cheek and falling into his outstretched arms.

"You knew I wouldn't let you do this without me," he said, holding her tight. "Today, every day, I'm here for you."

She dabbed the tears from her eyes, patted his arms, and

pulled away. Samantha and Tina shot through the employees-only door, scurried across the lobby, and hugged her simultaneously.

"Welcome back, Em," Tina said with a catch in her voice.

"Ditto that," Samantha echoed. "We've really been looking forward to this day."

"I still can't believe how they treated you," Tina said. "They're lucky you haven't filed some kind of claim against the company."

"That's not a route I want to take," Emily said, smiling at each one in turn. It was so good to see their faces, so reassuring to be in their presence. "I don't think a lawsuit would be good for any of us."

The four of them chatted quietly for a moment until Martin interrupted and tilted his head toward the hallway. "I know Tina and Samantha will catch up more with you later," he said. "Come on. I'll walk you to your office."

A few people shouted out greetings as they walked by. When Emily turned into her office, she was overwhelmed by a huge bouquet of flowers in pink, yellow, red, and orange, surrounded by lush greenery. Her hand flew to her mouth, and she turned to Martin.

"How did you know I dreamed you would do this?" Her eyes filled with tears and appreciation.

"Just a lucky guess."

She touched the flowers, inhaled their sweetness, and felt a calmness settle over her. "I've said it before, but I could not have gotten through these past few weeks, through the stuff at work and the stuff coming up from my past, without you." She looked at him and tapped the spot over her heart several times. "I should be giving you flowers."

His eyes grew misty, and he swallowed several times.

"I've got a meeting in five minutes, so I have to scoot," he said in a raspy voice. "But I'll see you at ten. In the meantime,

I'm sure you have lots of messages to review and calls to return, so I'll let you get to them." He hustled out the door.

She picked up the vase with both hands and moved it to the conference table, then returned to her desk. *I'm not going to dwell on what it feels like to be back in my office*, she thought. *I'm just going to figure out what needs to be done and try to let this day be as normal as it can be.*

She prioritized her phone messages and was about to tackle the stack of paperwork when the phone rang.

"Emily, it's Kathy Engle at Clifton Pharma. I heard you were coming back to work today and wanted to say hello."

"It's nice to hear your voice," Emily said. "I'm at my desk, looking through messages and trying to wrap my brain around the reports that need my immediate attention. It's good to be back. How are you?"

"I'm well, but I had to call and tell you how sorry I am over what happened." This wasn't the Kathy who laughed with her at the Clifton party in the hours before Pete Shelby groped her. This Kathy was all business in a way Emily had rarely heard before. "I'm annoyed like so many of the women who work with me. We're all disappointed Warren demanded your removal from our account. Word around the office is that Warren and Pete had a heated conversation, but if anyone knows what was said, they're not talking."

Kathy had the best intentions in calling, but Emily didn't want to get drawn into a conversation about what had happened. She wanted to focus on the present and ease out of the conversation as quickly as possible.

"I appreciate your call, and I'm sorry we won't be working together anymore," Emily said, taking the pink slip with Kathy's message from a couple of weeks ago, crumpling it in her hand, and tossing it into the waste basket. "But I need to move on and put my energies into the accounts I still have. I'm sure you understand." She was blunt, almost rude.

The line was silent for a moment. "I hear you. I'm just so sorry this happened. Perhaps we can get together for lunch one day."

"Perhaps, after a little more time has passed and this is well behind me. I don't want anyone at BAM or Clifton accusing us of talking business, but we've always had wonderful conversations about non-work issues, so I'd like to maintain our relationship. I just think we, or I, need to tread carefully."

"You're not thinking of taking any legal action, are you?"

Why did people keep asking her that? Did they think she had grounds for a suit, either against BAM or Clifton? Is that why Kathy called, to find out if she was going to sue Clifton? When Cara had brought up the possibility of legal action over dinner the other night, Albert had cautioned her against suing because it could backfire. After all, he'd reminded her, she'd slapped Pete Shelby in front of a lot of people, and he might counter-sue for assault. Albert advised her it would not be smart to invite that kind of trouble.

"No, I'm not. Just being careful. Thanks for calling, and I promise I'll be in touch."

The day started in slow motion, but then it flew by: her one-on-one with Martin, a quick welcome-back chat in the hallway with Chris, and more hugs than she could remember receiving in the office. She kept her focus on what was ahead, but, inevitably, other women at BAM stopped in to commiserate with her.

"Nice flowers," Tina said, poking her head around the corner. Tina lowered her voice as she walked into her office. "I heard you had a quick chat with Chris. How did it go?"

"No biggie," Emily said, rising from her desk and crossing the room to close the door. "I felt like he was walking on eggshells, and I'm good with that. I'm not suggesting he feels guilty for how I was treated …" she paused. "Well, maybe I am. In some ways, maybe he should feel guilty, although he was nice enough about giving me the two additional weeks off when I requested them. Of course, I'm still off the Clifton account and that won't change."

Tina sat in a chair across from Emily's desk. "But it's still wrong."

"I know." Emily remained on her feet, too agitated to sit.

"Several of us had an informal gathering at The Main Brew," Tina said, referring to one of their favorite pubs in Manayunk. "We drew up a list of concerns we want management to address, including creating a more professional environment and addressing the kind of inappropriate comments like Jeremy and Artie made during the Bryson account meeting." Tina pushed her bangs off her forehead and shook her head once. "I can't believe it's been a month since that meeting."

"Tell me about it. Four weeks feel like forever."

Tina nodded. "After our initial meeting, a few of us invited all female employees to a closed-door meeting here one afternoon. Chris got wind of it, not that we were trying to hide it, so he wasn't surprised when we approached him the following day. He's agreed to some sensitivity training for all employees."

"That's amazing. Good work."

"Thanks. Unfortunately, it came at your expense."

"I'll take the silver lining. I appreciate what you've done, and I'll be sure to thank Samantha next time I see her." Emily finally came around her desk and sat down. "Can you bring me up to speed on our accounts?" she asked, tapping the pile of file folders in front of her. She was one of those people who kept information about her accounts not only on her computer, but also as hard copies in file folders. Too many lost digital files had convinced her to always keep a hard copy.

Tina spent the next half hour updating her and answering questions. The two of them walked to the cafeteria for coffee, which Emily hoped would give her a jolt of energy. The fast-paced work environment reminded her she'd been on the sidelines for several weeks and had to focus hard to keep up; the end of the day couldn't come soon enough. She returned to her office with the coffee already half gone. Her phone rang the minute she sat down.

Laura got right to the point and spoke quickly. "Remember when you said if I wanted to go to the police and file a complaint against Stan, you would go with me?"

Emily smothered the sharp breath that stabbed her chest at the sound of Stan's name and the news that Laura had called to share with her. "Yes, of course," she practically whispered.

"I'm going to do it," Laura said. "I'm going to leave work a little early and talk to the detectives in the city's sex crimes unit. I can't sit by and do nothing, not when I might be able to stop what he's doing."

Chapter Forty-Two

"Thanks again for doing this." Laura jumped into the passenger seat, dropped her overstuffed bag on the floor next to her feet, then buckled her seat belt. She had dark gray circles under her eyes and her hands couldn't stop moving.

"I'm glad I could be here for you like I promised." Emily steered onto Columbus Boulevard and drove north. The Philadelphia Police Administration building, or the roundhouse as it was commonly called, was an easy drive from Flagstone's studios. "The other night it sounded like you would never go to the police," she said. "Do you mind if I ask you what changed?"

"In a way, nothing changed. With Stan, that is." Laura told her how Stan had been overly friendly with Shelley that morning in the studio, even though the young woman had asked him not to touch her. "She's just a kid out of college, and she looked so vulnerable when he joked with her and bumped her. It was easy to see how he could manipulate her." Laura wrapped her arms around her body for warmth and comfort. "I couldn't live with myself if he hurt her, or anyone else, and I could've prevented it."

Laura stared out the window, and Emily respected her apparent need for silence. After several minutes, they pulled into the crowded police parking lot and snagged a spot just vacated by a big van.

"When I called and spoke to an officer," Laura said, "he told me the Special Victims Unit is based in a separate facility in North Philadelphia. But, as luck would have it, the senior officer assigned to sexual assault investigations was in court today in Center City, so he said she could meet me here." Laura watched two officers escort a handcuffed man wearing gray sweatpants and matching shirt through the parking lot and into the roundhouse. "It's a little overwhelming to actually be here. Talk about an imposing building."

"It's probably meant to be, don't you think?" They watched the man escorted into the building until the door closed behind him. "What's the name of the officer you're meeting?"

"Actually, I don't remember." Laura squeezed her lower lip between her thumb and forefinger and frowned. "That's unlike me."

"Don't worry," Emily reassured her. "You have a lot on your mind. They'll tell us inside. You ready?"

The shakiness disappeared from Laura's voice, and she turned to Emily. "Yes, I'm ready. Let's do this."

They marched to the front entrance and told the officer behind the Plexiglass window the reason for their visit. After checking their drivers' licenses, he issued visitor badges and buzzed them into the lobby.

"Have you ever been here before?" Laura asked.

"Nope," Emily answered, looking around at the well-worn marble floors. "And it's not a place I want to visit often, either."

"Ditto."

"Laura Stricker?"

Both their heads whipped in the direction of the voice calling out. A woman in uniform approached them with an outstretched hand and a gentle smile.

"I'm Detective Jamelle Trench."

Laura identified herself and reached out.

The detective took Laura's hand in both of hers and held her gaze. "I'm sorry for what's happened to you and I'm here to support you in any way I can."

"Thank you. I appreciate the opportunity to meet with you. I hope it's okay that I brought a friend. This is Emily Archer."

"It's absolutely okay." Detective Trench greeted Emily and shook her hand. "Follow me. I've secured a room where we can talk."

Trench led them down a narrow hallway and opened the second to last door on the right. Emily expected to walk into an interrogation room, the kind they show on TV with a cold, scuffed linoleum floor, metal table, two metal chairs, and a two-way mirror that allowed others to watch their interviews from an adjoining room. Instead, Trench ushered them into a comfortable conference room with a round table and half a dozen chairs tucked in around it. The walls were decorated with scenic prints, the floor covered with thick carpeting, and a side table held a coffee machine, notepads, pens, and a box of tissues.

Trench opened a small refrigerator under the coffee machine and pulled out three bottled waters, handed one to each of them, and set the third on the table. "Please, have a seat." She grabbed a notepad and pen. "Let's begin with some basic info." Trench pulled out a chair and sat across from Laura.

Laura gave the detective her name, age, address, employer, and how long she'd been working at Flagstone.

"Okay, Laura," Trench said, leaning toward her. "That was the easy stuff. Tell me what happened, beginning with when and where. Give me as much of the backstory as you think is important. I'll hold off my questions until you're finished unless I'm confused."

Laura unscrewed the plastic cap from the water bottle and took a sip. "It happened almost two weeks ago." She explained how drinks with Stan after work led to dinner at her apartment and a sexual encounter she hadn't wanted.

"You told him no?"

"Yes, I did. He was kissing me, which I resisted, and he began pulling on my clothes, trying to get them off. I pushed him away and told him that's not what I wanted." Laura choked back a cry. "But he was so strong. I kept pushing him away. It didn't matter."

Emily got up from the table quietly and put the box of tissues on the table in front of Laura. She sat back in her chair and fought back an urge to cry.

Laura pulled a couple of tissues from the box and wiped her eyes, which remained almost closed as she recounted the attack.

"Tell me again, exactly how long ago this was. Less than two weeks you said?"

"Yes, it was a week ago last Wednesday."

Trench resumed taking notes. "How much contact have you had with him at work since then?"

"We work on the same program at Flagstone Productions, so I interact with him pretty much every day."

"And has he said anything about what happened that night?"

Laura took a deep breath and let it out slowly. Emily slid

her chair closer. Laura glanced at her and gave her a tight smile.

"I called in sick the next day, and he called to see how I was." Laura turned and looked at Trench. "I didn't pick up, so he left a message." She stifled a sob. "He said he hoped I'd had a nice time."

The detective raised her eyebrows. "He said that exactly?"

"Yes."

"Did you save the message?"

"No, I deleted it immediately. In hindsight, I guess I should've kept it."

"Has he asked you out for drinks since? Made any overtures?"

"No. I made it clear I wanted nothing more to do with him. He found out I told Cara what had happened. Then he got angry."

"Who's Cara?"

"My boss. The executive producer of *Fix It or Ditch It*."

"*Fix It or Ditch It*? That's the program you work on—the home restoration show? I love that show."

Trench's enthusiasm for her program brought a smile to Laura's face. "Yes, Stan is the new cohost. Cara's the EP, and also Emily's sister."

Trench nodded and looked again at Emily. "Okay, so, back to when this happened. Did you go to the doctor's or visit the hospital for a rape kit or physical exam?"

"I never gave any thought to doing that. I wasn't going to press charges, and besides, it wasn't a question of whether we had sex, it was that he forced me to. What good would a rape kit or exam for DNA evidence do?"

"It would confirm the presence of his semen or DNA in your body, on your person. Confirm that sexual intercourse had taken place." Trench spoke with calm determination. "Did he physically hurt you, bruise you, scratch you?"

"I had a bruise here, on my cheek, when his elbow hit me. I had red splotches and minor bruises on my face in a few places from where he pressed his hands hard against me."

"Did you scratch him?"

"Yes, when I was struggling with him and pushing him away from me." She explained where her scratches had left their mark on his face.

Trench was quiet as she looked over what she'd written and made additional notes. Emily glanced at the clock on the wall. It was five o'clock. They'd been there almost an hour. She wondered how much longer the detective was going to question Laura and what would happen next.

"I'm going to ask a couple of difficult questions, Laura, questions that will likely upset you, but I want you to trust me. I'm asking them for a reason."

"Okay." The hesitation in Laura's voice was clear. She glanced at Emily for encouragement.

"You said the two of you had been drinking that evening. Were you drinking more than normal? Could your judgment have been impaired?"

"I probably had a little more wine than I usually do. I had a couple of glasses of wine at the bar, then Stan opened a bottle at my house and poured us each a glass. I knew I didn't need any more wine, but I did drink some. I probably had another glass."

"It sounds like quite a bit of alcohol over what, two or three hours?" Trench asked. "How much did Stan drink?"

"I'd say it was closer to three hours. He had at least one glass of wine at my house and two drafts at the bar."

"Either at the bar or when you got to your house, did you give Stan any reason to believe you wanted to have sex with him? Were you flirtatious or—"

"Absolutely not."

"Are you confident you told him no in a way he could

understand—that he couldn't interpret your words or actions as playing hard to get?"

"What are you implying?" Emily said, rising from her chair and staring down at the detective.

Laura looked from Emily to Trench and started crying again.

"Emily, please sit down," Trench emphasized her words with a commanding look, then looked back at Laura.

"Emily, it's okay." Laura grabbed a couple more tissues and wiped her nose. "I think I know what she's getting at. Detective, this was not a 'date gone bad' as some people poorly characterize date rape. It wasn't even a date. It was two colleagues having drinks and dinner. I did not start something and then try to stop it. And I told him no. Strongly. Repeatedly."

Trench looked at Emily, who was still on her feet, and motioned with her head to return to her seat.

Emily lowered her body back into her chair, her eyes never leaving Laura.

"These are questions investigators will ask, and you need to be ready for them. Can you imagine how Stan will react once he learns you've filed a complaint?"

"He's already warned me to keep my mouth shut."

"That's typical." Emily blurted out the words before she could swallow them.

"Excuse me?" Trench glared at Emily. Laura turned to her and nodded. She was done telling her story. Time for Emily to tell hers.

"Is there something you want to say, Emily?" Trench prodded. "You're almost as tense as Laura. What's going on?"

The black and white institutional clock on the wall ticked off the seconds.

"Laura and I have something in common, unfortunately. We've both been sexually assaulted by Stan Hester."

"You what? You think you could've mentioned that earlier?" Trench's eyes shot back and forth between the two. "Are you also here to file a claim against Hester?"

"No. I can't. I was eighteen when he raped me." She fought back tears. "I'm in therapy to deal with the rape, and an attorney told me the statute of limitations has expired. I don't have a choice. I can't do anything about what Stan did to me." She pulled a tissue out of the box and wiped her eyes. "When I found out Stan had assaulted Laura, I knew I had to support her if she was willing to go to the police and press charges. We need you to help us."

Chapter Forty-Three

August 2004

Angela stretched out on the couch, adjusted the pillow around what she thought was her waist, and waited. She'd been doing a lot of that lately. Waiting for more contractions. Waiting for her water to break. Waiting for her baby to arrive. She'd read the articles her mother had given her and handouts from her gynecologist to understand what was happening to her body, and what to expect during the baby's birth. The doctor had talked with Angela and Mrs. Hargood about the possibility of a C-section because Angela's cervix was quite narrow, and the baby was above average weight. That last bit of news came as no surprise to Angela when she considered Felipe's broad shoulders and how she had to stand on her tiptoes and stretch her neck to kiss him. It figured the two of them would make a baby that was difficult for her to give birth to naturally.

Angela thought she was ready, but when the first contractions had hit, she'd yelped and bent over in pain. That was a week ago and contractions had been coming since then, never very close together. Yet. But she knew they would.

"Can I get you a glass of water?" Lacey asked, coming into

the living room and sitting on the chair next to the couch. Angela and Lacey had fought often and grown apart since they'd moved to Buffalo. Lacey missed her friends in Philadelphia, especially Emily, her other classmates, and her familiar surroundings of Central High School. Despite blaming Angela for ruining her life, Lacey still tried to help her when she needed it. It was just the two sisters now and they needed each other more than ever.

"No, thanks," Angela said. "I'm not putting anything else in my body until this kid comes out. I feel like a baby elephant."

"Like you would know how a baby elephant feels?" Lacey rolled her eyes.

"Trust me on this. I've become an expert on—oh, Jesus, Mary, and Joseph," she cried out, grabbing the arm of the couch and panting, struggling to remember the breathing exercises she'd learned in the pre-natal classes she and Lacey had attended. But it was difficult to focus on controlling her breathing when the pain felt like it was ripping out her insides.

Her mother rushed into the room. "Are you okay? That must have been a big contraction."

Angela nodded rapidly and sucked in air between her pursed lips, pushed it back out, sucked it in, pushed it out.

Mrs. Hargood plucked a tissue from the box on the table, knelt on the floor in front of the couch, and wiped the perspiration from Angela's forehead. Their eyes locked and her mother smiled. "It's getting closer to your baby's time."

Angela gasped and grabbed her belly as another contraction sent ripples of pain down the lower part of her body, places she hadn't felt such pain before even during previous contractions.

For the next hour, the three of them timed her contractions and helped Angela breathe through them, deciding after the last one it was time to go to the hospital. Lacey ran upstairs and came down a few minutes later with Angela's overnight bag and their mother's handbag. Angela leaned on her mother and sister as they walked down the hallway and out the front door.

Several hours later, the gynecologist came into Angela's hospital room and, after examining her, reported that her suspicions about a C-section were accurate. Angela looked at her mother, sure the fear was evident in her face.

"It'll be okay, honey. Lacey and I will be right here, waiting for you and your baby."

Minutes later, two nurses hustled into the room and began prepping Angela for surgery, checking the IV port in her arm, and telling her what to expect.

"Don't you worry. We're going to bring your healthy baby into the world and soon you will be able to hold your precious bundle." The anesthesiologist walked in, reviewed Angela's chart, and explained about the spinal anesthesia she would administer that would allow doctors to perform the C-section.

Everything after that was a blur. When she woke up later that day, she was too groggy to focus. She felt her mother's touch before she saw her face or heard her voice.

"Hi, my brave girl. Just let yourself sleep. Everything's fine. You have a baby boy, and he is healthy and so beautiful."

Her mother's face was close to hers as she spoke, and Angela was happy to hear her voice, happy to know her baby was okay. "What happened? I went to sleep. I wasn't supposed to sleep."

"There were complications and they had to use general anesthesia. Don't worry. You'll be fine. You need to keep sleeping."

"Can I see him?" she asked, her throat raw, her voice scratchy.

"Not yet, honey. Lacey's keeping an eye on him. You'll see him soon enough, but right now you need to rest."

Angela drifted off to sleep, listening to her mother and the nurses fussing over her, tucking the sheet a little tighter, pushing a strand of hair off her forehead.

The next time Angela opened her eyes, Lacey sat beside her bed, her arms just out of reach. Angela swallowed and tried to speak, but her voice was still hoarse. Whatever sound she made was enough to get her sister's attention.

"Hi, sleepy."

"Mmm." Her attempt at speaking wasn't much. She swallowed and tried again. "How long have I been out?" She flexed her fingers and stretched her neck from side to side.

"The baby's delivery was complicated. There was some bleeding and that's why they had to put you under. You've been dozing off and on for about twenty-four hours."

"Complicated? The baby?"

"Is fine. The baby is fine. He's so sweet. Wait until you see him."

She smiled. She had a baby boy. Then Angela caught her breath as a sharp pain struck her gut. "Hurts," she said.

"I know," Lacey told her. "The doctor said it would hurt for a while."

The door opened and Mrs. Hargood walked in with some baby blankets in her arms. Angela squinted and her mother came into sharper focus. Not just baby blankets, Angela suddenly realized. A baby. Her baby.

"I'll place him on your chest," her mother said, "but I'll help hold him. The doctor said you'll be weak for a couple more days."

Angela's eyes filled with tears watching her mother gently nestle the baby in her arms. He smelled sweet and his body warmed her. Her mother's arm wrapped around hers, and together they held this little boy who would change her life. Had already changed her life. He would need her for as many years as Angela had lived, and that thought slowed her racing pulse to a crawl. Her life was not her own now. Her mother had talked about the responsibility of having a child, of raising it, but it didn't really hit Angela until she looked at the sleeping face and the tiny fingers grasping her thumb.

Jesus, Mary, and Joseph, she thought. What have I done?

Chapter Forty-Four

"I hope I'm not calling too late."

Lacey's voice was so strained that Emily immediately put down her magazine and sat up.

"No, not late at all. What's up? You sound upset."

"I'm not sure what to do and I need someone to talk to about it. Timothy's asking a lot of questions about his father. Now that we're living in Philadelphia, and he knows we used to live here, that his mother dated a boy here, well, he wants to find his father. To meet his father."

"Do you think that's a good idea? You don't know how his father will react—if you can even track him down."

"I don't think it's about what I want. It's what Timothy wants. And needs. A boy needs his father. Any child needs their parents. Especially when one of them is not available."

Emily thought back to their conversation in the café a week ago. "You never finished telling me what happened to Angela. Did she go back to school after the baby was born?"

"Father pressured her again to give up the baby, but she remained steadfast in her refusal. Said she would rather die than give her son to a stranger. I'm so glad Angela didn't let

Father take Timothy away. He's a real blessing to my mom and me."

Emily could almost hear Lacey's proud smile through their cellphones.

"Angela always said she planned on going back to finish high school after the baby was about six months old," Lacey continued. "Mom had never worked, again because of the old-fashioned values of my father. We all pitched in with Timothy. Father was tough at first, but he grew to love his grandson. I had no energy for anything else since I was struggling with a loss of place, friends, even my identity. I went to school, did my homework, helped with Timothy, and kept my head down. My relationship with my sister was strained. We fought some and I blamed her a lot for my unhappiness." Lacey paused. "And then Angela disappeared. Mom said she left to run an errand one day and never came home."

"Just like that?" Again the hints that something happened to Angela, but her mother said she didn't know and Lacey had yet to say more, which had Emily's mind swirling with possibilities, many of them dark and ominous.

"The police searched a wide area and found the car, but there was no sign of Angela. A couple of weeks after she disappeared, I overheard my parents arguing in the kitchen. My mother kept pushing my dad. She asked him what he was hiding from her. Then I heard something I'd never heard before. My father crying." Lacey choked up and sniffed back tears. "I sat on the second-floor landing holding my breath. After a couple of minutes, my father said that just before she disappeared, he and Angela had a terrible fight. She had run from the room screaming that he didn't love her. I started crying too and slipped back into my bedroom before they realized I'd been listening."

Emily cupped her hand over her mouth and stared at the

floor, unable to find words. So much had happened to Lacey and her family, and Emily hadn't known any of it.

Lacey picked up the story again. "My mother was cleaning Angela's room and going through her things one day a few weeks after she disappeared. Mom discovered some pills in Angela's bedside table that turned out to be fentanyl. She also found a book on postpartum depression. Angela never told anyone what she was going through, the pain of the emergency surgery, the demands of being a new mother, a single teenage mother to boot. Apparently, she tried to handle the stress and pressure as much as she could by herself and hid a lot from us. You know, she was daddy's little girl. I can only guess, in some ways, she must have felt guilty for letting him down. Then postpartum issues on top of that. Then an addiction to fentanyl." Lacey's voice shook and she covered the phone while she found a tissue and blew her nose. "Sorry about that. To this day it brings me to tears when I think about how overwhelmed and alone Angela must have felt. I wish I had known. I wish I could have helped her. I wish I hadn't been so mad at her so often."

"How much has Timothy been told about what happened to his mother?"

"We've been vague because we don't know all the details. Can't know. But the same might not be true about Timothy's father. Timothy said tonight he might never be able to know what happened to his mother, but now that we're living in Philadelphia, why can't he look for his father? Learn about how his father and mother met. And I didn't have a good answer for him."

"Do you know who the father is?"

"Father forced Angela to tell him the boy's name. One day Angela told me his first name was Felipe, but she made me promise never to tell anyone else. And never to contact him. As if I could find him by his first name in a city this size. So do

I honor my promise to my sister, or do I help my nephew find his family here in Philly?"

Lacey's father. He forced his family to move from Philadelphia. Why did they move back? "How is it you are here now if your father wanted you to leave Philadelphia for good?"

"Father died a few months ago. He had a massive heart attack. Some people from his company came to Buffalo for the funeral, and one woman I'd met over the years knew I was a teacher. Knew we used to live here and that I went to Central. She had a child at Central, had heard of a sudden opening, and told me that if I was interested, I should contact the school district. I applied immediately. Asked a few people at Central and in the district's administration for favors, and I got the job. So not long ago, Mother, Timothy, and I moved back to Philly."

Now that Emily was up to date, it was time to back up to the beginning of the conversation. "So Timothy's father is named Felipe? You don't know his last name?"

"No, Angela never told me, and my mother can't remember it."

"There are, what, forty or more high schools in Philadelphia?"

"More like fifty or so. Plus charter schools. Plus the Catholic schools. There could be eighty schools for high school students in the city and my head is spinning thinking about searching for a Felipe in all of them."

"Wow, I had no idea. It'd be like finding a needle in a haystack."

"I did make an attempt. I went to the library at Central after class one day and looked in the yearbooks. I found Angela's photo in a yearbook from her sophomore year. So I checked yearbooks a couple of years before and a couple of years after and found six students named Felipe."

"That's a start, I guess."

"What do I do? Call them up and say, hey, I'm Lacey Hargood. Did you date my sister, Angela in 2003?"

They were both quiet, wondering how those conversations might go. How many of the Felipes would hang up? How many of them were no longer alive? How long would it take to track down Timothy's father?

"I know it won't be easy, and I'd be willing to help, but if you know the first name of Timothy's father, and you might be able to track him down, admittedly with some work, how can you deny them the opportunity to meet?"

"I'm afraid Timothy will be rejected, his father won't want any part of his life. He probably doesn't even know he has a son. What if he's married with kids of his own and wants no part of an illegitimate child from his past?"

Emily understood why not knowing how things would turn out with Timothy's father upset Lacey, but she also knew it was difficult to hide from the past. And not always healthy.

"I understand wanting to protect Timothy, but he's on the verge of becoming an adult. I'm not a mother, but I think it's only fair to help Timothy find his father." Emily hoped she wasn't pushing, but Lacey had called her for a reason—to talk about what to do. "Did your mother keep Angela's personal items? Maybe you could go back through them. See if she ever wrote down Felipe's full name. I think it's worth trying to find him. Sometimes you can avoid the past and sometimes you can't. It might be healing for all of you."

Chapter Forty-Five

Delivering bad news was never easy. Cara was relieved the pressure wasn't on her and Jessica this time as they made their way to Jim's office. He didn't waste time with small talk.

"Detective Trench from the Philadelphia police sex crimes unit called me and requested a meeting," Jim said, running his hand through his short-cropped hair, a nervous gesture Cara recalled seeing only when he was about to deliver serious financial news and word of possible layoffs to the staff. He waved her and Jessica over to his conference table, then sat next to Flagstone's co-owner, Aaron. "The detective said one of our employees accused Stan of sexual assault. Rape. Given our past discussion, I am guessing the woman involved was Laura. Were either of you aware of this?"

"Laura told me what happened," Cara said, "but she said she had no intention of going to the police." The last time she saw Laura was when the producer walked out of the studio after the promo shoot.

"Well, something changed her mind, and now police are coming here to talk with Stan, to get his side of the story."

Jim's hand shook when he reached for his mug of coffee, so he grabbed it with both hands. Sweat beaded on his upper lip. His face was flushed as if he'd just finished a thirty-minute cardio workout.

Cara was relieved Jim was upset. That meant he understood the implications of Laura's trip to the police and the ramifications of Stan's behavior. Aaron, on the other hand, was typically distant, the guy who preferred to stay in the background. He was Flagstone's numbers guy, more comfortable alone in front of his computer than dealing with staff issues or people in general.

They had just started to talk about how to handle the situation when Jim's phone buzzed.

"Please bring them to my office," he told his assistant. He replaced the receiver and strode toward the door. "Let's hear what the police have to say."

Trench introduced herself and Officer Toni Farrelli, also of the city's sex crimes unit, then asked if they could speak to Jim and Aaron alone. Cara and Jessica left the room and were talking in the hallway when Stan rounded the corner and lumbered past them. He threw a glance in their direction, his jaw tense, his mouth trying—unsuccessfully—to form a smile. He moved past them quickly and disappeared.

"Boy, I'd give anything to have a hidden microphone in Jim's office," Cara said, the executive producer in her automatically thinking about how to capture information.

"We'll learn soon enough, I think. I'll talk with you later."

Jessica left her standing in the hallway, staring after Stan and wondering what he was telling his bosses and the cops. Not that Cara couldn't guess. Just thinking about him sitting there, denying what he did to Laura, stirred up the anger inside her again. What he did to Laura. What he did to Emily. The very thought ... A rumbling noise rose from the pit of her stomach. It began as a little tremor and grew quickly. The urge to throw up raced up her throat, and she clasped her hand over her mouth. She pressed her other hand against her stomach, leaned back against the wall, and willed her body to calm down. After another minute, she pushed away from the wall and shuffled back to her office.

Half an hour later, there was a knock on her open door.

"Laura, come on in." Cara motioned to the empty chair in front of her desk.

"I can't," Laura said, looking to her left and right and dropping her voice to a near whisper. "The police want to talk with me. Again. Now." The pen between Laura's thumb and forefinger danced with nervous energy. "Will you come with me?"

"Of course. Will they let me?" She stood and reached for her cellphone.

"Detective Trench let Emily sit with me last night when I went to police headquarters."

Cara tried to hide her surprise. "I didn't know you went to the police. That is, not until Jim told me this morning."

"After watching Stan with Shelley yesterday ..." Tears filled Laura's eyes, and she looked at the floor.

"Oh, Laura. I'm sorry this is happening to you." Cara hurried across the room. "Of course, I'll come with you. Where do they want to meet?"

"Jim's office."

"Do you want some coffee? A glass of water?"

Laura shook her head.

"Okay, let's go."

"Laura, how are you today?" Detective Trench asked as soon as Cara and Laura walked in.

"I'm okay. This is Cara, the executive producer I told you about who works with me on *Fix It or Ditch It*."

"Laura said she thought it would be okay if I join her."

"You're Emily's sister?"

She nodded once. Jim tilted his head and raised his eyebrows, his movements seemingly asking why the detective knew who Emily was, why her sister was involved in this situation with Laura and Stan.

"Later," Cara mouthed to him.

"Do you want to meet here or in the conference room?" Jim asked.

"Which is more private?" Trench said.

"Definitely here."

"Then we'll stay here. Just the four of us, if you don't mind." Trench motioned to Officer Farrelli and the two other women in the room.

"Sure. Take as long as you need." Jim walked out, followed by slow-stepping Aaron.

Trench introduced Officer Farrelli and they settled into the couch and comfortable chairs in front of the windows overlooking a well-tended spot of land between the building and the nearby line of deciduous trees. "Have you had any second thoughts about filing the complaint, or any additional information you want to share with us?"

"I'm fine, and no, I am *not* changing my mind. I knew when I started this that I wouldn't back down, no matter how unpleasant it got."

"Officer Farrelli and I just finished questioning Mr. Hester. As you expected, he said the sex was consensual."

Laura listened with a steady gaze and tight lips. Her feet were planted firmly on the floor, and she sat tall in her chair. Cara admired her determination.

"While we were talking with Mr. Hester, we noticed a few scratches on his face and neck. You said you were aware that you'd scratched him?"

"Yes, as I was pushing him away from me." She closed her eyes for a moment and took a deep breath. Then she looked back at the detective.

Trench tapped her phone on and continued to speak while she searched the device. "You said the assault was almost two weeks ago, so I didn't expect to see bright scratches on Mr. Hester's face today. He was wearing makeup when he met with us, but even with the makeup, I saw scratches. After he removed the heavy foundation, at our request, Officer Farrelli and I took some photos."

Trench set her phone on the coffee table and used her fore-finger to spin it around so Laura could see the image.

Cara leaned in as well.

"This is a photo of his left cheek. You can see faint remnants of a scratch. Do you see it?"

Laura nodded. "That's where I caught him with my fingernails. I noticed that scratch the following week when it was slightly red and had a thin scab over it."

"He told us just now that you did scratch him, but he claimed you scratched him during sex that got a little rough."

"That's a lie," Laura said.

"Yes, that's a lie," Cara echoed. "Or else what he told me about getting those scratches while jogging in Fairmount Park is a lie. Both can't be true."

"When did he tell you that?"

Cara described her conversation with Stan in his office the day after Laura's assault. Trench asked Officer Farrelli to make a note to follow up with Stan, then she reached over and swiped her finger across the phone screen, revealing another image.

"What about this photo of scratches just under his jawline on the right side of his face?" She paused, swiping her finger across the phone again. "And this scratch near his hairline, also on the right."

Laura studied the photos, swiping them back and forth. "These look newer to me."

"Could you have caused these scratches as well?"

"I don't know how I would've managed to reach him there." Laura closed her eyes to focus on the memory. "He had my left arm pinned against the couch, almost underneath me. I don't know how I could've reached around with my right arm and scratched him there." Laura looked up at the detective and searched her face for information.

"Have you noticed these scratches under his makeup the last few days?" Trench kept her voice soft and gentle, prodding Laura, but not leading her.

Cara looked at the images as Laura reviewed them again and tried to recall seeing the scratches on Stan. She thought back over the past several days. The *Fix It* crew hadn't been shooting many on-camera segments, in studio or in the field. But she did recall one day last week when she bumped into Stan in the hallway and noticed he'd been wearing makeup more often around the office. That was unusual.

"I can't say for sure," Laura said. "Honestly, I've been trying hard not to look at him unless I really have to."

"I do think Stan's been wearing makeup more than usual," Cara said. "Even on days he wasn't scheduled to appear on camera. And the day after he and Laura went out, I was in his office and saw those scratches on the left side of his face. They were red and puffy. That's when he told me a tree branch caught him while he was jogging."

Trench nodded and pointed to the last two photos on the screen. "And these?"

"I don't remember seeing those that day." Cara nodded at the photos, then looked back Trench. "Matter of fact, I can almost guarantee he didn't have those the day after he assaulted Laura."

"How can you be so sure?"

"I'm a detail person," Cara said. "It's key to my job. I analyze images, scripts, people on camera, video. I look at everything very critically. And very closely. I recall seeing the scratches on the left side of his face the day after he and Laura went out. I'm quite sure I didn't see those scratches in the other photos."

Laura stared at Cara, mouth open, lines forming around her eyes and forehead as what Cara said registered with her.

"So, if I didn't scratch Stan there," Laura asked, "who did?"

"I don't know," Detective Trench said, retrieving her phone from the table and putting it in her chest pocket next to her two-way radio. "But Officer Farrelli and I are going to find out."

Chapter Forty-Six

"He was questioned by the police, but nothing happened?" Emily tried to keep her voice even so the hysteria in her heart wouldn't reach her mouth. "The police didn't take him in and charge him? How can that be?"

"It's what we feared and expected." Cara told her what happened at Flagstone with Detective Trench and Officer Farrelli, then asked about something that had been bothering her. "I didn't know you were at police headquarters with Laura yesterday."

"Sorry I didn't mention it." She rested her elbows on her desk and switched the phone to her other hand. "I was exhausted when I got home and just didn't have it in me to call or text. Sorry," she repeated.

"I understand, but I was caught off guard when Laura told me." Papers rustled in the background, then Cara continued. "There was an interesting development though."

"What? Is it good news?"

Cara told her about the scratches on Stan's face, scratches Laura said she could not have caused.

"Could they be from the Delancey Street victim?"

"I don't know, but Detective Trench said she and Officer Farrelli are looking into it."

"I wonder how they are going to do that." Emily flashed back to the earring she found in the trash bag from Stan's dumpster—probably, maybe, hopefully, from the bag he threw into the dumpster—and wondered again if she should take it to the police. Why didn't she rush off to tell them? Why did she hesitate? What was she afraid of? That they wouldn't believe her? That they would yell at her for contaminating evidence? Well, she had, hadn't she? But she had found a clue that could be important. Could be, she tried to remind herself. She didn't really know if the earring belonged to the injured woman. And if it didn't, the cops would probably reprimand her, tell her to keep her nose out of a police investigation, and she'd be back at square one. She couldn't afford to be wrong, so first, she needed to find out whose earring she found. And how was she going to do that?

"I have no idea," Cara said.

Her throat seized, and she almost dropped the phone. Had she been thinking all those things about the earring, or did she say them out loud? She hadn't told Cara about the earring yet, didn't want her and Albert to criticize her for what she'd done. What she had to do. Her brother-in-law couldn't understand the ferocious drive within her to find evidence against Stan. Her sister understood but didn't like Emily running off and playing amateur sleuth. But Emily had to act. Had to help put him behind bars for attacking someone else because she couldn't have him arrested for raping her.

"No idea about what?" Emily's muscles tensed while she waited for Cara's answer.

"Weren't you listening?" Cara asked.

"Sorry. Like I said, it was a stressful night, and my brain is tired. My mind went off on a tangent."

"About what?"

Thank goodness. She'd only been thinking, not talking out loud.

"I'm upset the police didn't arrest Stan," Emily said. "I knew it was a long shot, but I guess I was hoping they would charge him. I'm fighting a losing battle trying to think about anything else right now."

"I understand. This is a complicated situation that just got messier."

"How so?"

"After the police left, I had a battle with Jim and Aaron. They suggested we take Laura off *Fix It or Ditch It*, at least temporarily. Aaron went so far as to say perhaps she should be removed from the show. Period."

"Are you serious? That wouldn't be fair to her."

"No, it wouldn't, and she already told me she wouldn't give up the show. That was before she filed the complaint, so, yes, the situation is more complicated now."

"Still, removing her, even for a short time, would be perceived as punishment. Why not replace him for a few weeks instead?" Why was the man in these situations so often protected and the woman treated unfairly? Emily decided not to dwell on that dynamic again or she'd stir up the anger and frustration she'd been working so hard to control.

"The idea of taking Stan off the show was shot down immediately by Aaron. He said, and I quote, 'We can't take the star off the show just become someone claims she didn't like the way he had sex with her.'"

"Please tell me he didn't really say that." Emily tapped the heels of her feet, first the left, then the right, then back and forth again and again to calm down.

"I wish I could. At least Jim cut him off and said no one was being taken off the show right away. He wants to let things 'cool down,' as Jim put it. Jim is clearly the more sensitive one in the room and I'm grateful he is taking this seriously."

"I don't know how you deal with Aaron. I would've pulled my hair out if I'd been sitting in those meetings."

"It's been a difficult day, and that's putting it mildly," Cara said. "I know we hoped the police would arrest Stan, and they still might. But we've got to let them do their work."

Emily sighed. "I suppose so."

They hung up after promising to talk the next day.

Just let the police do their work, Emily thought. She drummed her fingers on her desk. *What if I've already done their work for them? What if I discovered evidence linking Stan to the victim? How can I find out if that earring belongs to her?*

She turned to her computer and consulted the local news websites, but there was nothing new about the attack on the Delancey Street woman. She read over the initial story again. Halfway through the article, she stopped and instinctively picked up her pen. The Anchor Bar & Grill was on the water-front off Columbus Avenue just below Spring Garden. Two of the woman's friends said they last saw her leaving with the man who offered to drive her home. She made some notes, then picked up the phone.

"I need your help," she told Martin as soon as he answered. "Do you want to grab a drink with me at the Anchor Bar & Grill?" She held her breath, hoping he would say yes.

"The Anchor? On the Delaware River? Is this for a client?"

"Uh, no. Actually, I'm trying to track down a clue about the Delancey Street woman."

"And you want to go to the Anchor because ..." His voice trailed off.

"Maybe I can find her friends or someone else who saw the guy she left with." It took so long for Martin to answer, Emily was sure he was going to turn her down.

"It's a long shot. Besides, don't you think the cops would've tracked down the woman's friends and looked for the guy who hurt her? And they would've scoured the place where they found her that night."

"Maybe, but they don't have—" Emily stopped herself from mentioning the earrings. She hadn't told anyone yet. Should she confide in Martin?

"They don't have what?"

"My charming personality," she laughed and waited for his response.

"I can't tonight. Ramón and I have plans," he finally said. "How about tomorrow?"

She couldn't hide her disappointment, but Martin had been too good to her to push. She agreed to wait until the following evening.

"Promise me you won't go there alone tonight." He waited for her answer. "Em?"

He knew her too well. She struggled with the desire to find clues implicating Stan and summoned up all the strength she could to respond. "I promise."

"Now say it as if you mean it."

She laughed again, despite herself. "You're so tough on me."

"That's because I know you too well. Promise me." The levity in his voice was replaced by a firmness she rarely heard.

"I promise. I won't go tonight without you."

"Good. See you tomorrow."

Emily checked the time on her computer monitor. Wow, it was already well after five. How much time had she spent poking around the internet, thinking about collecting evidence against Stan? She packed up her bag and walked out to the parking lot. After she turned onto Main Street, she fought the urge to keep driving straight into the city. Reluctantly, she steered left and headed toward home.

"Boy, do I need a distraction," she said as she looked out the window for pedestrians before making a turn. "I need to get out of my own thoughts, or I'm going to drive myself crazy." She turned on the radio and was about to push the button for one of the area's rock stations when the anchor's deep voice from the all-news station filled the car. His first words piqued her interest, and she raised the volume.

"Police in New Jersey just confirmed the man who assaulted and murdered the young mother of two last month near Trenton had a history of violence and spent more than a decade behind bars. He was released from prison only two days prior to the attack."

Emily pounded the steering wheel and screamed so loud she drowned out the radio. How many more women had to suffer at the hands of violent men? She spun the wheel and took the next right toward the Anchor Bar. And she asked Martin to forgive her for breaking her promise.

Chapter Forty-Seven

The deep, thumping bass and pounding drums caused Emily's pulse to speed up as she approached the main entrance of the Anchor Bar & Grill. Her mind swirled with images, wondering what it had been like the night the woman from Delancey Street was here. Emily stood in the last place the poor woman was seen. Stan may have parked where Emily did. Her nerves tingled with energy and fear. What if he was here now? Drinking and eyeing his next victim? What would she do? How could she prevent herself from lashing out at him?

"Whoa, girl," she whispered under her breath. "You're like a runaway freight train going downhill. Chill."

She stepped inside and her head swiveled from side to side, taking in the large room with a small band in the front corner away from the door and tables organized in small groups around the dance floor. Next was the rectangular bar, surrounded by tall captain's chairs and providing a buffer between the drinkers, dancers, and diners. The dining room on the other side overlooked the Delaware River through three walls of windows.

What a relief. Stan was nowhere in sight. But this could be his kind of crowd. The people who were perched on their barstools were better dressed than those who stopped in other neighborhood bars on the way home from work.

The maître d' stand, which held a phone, menus, and the book of reservations, stood empty. The bar looked more promising anyway, so she walked over and found an empty stool. At least two bartenders pulled drafts from a dozen taps and made specialty cocktails inside crystal shakers jammed with alcohol and ice cubes. The thirsty crowd kept them busy, and it was a couple of minutes before someone noticed her.

"What can I get you?" In one motion the bartender collected the tip left by the last patron and gave the bar a quick swipe with his towel. He slapped a napkin down on the mahogany surface in front of her.

"I'm looking for information, not a drink." She asked if he remembered seeing the Delancey Street victim the night she disappeared.

"Who are you? You don't look like a cop, and besides, they've already been here asking questions."

"I'm not. I'm a friend of her family," Emily lied. She was getting pretty good at lying and didn't know whether to feel proud or ashamed. Her parents had taught her about the importance of honesty when she was young. But what was the harm of one little white lie on the path to finding important information?

He looked her over for a moment while he thought about her request, saw a man out of the corner of his eye motioning for another beer, and nodded.

"She was in here regularly, but not often if you know what I mean. A couple, maybe three times a month with friends, mostly for dinner, but sometimes they'd grab a table in the bar and hit the dance floor. She seemed nice enough. All of them did. Is she still in the hospital?"

"I've been told she's more responsive to people when they talk to her, but she still hasn't said a word." That part was the truth. She'd heard it on the radio.

"It's awful what happened to her, but I'm not sure how I can help you."

"I'm trying to find her friends, to see if they knew who the man was, the one she left here with that night."

Another customer lifted his empty beer glass in the bartender's direction. Music poured from the band's double-tiered speakers; empty bar stools were getting scarce.

"Give me a minute so I can take care of my customers. I'll also look around to see if I recognize anyone she might have been with. I didn't see anyone when the police came in seeking information, but perhaps you'll be luckier."

She half-sat on the stool, half-leaned against the bar, watching drinks being poured and sipped, tabs tallied on the digital pad, paid with one plastic card after another. It was almost five minutes before the bartender broke free and returned.

"I think there are two women seated in the restaurant who are her friends. They're at the first table on the left next to the windows."

She thanked him and dropped a ten on the bar. The table where the two women sat held four place settings, but only two chairs were occupied. Emily introduced herself.

"Is Nicole okay? She didn't take a turn for the worse, did she?"

Finally, a name. Nicole. The cops hadn't identified her because of the standard protocol of not naming sexual assault victims. If these women knew Nicole's name, they must know more.

"No, no, she's not getting worse. Matter of fact, she's been more responsive, so people are hopeful she'll regain conscious-ness soon." Emily reassured them and again explained that, no, she wasn't a cop but a friend of the family trying to help find out who attacked Nicole.

"Do you mind if I join you for a minute? I'm desperate for information about what happened to Nicole that night." She didn't wait for an answer before she pulled out one of the chairs and dropped into it. They shared names, and then Emily started firing questions.

"Do you remember what happened that night? How did Nicole meet the man she left with? And can you describe him?"

Michelle and Kiki looked at each other.

"It was last Friday," the blonde woman, Michelle, said. "Nicole wanted to come here after work because she was having a tough week and wanted to get lost in the Anchor's signature Cocoa Coconut martinis. We sat in the bar side, the three of us, at one of those tall tables. This guy looked over at us several times, and Nicole started flirting with him." She paused and took a sip of her drink. "He walked over and asked if Nicole wanted to dance. She jumped out of her chair, and they danced for several songs. When she returned to the table, he joined us."

"Had you seen him in here before?"

"No, it was the first time any of us had seen him here," Kiki, the one with shorter brown hair said. "We talked about it when we first spotted him at the bar, how nice it was to see a new face."

"Can you describe him?" She tried to keep the anxiety and excitement out of her voice, but it was difficult to hide. These were people who might be able to identify Nicole's attacker, maybe even the earring Emily had found.

"He had dark hair, swept back with some gel," Michelle said. "I remember that because, before he came over to our table, we were trying to decide if it was gel or whether his hair was wet from showering after working out at the gym."

"Did he have six-pack abs or lumberjack arms? You know the way people describe guys who work out a lot?"

"No major muscles," Kiki said. "He was about average build and height and wore black, thick-framed glasses, you know, the kind everyone on the cable news shows is wearing."

She frowned at the mention of glasses. Stan didn't wear glasses in any of the publicity photos she'd seen online. She jotted some notes on her cellphone.

"And he looked like he had just left work—a professional guy," Michelle added, "because he was wearing dress slacks. He also had on a nice shirt, light-colored with baby blue stripes." She paused for a moment. "And no tie, although most men remove their tie before they walk into a bar." She turned to her friend. "Isn't that right, Kiki?"

"Yep, that's pretty much what I remember."

Emily thanked them for the description. "Can you tell me if Nicole was wearing earrings that night?" She reached into her pocket and pulled out a plain white envelope. She opened it and took out the plastic bag.

Michelle gasped. "Oh, my God. That's—" she clamped her hand over her mouth and tears filled her eyes.

Kiki grabbed Michelle's hand, never taking her eyes off the earring. "Can I look at the earring more closely?"

"Just don't take it out of the bag," Emily said, handing it to Kiki.

Both women stared at the earring.

"Nicole's mother gave the earrings to her last month, for her twenty-ninth birthday," Michelle said. "She loved them so much, they're practically the only earrings she's worn since then."

"She had them on that night?" Emily asked.

"Yes," they said in unison.

"Where did you get it?" Kiki asked.

"I'd like to know that, too," a familiar voice said from

behind Emily, dropping a hand onto her shoulder and squeezing too hard to be friendly.

Chapter Forty-Eight

Emily's heart raced faster than the last time she stayed up all night reading the latest psychological thriller. Her thinking screeched to a halt. She didn't dare turn around, so she kept her eyes on the table in front of her and willed herself not to panic. That was almost impossible given who stood behind her. She hazarded a quick glance across the table. Michelle's and Kiki's questioning eyes darted from Emily to the two women who had just arrived wearing navy polyester pantsuits and exuding power, control, and more than a little intimidation.

Officer Farrelli stepped close to the table and opened the left side of her jacket, revealing the badge tucked into the waistband of her slacks. "I'm Officer Farrelli. That's Detective Trench. We're with the Philadelphia police sex crimes unit."

"Are you also here to ask us about Nicole?" Michelle directed her question at Officer Farrelli, but it was the detective who responded.

"Right now, I'm more interested in finding out what Emily is doing here and where she found that earring."

Trench's questions came over the top of her head, forceful enough to prickle her scalp with a blast of heat.

"She said she's a friend of Nicole's family, and she's trying to find the man Nicole left with the night she was attacked," Michelle said.

Trench's hand squeezed a little tighter. "She's not."

"Then who is she?" Everything on Michelle's face—her forehead, her eyes, her nose, her mouth—wrinkled in confusion.

"Officer Farrelli will explain, and she's going to ask you some questions," Detective Trench said. She reached over and took the plastic bag with the earring out of Kiki's hands and dropped it into the front pocket of her jacket. Then she pulled Emily to her feet. "You're coming outside with me."

Emily tried to assess how much trouble she was in as Trench led her through the bar and out into the parking lot. An unmarked police car sat in the emergency zone. A light breeze off the Delaware River fed the chilly night and rustled the dying leaves on the trees. She shivered from the cool air and the realization the evening wasn't turning out the way she had planned.

"You've got some explaining to do." Trench stopped beside the white car, its rack of red and blue lights on the roof the only outward sign it was a cop car. The detective positioned Emily with her back to the car and left her little room to move. "What the hell are you doing here talking with possible witnesses? How did you come into possession of this earring, and what, if anything, does it have to do with the Delancey Street victim?"

The time for being hesitant to tell police about the earring was over. "I found the earring in a bag in a dumpster in the parking lot of Stan Hester's condo."

"Details. I want details, and don't leave anything out."

Trench spit orders at Emily like she was a new recruit who'd screwed up. The screwed up part was right at least.

The cop was probably three inches from her face, and Emily tried with no success to back up farther against the car to get some distance between them. She filled Trench in about seeing Stan cleaning his car and tossing a small white trash bag into the dumpster that she later retrieved and discovered the earring.

"And did you, at any point, think about contacting police so we could check the dumpster?" Trench's eyes bored into hers.

Emily's throat was so dry she couldn't swallow. "No," she said, the word barely coming out of her mouth. "I wanted to grab the bag before it was hauled off by a trash truck and lost forever. I didn't think about anything except I had to do something to get it in case it was important."

"And when you found the earring in the trash bag, why didn't you contact police then?"

"It didn't seem like enough evidence."

"It wasn't. Isn't. That's why people let us do the work we're trained to do. So we can search for the evidence and connect the dots that can link a suspect to a crime. Did you think about that?"

She looked at the Detective and bit her tongue; she didn't have a good answer. Was it even a question?

"And how did you learn her name is Nicole? It's not public knowledge."

"From her friends."

"Who you spoke with while you were trying to conduct your own investigation and interfering with the police's."

Trench's face was so close to hers that Emily saw the redness in the Detective's tired eyes and the blood vessels in her cheeks.

"Is Stan Hester's name on the trash bag?"

"No."

"Then how do you know that it's his?"

"Because the bag also contains menus from restaurants in the Tampa area, and Stan just moved here from there."

"Millions of people visit Florida every day, including the Tampa area for Busch Gardens, Bok Tower, Adventure Island, and all those other places that compete with everything Disney, Universal, and Sea World offer in Orlando." Trench ran out of breath trying to recite some of Florida's tourist destinations. "Millions of people. Probably tens of thousands of them from the Philadelphia area. You think maybe someone else could have Tampa-area restaurant menus in their possession?"

"Maybe in rental cars, but—"

"Stop, Emily. Just stop." Detective Trench closed her eyes and rubbed her forehead with her fingers and thumb. Car doors slammed shut, and laughter drifted across the parking lot—more customers for the bar and the restaurant. As soon as the latest arrivals disappeared inside, the lot was quiet again except for the low hum of traffic on the nearby roadway. And for the footsteps coming closer and closer.

"Emily?" Martin called out. He and Ramón hurried over to where she and Trench stood. "Emily, you promised you wouldn't come here alone."

"Excuse me, sir." Trench took a couple of steps toward Martin and put her arm out to stop him from coming closer. "Who are you?"

"Martin Gilbert. Emily's friend."

"After what she's done tonight, she's going to need one."

"Em, what did you do?"

"I talked to Nicole's friends and showed them the earring to see if they could identify it."

"What earring? And who's Nicole?" Martin tried to follow the conversation, but his brain couldn't get past his steaming anger at her for going alone to the Anchor Bar, for breaking her promise.

"Your friend apparently found an earring that may be connected to a crime." The detective lowered her arm and turned back to Emily. "You contaminated evidence that might've led to the conviction of a perpetrator of an attack that almost killed a woman."

Martin stared at Emily in disbelief.

"Or I may have found evidence of the guy who did it." Why didn't Trench see her side of this?

"But it won't be admissible!" Trench said, her face bright red, her hands balled into fists. Suddenly, Trench stopped. Looked down. Took a few deep breaths and looked like she was counting to ten. She regained control and resumed speaking. "You may have screwed up any case we could've had against Stan Hester if he is the person who attacked Nicole. Don't you ever watch TV crime shows? You should've told us you found the earring in the dumpster. I could have you arrested for interfering with a police investigation."

Detective Trench stepped back, reached behind her back under her jacket, and pulled out her handcuffs. "Not only *could* I arrest you, Emily Archer," she said, her voice loud and commanding, "I *am* arresting you."

Emily's eyebrows shot up. Her face turned white. She looked to Martin and Ramón for help, but they looked just as shocked. Trench turned her around and pushed her up against the police car while securing her hands in plastic handcuffs.

Chapter Forty-Nine

She found herself in a room that wasn't nearly as nice as the one she was in the last time she'd visited police headquarters. Of course, this wasn't a visit, not when she was under arrest. Charged with a crime. For the first time in her life. Sitting alone in this cold room on an uncomfortable metal chair, her arms resting on a metal table, her heels tapping on the hard linoleum floor that looked like it needed a good scrubbing, she thought about what had brought her here. And who.

Stan. She was here because of him. Because of what he'd done to her. She started going down a familiar path of feeling like a victim and willed herself to stop. She didn't want to be a victim anymore. That's one of the reasons she'd been encouraging Laura to file a complaint against Stan, and why she was trying so hard to find evidence against him for attacking the Delancey Street victim—Nicole. She couldn't get justice for what Stan did to her, so she was working hard to get justice for Laura and Nicole. She wanted to help stop Stan and prevent the women from feeling like victims. They weren't victims. They were survivors. Every one of them.

She didn't want to admit it, but she understood what Detective Trench had said about the evidence. A burning sensation rose up from her stomach and caught in her throat when she considered she could have ruined a case against Stan. Maybe Trench was right. She should have gone to the police sooner. Should not have gone off on her own. But she knew in her heart she couldn't have stood by and done nothing. Stan was hurting women. He had to be stopped. She swallowed, but the bad taste in her mouth remained.

The big two-way mirror on the wall in front of her stared back at her. *Who's watching me?* Trench had asked her if she watched police shows, if she didn't have at least a basic under-standing of crimes and evidence, if she didn't know something about police procedures. Well, she'd seen some TV programs involving police and knew enough. Cops stood on the other side of that mirror and watched the person sitting where she was. What was worse? Seeing someone watching you, or not seeing them but knowing they're watching you? *Careful, Em,* she thought, *you're sounding a little loopy. Well, that's what happens when I'm forced to sit in here and wait for help. Albert will get me out of this place and this mess. I know he will.*

Just before Trench had pushed her head down and eased her into the back seat of the police car, Emily had shouted to Martin to call Albert and tell him to meet her at the police station. Albert would be here soon, but he wasn't going to be happy to see her.

Five minutes later, the door opened, and Albert stepped inside, wearing slacks and a collared, button-down shirt with a tie. He thanked the police officer on the other side of the door and walked over to the table without looking at her. This was bad, to not even glance her way. He set his briefcase on the table and pulled out the metal chair across from her, but he didn't sit. He put his hands on the back of the chair and leaned forward. Then he looked at her.

"What the hell were you thinking?"

"I was just—"

His eyebrows arched and he put a finger to his lips. "Don't say another word."

She knew he was angry, but she was tired of people asking her that question. Especially when they wouldn't let her answer it.

"Detective Trench told me what you said about finding the earring. It could connect Stan to the Delancey Street woman, but it doesn't matter if the evidence is not admissible in a court of law. I told you that the first time you pulled bags from the dumpster."

She wanted to tell him she understood, that Trench had already read her the riot act before she arrested her, but Emily bit her tongue and tried to sit still and listen.

"You're being charged with tampering with evidence. It's a second-degree misdemeanor charge and could land you in jail for a year. Cost you five thousand dollars or more in fines."

"Do police believe the earring is evidence against Stan?"

"Detective Trench didn't fill me in on the particulars of their case, but did you hear what I said? You interfered with a police investigation. Tampering with evidence is serious. Jail time. A fine. A criminal record."

"Does anybody care that I may have discovered evidence linking Stan to Nicole?" Her voice shot up another octave. "The earring might prove she was in his car, that he was the person who assaulted her."

"That's all you can think about. Try thinking about how he might get away with it—if he did it—because you ruined evidence that could convict him. Think about that, I mean really think about that for a minute." He pulled the chair out a little farther and sat, smoothing his tie and snapping his shirt cuffs.

Emily had never seen Albert so angry. She wanted to stop

the tears that began filling her eyes, but she couldn't. All she wanted from the moment she remembered how Stan had raped her was to hold him responsible. He had done something awful to her, something that wounded her physically and emotionally and she would never be the same. And Stan? He was walking around, getting on with his life, like he hadn't a care in the world. It wasn't fair.

"I'm sorry," Emily said. "You can't possibly understand. You can't—" Then her tears came hard and unrelenting. Sobs racked her body. Albert pulled a white handkerchief out of his pocket, shook out the creases, and handed it to her. She looked at his face and saw his anger melt into sorrow.

"I'm sorry for what happened to you, Em," he said, his voice soft and loving. "If I could make your pain go away, I would. If I could build a case and put Stan Hester behind bars, I would. But I can't. And you can't either. You've got to stop taking things into your own hands, okay? You're making a mess of things and alienating the police. If you promise to stop interfering, I think I can get Detective Trench to reconsider the charge. But you've got to promise me."

She thought again about how she broke her promise to Martin to stay away from the Anchor Bar and how she was going to have to figure out how to apologize. She couldn't make another promise and break it. Albert was going to help her; she had to promise to butt out of this investigation and mean it.

The door to the interrogation room opened, and Detective Trench marched in. Albert rose and stepped away from the table, but Emily kept her seat, her head down, trying to stop the tears and hide the pain.

"Your brother-in-law posted bail." Trench took the chair Albert had vacated and dropped a file folder on the table next to his briefcase. "While I really don't want to see you in custody, I'm sort of sorry he did, because you're a loose cannon. You are obstructing our investigation. You should remain locked up to keep you out of our way so we can build a case with the evidence we need to get a conviction in a court of law. Because that's how the system works, Emily."

Emily gulped her tears but couldn't look at the detective. She braced for another lecture, but she wasn't ready for what came next.

"Emily, I told you the other night, I'm sorry Stan Hester raped you. I've worked in the sex crimes unit for fifteen years now. I understand how a sexual assault can leave a woman broken and seeking revenge. But vengeance outside the law often backfires and doesn't bring the kind of closure that heals. Trust me on this."

Trench picked at an old piece of masking tape on the table. "I understand your motivation, but you went about it all wrong. I already told you how much you've ruined potential evidence, and I suspect your brother-in-law has explained that to you as well." Trench started to say something else, then reached across and tapped her fingers on the table in front of Emily. "Look at me, Emily."

She wiped her eyes one last time, raised her chin, and met the detective's eyes.

"If Stan is a sexual predator, I want him behind bars as much as you do. We have the same goal, but you need to remember you are not in charge. I am. Do you understand?"

She nodded quickly and squeezed the handkerchief in the palm of her hand.

"You stay out of the way, and I promise, I'll do everything in my power to get Stan Hester off the street."

Chapter Fifty

"I am so mad at you," Martin said as soon as Emily walked into her living room, trailed by Albert and Detective Trench. Earlier in the evening, Martin and Ramón had picked up Emily's car at the Anchor Bar and driven it to her place. They used the spare key Martin had to let themselves in.

"I know you are. You have a right to be. I'm sorry."

Martin wouldn't accept a hug, but Ramón did. She'd ruined their evening and betrayed the trust of her closest friend.

"Your car's halfway up the block. Your keys are on the table in the hallway." Martin stood and strode toward the front door.

"I know it's late, but will you wait a minute while Detective Trench and I collect something from the kitchen?" She pleaded with Martin. "I'd really like to tell you what happened, why I broke my promise to you."

Ramón pulled Martin back down on the couch and handed him his cup of coffee. No one would be getting much sleep tonight. She thanked them, then hurried to the kitchen.

"Here it is," she said, opening a lower cupboard door next

to the refrigerator. She pulled out her gardening gloves, but Trench was way ahead of her. The detective's right hand was already encased in blue latex, and a crisp snap confirmed she'd put another glove on her left hand.

"I'll take it from here." Trench reached in, slid her right index finger through the openings of the small white bag, and lifted it out of the cupboard. "Did you open it here in the kitchen?"

"No, I was sitting in a chair by the table on the patio out back."

"Show me."

She flipped on the switch, bathing the gray slate patio in light, then led Albert and Detective Trench outdoors. The small patio and postage-sized lawn were surrounded by a wooden privacy fence. At three in the morning, their voices were the only sound.

"Where did you look at the bag's contents?"

"I sat at the table, in that chair." She walked over and eased herself into the chair to show exactly where she'd been.

"Did you dump the contents of the bag out on the table? Or on the patio?"

I'm not that stupid, she almost said before biting her tongue. This probably wasn't a good time to engage Trench and Albert in a discussion about her ability to make intelligent decisions.

"No, I didn't dump the contents anywhere. First, I put on my gardening gloves, which are part rubber. Then I untied the knot and peered inside."

"The top of the bag was knotted?"

"Yes."

"Like it is now?"

"Yes."

"Nothing could have fallen out?"

"No. I don't think so."

"Then what did you do?" Trench kept her distance from the table and bent down low, tilting her head and running her eyes over the patio.

Emily explained how she'd pulled out a few restaurant menus and some trash, including wadded-up papers from the bottom of the bag. "And then, still holding some of the menus and papers, I dropped my hands to my lap. That's when I heard a ping. Something dropped onto the patio."

"Where?"

"Right here." She pointed to the area directly in front of her feet.

"Don't move." Trench examined the patio, then came around behind her and scanned the glass tabletop. "Have you been out here since you checked the bag?"

"No, this is the first time."

"Okay, get up," Trench said. "It's too late to bring the forensics guys out now, but I want you to stay off the patio, stay away from the table. Don't touch anything. We'll be out here first light of day to sweep it for any fibers that may not already have been carried away by the wind."

Emily rose from the chair and looked at where she planted her feet on the patio to make sure she didn't step on anything obvious. The three of them traipsed back into the kitchen. She flicked off the outdoor light and locked the kitchen door.

"I'll see you by seven in the morning," Trench said, holding the small trash bag in her hands and walking toward the front of the house. "Don't go back to the Anchor Bar. Don't try to track down Stan Hester." Trench stopped, turned, and looked at Emily. "Don't. Do. Anything. Stay out of our way."

Albert let the detective out then returned to the living room.

"Before I leave, Emily, I want to reiterate what Detective Trench said. Let the police do their work. They didn't drop the charges against you. They let you out on bail because I told them I would make sure you wouldn't do anything to impede their investigation. Anything else, that is. So don't. Because if you do, they'll throw you in jail again, and I might not have such an easy time getting you out. Understood?" He didn't wait for an answer. "Goodbye."

The remaining three sat in uncomfortable silence until she found her courage.

"Martin, I'm sorry," Emily began, her voice unsteady and unsure. "I had every intention of going home after work. Naturally, I was tempted to drive to the Anchor Bar, but I headed home after I left BAM. Honestly, I did." She twisted the gold and pearl ring on her right hand and looked at Martin through misty eyes. "Then I turned on the radio and heard a news report about a guy who sexually assaulted and murdered a woman just two days after he was released from prison. It's like he couldn't wait to get out and attack again. It made me so angry. My pulse raced. My heart pounded like crazy. Before I knew it, I'd set my sights on the Anchor Bar, determined to find the woman's friends. To stop whoever hurt Nicole from attacking anyone else." Her eyes pleaded with him. "I'm sorry I broke my promise, I really am. Please forgive me."

Martin pressed his lips together and took several quick gulps of air. "Tell me what happened. Not just last night. Before that. Start with finding the trash bag Detective Trench took with her."

About fifteen minutes later, she wrapped up her story and leaned back against the chair, the energy drained from her body. "That's all of it."

"You dug around the trash in Stan's dumpster? That's a side of you I didn't know existed." He smiled and the tension in the room finally broke.

"It's not something I'm going to put on my résumé," she said.

"Yep. Not really a marketable skill." Martin stood and stretched. Ramón rubbed his eyes and got to his feet.

"I'm sorry I ruined your evening. I hope you weren't doing anything special." She raised her eyebrows and gave a tentative smile.

Martin looked at Ramón and sighed. "Dinner at Devon's on Rittenhouse Square. Tickets to *Hamilton*. Orchestra. Center section. Row six."

She gasped. "Oh, jeez, I know those tickets are hard to come by."

"Hard to come by? More like impossible. The show closes in two weeks."

She bit her lip and willed the tears to stay inside. "I'm sorry. I'd do anything to make it up to you."

"That's probably impossible." Martin's brisk tone let her know he was still angry. Both men walked toward the front door. "I love you, Emily," Martin said, opening the door and stepping over the threshold. "But I can't help but be angry at you right now. So please stay out of trouble. Start jogging. Take up rowing on the Schuylkill River. Meditate. Do what you need to in order to get Stan Hester out of your head."

They walked down the steps and turned left.

"Yeah, right. Get Stan Hester out of my head. That's easier said than done," Emily said, closing the door.

She went upstairs, changed into her pajamas, and fell into bed. Her mind was too agitated for sleep, and since she couldn't act on her thoughts, she spent the next few hours thinking of what she *wanted* to do instead of actually *doing* it until the morning pushed her into another day.

Chapter Fifty-One

The police arrived just before seven, declined her offer of coffee, and quickly went to work, wearing latex gloves, meticulously sweeping the patio with a hand broom they'd brought, and putting what they collected into a sterile bag. Then they were gone. She shed her jeans and sweatshirt, dressed in a navy pantsuit, and drove into the city for her session with Mandy.

Returning to work had forced her to scale back her therapy sessions to once a week. While she knew she'd done a lot of good work with Mandy processing the trauma of Stan's attack and some other traumas, she still suffered from PTSD. Didn't her aggressive behavior and arrest prove that? And how was she going to explain the arrest to Mandy? She mulled it over during the drive and decided the best approach was probably the blunt truth.

"That may be a first," Mandy said after Emily finished telling her what had happened. "At the end of our session last Thursday, which seems like an eternity ago, I told you that I worried about what you might do next. Even so, you getting arrested never crossed my mind."

How could Emily explain her impulsive decision? She knew she reacted strongly to the horrific news story about the man arrested in New Jersey, but Stan Hester had been in her sights for a few weeks.

"It's like I was driven to do what I did," she said, trying to defend her actions.

"It's not *like* you were driven, Emily. You *were* driven, *are* driven. You act impulsively, sometimes recklessly, without regard for your safety. You also fail to consider how your actions will affect others. For example, the police investigation." Mandy removed her reading glasses and put them on the table next to her chair. "You're on a vigilante crusade here, Emily, and you could get hurt. Yes, physically, but of equal concern to me is what this is doing to you emotionally."

Mandy waited for a response, but Emily didn't know how to explain her actions beyond what she'd already said.

"Let's see how we can work with this." Mandy put her notepad on the coffee table next to her glasses, unzipped the leather bag, and pulled out the tappers. "Gray one in your left hand, black one in your right," she reminded Emily. "Before I turn them on, let's identify the trauma and a specific target. Where do you want to begin?"

"I would say sitting in the bar, listening to Laura tell me how Stan attacked her. Laura didn't go into graphic detail, but when I was listening to her, it was like Stan was attacking me all over again."

"That's exactly what I feared would happen."

"I get it now, but even though listening to Laura triggered me, I would do it all over again. She needed someone to talk with, someone who understood what she went through."

"What emotions do you feel when you think about your conversation with Laura?"

"I heard her talk about what Stan did to her, but my mind kept flashing back to what he did to me. I was scared." The words came quickly, her legs bounced up and down so much, she couldn't stop them. The hard tapping of her feet shot all the way through her body and into her shoulders.

"What is your level of upset?"

"It's about an eight." She squeezed her fist around the tapper and rubbed her hand over the upper part of her chest, trying to find an outlet for her nervous energy.

"That's pretty high." Mandy paused, grabbed her notepad, and wrote something down. "And what is your negative belief?" she asked, while still making notes.

"It could happen to me again. I could be a victim again. I might not be able to stop it."

"What would you rather believe?"

"That I'm strong enough to defend myself. Smart enough to identify a dangerous situation and keep out of it." She squeezed her eyes tight. "Sometimes I'm afraid I won't recognize when someone's trying to hurt me. I guess I'm not sure I trust my judgment."

"Remember the night you were in the bar in Manayunk and walked toward your car alone, when you feared you were being followed?"

Her eyes popped open, surprised at the switch of topics. "Yes, that happened shortly before I came to see you."

"What did you do then, when you were afraid?"

Emily thought about how scared she had been, and how she asked the woman who'd come out of a bar with her friends to walk her to her car. She had recognized it could be dangerous to continue on alone that night and wisely sought help from others.

"Maybe my instincts are better than I think," she acknowledged.

"Let's begin there. Think about how you felt the danger and asked for help."

Her hands vibrated around the tappers. She remembered

hearing footsteps. Then spotting the two couples and feeling relief when they walked her to her car.

"I can ask for help," she said, a wave of relief washing over her body as she looked at Mandy. "And I can identify dangerous situations. I did that night."

"Good. Close your eyes and think about that a little longer."

A few minutes later, Emily's mind was clear and her body stronger. Her feet remained flat on the floor. She sat up straighter and rolled her shoulders.

"What is your level of upset about that night now?"

"It's back to a two."

"And that's where we left it when we processed the memory of Stan assaulting you. Good job, Emily. Let's work on the conversation you had with Laura about Stan, but first, what did she say when you told her Stan had attacked you more than a decade ago?"

She briefly filled Mandy in on her meeting with Laura.

"Okay, then let's work on your conversation with Laura about what Stan did to her."

Emily was more than ready. They worked on her memories of Stan's attack on Laura until her level of upset was down to a three.

"That's pretty good," Mandy said. "We're nearing the end of our time. I'm going to slow down the speed of the tappers. Think of your safe space for a bit, and we'll send you out of here on a positive note."

A short time later, she handed the tappers back to Mandy. Her arms felt stronger. When she stood from her chair, her legs lifted her easily.

"I really do feel more in control now," Emily said. "Strong enough to take care of myself, to keep myself out of danger." She paused. "But I also recognize things do happen. Things out of our control."

"And how does that make you feel?"

She shrugged her shoulders. "I suppose it's useless to try to control everything, isn't it?"

Mandy smiled. "Some people spend a lot of time worrying about what will happen. It's wasted energy and lost time."

"I'll just have to accept there are certain things in life I can't control, like flying when the plane hits turbulence and I get scared. But I can control staying alert, being careful about who I'm around, and avoiding men who scare me or situations where I feel vulnerable. I can protect myself from thinking like a victim, becoming a victim."

"You did a lot of good work, today, Emily. I hope you feel proud about that. Let your mind and body absorb how resilient you are. I'll see you next week."

When her feet hit the sidewalk, Emily had a swagger and a confidence that she hadn't felt in weeks. She couldn't help wondering what was going on with the police investigation, but coming out of Mandy's office, she promised herself she would stay out of their way. And hoped she was getting better at keeping her promises.

Chapter Fifty-Two

The session with Mandy left Emily stronger and compensated for her lack of sleep. There were still moments that came at her when she least expected it, when the raw emotions of Stan raping her stopped her cold. But thanks to the EMDR work and her ability to lock away upsetting emotions in her container, even those memories never overwhelmed her. She was feeling less anxious, less tense, and she told Cara right after she answered her sister's call.

"You sound pretty upbeat for someone who was arrested and spent half the night with the police. And Albert."

"Yeah, about that," she said, "I'm sorry I dragged Albert away from home and kept him until the early hours. I really appreciate that he came to help me out. Literally, to help me out of jail."

"Corporate lawyers don't spend a lot of time at police headquarters, you know, so it's not like Albert's a regular there, but I'm glad he could bail you out. The reason for your arrest, though, this impetuous behavior—"

"I know. I know." She interrupted Cara to save herself another lecture. "I've been reprimanded by the cops, by

Albert, Martin, and even my therapist chastised me this morning for acting rashly. I heard them all. I had a great session with Mandy, and I'm turning over a new leaf, staying out of the cops' way."

"A lot of people will be glad to hear that."

"I'm sure. So, is there anything new there with Stan today?"

"I thought you just said—"

"I said I would stay out of the cops' way. I didn't say I'd lost interest in the investigation or what might happen to him."

"Just don't, you know, do *anything*," Cara said in her big sister's lecturing voice. "If you're tempted to do something about Stan, or Laura, or the Delancey woman, remember, whatever you're contemplating, it's a bad idea. I repeat, a bad idea. Then don't do it."

"I'm prepared to stay out of the police's way, Cara, believe me, but I have this excess energy and don't want to go home and pace. Can we get together for a drink or dinner?" Emily wasn't in the mood to play aunt this evening, but she did want to spend time with Cara and make nice to Albert. And that was preferable to going home alone where she might think her way into trouble.

"Albert dropped the kids off at his mom's this morning because he's working late, probably till midnight or something, there's a big case coming up. I wasn't sure what the day would hold for me, so the kids are staying there overnight. Dinner and a drink sound wonderful, not necessarily in that order. It's also been a tough few days here."

"I'm sure it has been. You can fill me in when I see you. I'll be at Flagstone in thirty minutes or less."

Emily snagged a spot in the first row, close to Flagstone's front entrance, then texted Cara. Music bounced around the car from the windshield to the back of the SUV; she pounded the steering wheel to the beat and allowed a big smile to play across her face. Fall days this warm and sunny didn't come around often, so she rolled down the window and inhaled the fresh air.

Cara came out of the two-story brick building, spotted her immediately, and waved. Before the door closed, Stan stepped out. He was practically on Cara's heels. Emily hadn't seen Stan's car when she drove into the lot and couldn't locate it now, but it must be behind her. He passed by Cara and headed right for Emily. Her hands froze on the steering wheel.

He saw her before she could hide. Or drive into him. Which she considered for a nanosecond, but then, as Cara had suggested earlier, if something seemed like a bad idea, don't do it. So she looked down and prayed that Cara reached her car quickly.

"You!" Stan yelled at her. "Are you stalking me now?"

Emily's head shot up, and she met Stan's angry eyes. She held her breath. Tried to control her hands on the steering wheel, which were now shaking.

Cara came up behind him.

"Calm down, Stan. Emily is here for me."

"You know her? She accused me—" he stopped himself from saying too much.

"She's my sister."

His eyes darted back and forth between them as he made the connection. "So that's what's going on. You're ganging up on me." His hands balled into fists. "Did you two push Laura to go to the police and file a complaint against me?"

"Be careful making accusations without the facts, Stan." Cara put her arms up in front of her to warn him to back off. He brushed them away with such force, one of her hands hit the front of Emily's vehicle. Cara cried out and grabbed her arm.

Emily shoved her door open and jumped out. "Cara,

you're hurt." She tried to push around Stan, but he blocked the way. Emily glared at Stan, and Cara bent over in pain.

"What's going on out here?" Jim ran out the front door toward the three of them, waving his arms. "Cara, are you okay?" Jim leaned over to look into her eyes.

"Stan pushed my arm against the car. I don't think anything's broken, but it hurts." She hunched her shoulders and held her hand out for Jim to see. He looked at her hand, then at Stan, then spotted Emily.

"Emily, what are you doing here?"

"I came to pick Cara up for dinner, but after what Stan just did, it looks like we're going to urgent care instead." Emily tried to reach out to Cara again, but Stan pinned her against her car.

"Okay, everyone. Let's take a deep breath. Stan, why don't —" Jim stopped abruptly and turned his head toward the sound of approaching sirens.

Stan's head whipped in the same direction. He brushed Emily aside and walked quickly toward his car. Two police cars raced into Flagstone's parking lot. The first one stopped near where Emily, Cara, and Jim stood; the other car spun around and blocked the parking lot entrance.

Detective Trench hopped out of the passenger side of the first car and raced to Stan's side. Officer Farrelli got out from behind the wheel and watched.

"Stan Hester," Trench said, flashing her badge and waving a piece of paper in his face. "We have a warrant to search your car. Stop where you are and hand over the key."

Stan gave a quick look around and realized there was no place to go. The detective held out her hand.

"What right do you have to search my car?" His hands rested on his hips.

"I have the right according to this warrant, signed by a judge less than an hour ago, based upon evidence we have implicating you in the attack on the woman at Third and Delancey on October 26." She reached out and gave him the document with the hand that wasn't waiting for his key.

Stan scanned the document, then stared down Trench with stone-cold eyes. "I'm not responsible for what happened to that woman." He stopped abruptly, realizing he probably shouldn't say much. "Are you arresting me?"

"No, sir. If I was arresting you, I'd be putting you in hand-cuffs. Right now, we're here to search your car."

Employees continued to walk out of the building. People slowed upon seeing the flashing lights and stopped, many looking at Stan and Trench, others taking in the car blocking the exit.

Emily held her breath.

Stan reached into his pocket, removed the key to his car and repocketed the rest. He handed the key to Trench.

"Where's the vehicle?" the Detective said, looking around the lot.

"Back there." He waved his arm. "If you have a warrant, you probably know what it looks like."

Jim walked over to diffuse the tension. "Detective, perhaps Stan and I can wait in my office while you conduct your search. Is that okay?"

Trench gave her assent with a quick nod. As the men walked back inside the production company, two officers who had been in the second car approached, wearing latex gloves and carrying several items, including plastic bags and what appeared to Emily to be a small vacuum cleaner.

Trench led them two rows deeper into the parking lot to a black sports car. She beeped the car doors open, and the offi-cers went to work.

"What happened to you?" Officer Farrelli asked Cara.

"Stan shoved me hard, and my arm hit Emily's SUV."

"Let me take a look."

While Farrelli examined Cara's hand, and the two evidence cops searched Stan's vehicle, Detective Trench walked over to where Emily stood just behind her car and away from the others.

"What're you doing here?" The demanding tone in the detective's voice made it clear she wasn't asking out of idle curiosity.

"I came to pick up Cara. We're going out to dinner. At least we were."

"What happened to Cara?" Trench asked after a quick glance.

Emily explained.

They said nothing for a moment, both watching the officers at work. The driver and passenger doors of Stan's car were open. So was the trunk. A cop knelt on the ground on each side of the vehicle, looking in the front seats and in the back.

"How did you manage to get a search warrant anyway?"

Trench looked at her sharply and raised her eyebrows.

"Just asking for a friend." Emily smiled and thought she saw the slightest upturn on the corners of Trench's mouth.

"Nicole regained consciousness."

"Really? That's great news!"

"Yes, it is. She can't remember much of the evening yet, but she remembered enough to give us a description of the man who drove her home, a description that matched what her friends at the Anchor Bar told us." Detective Trench reached into her back pocket and pulled out a piece of paper. She unfolded it and showed it to Emily. "Your eyes only," she warned. "Do you recognize this man?"

Emily scrunched her eyes and leaned closer to the police sketch of a man with slicked-back hair and black-framed glasses. "He looks a little familiar, but no, not really."

"What about now?" Trench showed her another drawing with the glasses removed and the hair, while not exactly combed out, had almost no gel in it. The jawline was more defined; the hard eyes dark.

Emily's eyebrows shot up. "Oh, jeez, that's Stan."

"Yes, it is."

"If Nicole said he was the guy who attacked her, why don't you arrest him?"

"Evidence. We need evidence. Remember? And we hope to find it in his car."

They stared again at Stan's car and the two officers inspecting it inch by inch.

"We haven't circulated these composite images, so don't tell anyone about them. Not Cara. Not Laura. No one."

"I won't. I promise." Ouch, there was that word again. "I mean it, I really mean it," she reiterated. "But tell me this. Last night, you arrested me for tampering with evidence, and now you're updating me on the police investigation and showing me an image that implicates Stan. What gives?"

"I may be a tough cop," Trench said, then added, "No, I *am* a tough cop. But I'm also a woman. I'm as eager to find Nicole's attacker as you are. We're on the same team, Emily. We both want to catch the bad guy."

"Detective Trench, can you come here?" one of the cops shouted and motioned her over.

Emily followed Trench, not getting the message yet about sitting back and waiting. The police officers conferred, and one of them showed Trench a piece of paper. He held it in his latex-protected hands. It looked like a receipt, the kind of credit card receipt you get at a restaurant. Or a bar.

"Where did you find it?" Trench asked.

"Between the front seat and the console. It might've fallen out of his pants or jacket pocket when he pulled out his car key. As you can see, it's slightly crumpled."

The cop looked at Trench, then shifted his eyes to Emily. Trench whipped around.

"Not a word, about this, Emily. And back up. Go stand behind your car, or better yet, why don't you see how Cara's doing?"

She hustled toward her sister and Officer Farrelli. But her mind was spinning on what she'd just seen and heard. Could that receipt place Stan at the Anchor Bar that night? That would be pretty damning evidence, wouldn't it? That, combined with Nicole and her friends identifying Stan from the composite, could be enough to arrest him, couldn't it? She rubbed her hands together and smiled, giddy at the thought Stan could be behind bars before the night was over. Her glee was abruptly interrupted by Detective Trench's next question.

"Farrelli, where's Mr. Hester?"

Officer Farrelli looked around. "Last I saw, he was walking into the building with Jim."

Emily looked around. Jim stood just outside the entrance to the building. Alone.

Chapter Fifty-Three

Detective Trench rushed toward Jim. Emily couldn't help herself. She followed.

"Where's Mr. Hester?"

"He said he had to go to the restroom. I walked him there and told him to meet me out here when he was finished." Jim shifted his weight from one foot to the other and scanned the parking lot.

"How long ago was that?"

He pulled out his cellphone and checked the time. "Maybe five minutes." Lines of worry grew deeper around his eyes. "Maybe a little longer."

"How many ways are there out of the building in addition to the front door?"

"One in the back and an emergency door on the side facing the river."

"Officer Farrelli," Trench shouted. "Inside with me." She tapped Jim's shoulder. "Show me the restroom where you left him and the exits. Everybody else, stay put out here." The detective shot Emily a no-nonsense look.

The cops and Jim went inside, and Cara came up beside Emily.

"Are you okay? How's your arm, your hand?" She reached out to inspect her sister's injury, but Cara kept her left arm safely wrapped against her body.

"Officer Farrelli said nothing's broken, but she recommended I get it checked out when we're done here."

"That could be a while."

"I know. It's okay."

"Do you want to sit in my car?"

"I'd rather stand near the front door where I can watch Stan come out in handcuffs," Cara said, her eyes glued to Flagstone's entrance.

Emily smiled. "Me too."

As they turned toward the front doors, Cara tapped Emily's arm. "Look, Laura's over there with Shelley. Let's tell her what's going on."

In response to Laura's question, Cara explained how Stan had flung her arm away and into Emily's car.

"I heard the shouting when I walked out of the building," Laura said. "But I wanted to stay far away. I've been watching from here with Shelley, trying to see as much as we could. Why did the police go inside?"

If anyone deserved to learn about the unfolding events involving Stan it was Laura, but Emily couldn't tell her what she'd learned. Not yet.

"Detective Trench said they got a warrant to search Stan's car," she said.

"How? Why?"

She couldn't lie either. Not this time. "I can't say. Detective Trench will explain everything as soon as she can."

Laura held her eyes but didn't ask any more questions.

"Come on, let's wait over there with the others." Emily led

them to where Flagstone employees were standing on the sidewalk.

A few minutes later, Trench strode out the door and quickly approached the two officers searching Stan's car. They spoke for a moment, then the two evidence specialists collected their plastic bags and little vacuum cleaner, closed up Stan's car, and locked it. They put their materials into the police car, and one of the cops backed it up so the car was only partially blocking the entrance. He stood next to the vehicle, arms crossed over his body. The message was clear: no one was leaving. The other officer joined Trench at the far end of the parking lot, which ended about twenty feet from the Delaware River.

The detective pointed, and the cop took off running north on the trail that hugged the river. Trench walked back without saying a word and disappeared around the side of the building closer to the road.

Dozens of pairs of eyes were no longer casually curious. The few people still left inside Flagstone peered out the windows. Everyone else gathered on the front steps or in the parking lot, watching and waiting.

Another blast of sirens seemed to come out of nowhere and quickly grew louder. Two police cars crossed the median of the busy roadway and raced into Flagstone's parking lot. Officers jumped out of the vehicles and hurried toward Trench. Seconds later, two of the cops ran into the building.

"Who are they searching for and why?" someone just to Emily's right asked. He was about the last employee to exit Flagstone.

All eyes turned toward Jim. "They're looking for Stan," he said. "I'm not at liberty to say why. We have to wait for the police to do their work."

Almost an hour later, after the police had returned to Flagstone and interviewed the employees to learn what they knew, people were allowed to climb into their cars. It was well past dinnertime, and many of their questions remained unanswered, including the most pressing question: where did Stan Hester go?

As the others trudged home, Emily, Cara, and Jim followed Detective Trench and Officer Farrelli inside and sank into the lobby couch and chairs.

"The building's as secure as we can make it," Jim said in response to a question from Trench. "Employees have ID cards they swipe across a security pad for access. There's one pad next to the main entrance and another access point in the back where our crews park their vehicles to load and unload their video gear. That's the spot I showed you when we first searched the building."

"We've stationed an officer out back to guard that entrance and another officer out front to watch the rest of the building and Stan's car," Trench said, nodding. "If he comes back here, we'll get him."

"Do you have any production crews still out who might return this evening?" Officer Farrelli fired her question without taking her eyes off her little spiral-bound notepad where she was writing as fast as she could.

Jim shook his head. "All the crews are back in-house, and we don't have any staff coming in overnight."

"Do you know how Stan got away? Where he went?" Emily had been sitting still and listening silently for as long as she could.

Trench looked at each of them, first Emily, then Cara, then Jim. "For your ears only," she said, and everyone indicated they understood.

"Apparently, as soon as he left Jim's office, he exited the building through the back entrance. A cameraman," Trench referred to her notes, "Felipe Santiago was unloading his gear. Stan rushed out the door, and Felipe asked him where he was going. Stan said he needed some fresh air and was taking a walk on the Delaware River Trail."

Emily quickly turned to Trench. "Did you say Felipe Santiago?"

"Yes. Why?" Trench's eyes bored into Emily's. "Do you know him? Is there some relevance?"

"No, sorry for taking us off track. Thought I knew his name from high school."

Cara studied her sister's face almost as much as the detective did. The silence had almost become uncomfortable, then Trench resumed her report.

"As I was saying, Stan told Felipe he was going for a walk on the river trail."

"So he disappeared up the trail?" Jim asked.

"Not completely," Trench said. "An employee of Pep Boys just up the road said a man matching Stan's description came into the store about ten minutes after Felipe saw him disappear. The clerk described the man as a little nervous, said he kept jerking his head around, looking over his shoulder. According to the clerk who checked him out, the man bought sunglasses and a black cap with the Quaker State logo on it. The clerk said he was in a hurry, that he ripped off the price tag and put the hat on as soon as the clerk scanned the barcode. Apparently, he didn't take his receipt or change before he donned the sunglasses and rushed out the door. That's the last time anyone reported seeing Hester. We've got no idea which direction he headed or where he's going."

Chapter Fifty-Four

Late October 2004

Angela couldn't stop crying. She didn't remember crying this much over Felipe, not even when her father forced the family to leave Philadelphia, but the tears kept coming and coming and she wrapped her arms around her chest to hold herself together. When she opened her eyes, she watched pieces of her floating away, drifting up and up into nothingness. One time she tried to grab the pieces before they flew too high above her, but her arms wouldn't reach that high, so she kept them wrapped around her body so no more pieces of her would escape.

The baby cried all the time. He was hungry. He was wet. He had pooped. He didn't want to be alone. He wanted to be held. He wanted. He wanted. There was no time left for her. No sleeping. No watching TV unless she was holding the baby. No time to stare out the window and dream her dreams. Dreams she'd once had about going to college, becoming a teacher, getting married. Her dreams were replaced by this wriggling baby, now almost two months old, who never seemed to get enough attention. Her mother helped a lot and Lacey did when she could, but Lacey was in school all day and doing homework most nights. Lacey still resented her for making the family move, but she was making friends in school now and building a life here, while Angela felt her life drifting away.

She realized the idea of a little baby sounded better than actually being the single teenage mother of a little baby twenty-four hours a day. What she wouldn't give now for a trip to the mall with her friends to look over the latest nail polish colors or flirt with the boys. Would she ever do that again? Would her life ever be normal again?

During an appointment, a few weeks after the baby had been born, the gynecologist asked how Angela was doing and she couldn't bear to tell her the truth. She'd seen other new moms in the waiting room cooing to their babies and practically drooling over them. The love for their babies was written all over their faces. How could she admit to her doctor she didn't feel that way toward her baby?

"Is the baby waking you up much at night?" the doctor had asked, and Angela said it wasn't too bad, didn't tell the doctor that some nights she wanted to scream when the baby began crying instead of getting out of bed and feeding him.

"How is the pain now from the surgery? During our last appointment, you asked me to renew the Vicodin prescription and I explained you need to be careful because it's an opioid and very addictive. Do you remember our discussion?" The gynecologist looked up from her computer screen, her eyes searching Angela's.

Yes, of course, Angela had remembered the conversation. She panicked when the doctor said she couldn't have any more pills. Angela had winced in pain when the doctor examined her, apparently a good enough actress that the doctor renewed her prescription, "Just one more time," she'd said, and Angela knew she'd have to find another source for the pills because that was the only thing holding her together.

One day she went to a little grocery store in a neighborhood that would have appalled her parents. The corner
grocery was next to a bar where a lot of guys hung out and
played pool. Angela walked into the bar, asked around as
discreetly as she could, and talked a guy into giving her a
fentanyl. Then he sold her some. And then she had to go there
every week, using spending money she told her mother she
wanted for baby clothes and stealing bills out of her father's
wallet when he left it on the dresser.

Now she panicked every time she had to figure out where
to get money to pay the pill guy. Every once in a while, during
a semi-lucid moment, she realized she was addicted but had no
idea what to do about it. And instead of the fentanyl making
her feel better, she was floating away into nothingness more
and more often, no longer fearing where it went because any
place was starting to look better than where she was. How
much longer could she do this?

Angela wiped her tears on her sleeve and stopped crying
long enough to ask her mother to watch Timothy while she
went for a drive and got some fresh air. She backed out of the
driveway and as soon as she put the car in drive and rounded
the corner, she began to cry again, the desperation of her life
too much to bear. She sobbed, closing her eyes for a second.

A loud beep startled her, and she pulled the steering wheel
to the right to get back in her lane, narrowly missing the car
coming toward her. Maybe she should pull to the side of the
road. Then she spotted a sign for a county park up ahead. She
pulled in the entrance. Pulled all the way to the end of the
parking lot, put the gear in park, and turned off the ignition.
Most trees had given up their leaves, their tall trunks a stark
contrast to the bright blue sky.

The warm temperatures and bright sunshine followed
three days of non-stop rain, leaving the usually quiet creek
churning with fast-moving waters. Angela got out of the car

slowly and trudged along a muddy path drawing her closer to the creek. She was so tired. Something had to be better than this.

Bending over, she picked up a stone and put it into her coat pocket. She held one of the stones in her hand, turned it over and wished swallowing the stone would make her happier the same way the pills did. She wiped the dirt off of another stone as she picked it up and put it into her pocket. Then a larger stone. The stones became larger under her feet as her path took her from the edge of the creek into its shallow waters, which Angela didn't notice until the cold water chilled her feet.

Rocks. Pills. No more pain. No more crying baby. It was Angela crying now, tears clouding her vision as she stepped on one flat piece of rock in the creek, then another, each step taking her farther away from land. She turned and looked upstream, where the creek was littered in rocks. Downstream, the water flowed unobstructed, faster and faster. Angela stood in the middle of the creek where the rocks disappeared, where the water grew deeper and swirled in pools.

Angela reached down to touch the water and connect to it, but the motion threw her off balance and she slipped again, only this time there wasn't another rock to step onto. Her arms flailed and she spun halfway around and dropped, pulled down by pockets of stones and memories of pills. She cried out in pain when her head hit a rock. The water rushed around her, the current pulled her along, and the weight of her coat prevented her from floating. Swirling pools of deeper water appeared on one side then the other as the creek rushed toward the river, slowly pulling her under. With no more physical strength or emotional energy to keep fighting, she gave in to her fate. The last thing she saw as the creek water washed away her tears was the face of her little baby.

Chapter Fifty-Five

Emily's eyes glazed over as she tried for the third time to review the edits to the marketing plan she'd been studying for the last hour. All she could think about was Stan. Where was he? Did the cops have a beat on him yet? How do investigators track down someone determined to disappear? And how often do people disappear successfully? Would Detective Trench call her with an update? She couldn't think about the answers to her questions because, as soon as one question ended, she immediately thought of another.

Then there was the other topic vying for time in her head. Lacey and her nephew Timothy, and what happened to Angela. It was such a tragic story with no closure for the family. But the newest piece of information was the one she had trouble putting aside. Felipe Santiago, the cameraman at Flagstone. She didn't know how old the guy was, and it was a big jump to think he could have been the boy who dated Angela. Fathered her son. But Flagstone's Felipe was another lead she could check out for Lacey. Maybe with Cara's help.

After the meeting with the police when Stan had disappeared last night, she and Cara were too exhausted to go out to dinner. Cara wanted to go home and put ice on her hand, so Emily drove them both to Cara's where she made dinner, poured wine, and explained why she'd reacted the way she had when police mentioned Felipe's name.

"And you think Felipe could be Timothy's father?" Cara had asked her.

"Lacey and I are tracking down every Felipe we can find, so he's another possibility. I think it's worth checking out. Don't you think he'd want to know?"

"It's difficult to say," Cara said.

"Is he married? Does he have any children?"

Cara squeezed her eyes and fought her tiredness for information. "I don't know. He works on other shows, not on any of mine. I mean, I know him from seeing him around the office, but not that well."

"Is he about our age?"

"Maybe. I guess he could be. I don't know."

"Could you check with personnel?"

"Emily, you can't go poking into someone's private information just because he has the same name as someone who may be connected to someone else more than a decade ago. That would be such an intrusion. Look, I'd like to help Lacey as well. I remember Angela. We had different interests, so we weren't friends. But I saw her around high school and in our neighborhood. Still, you know, I can't do something improper, maybe illegal. I can't."

And that's how they'd left it. By the time Emily had gotten home, she was too exhausted to call Lacey, and then the morning came rushing at her so there was no telling when she'd have time. Mostly, Emily just wanted to get through the day. It had been a stressful week and she was so glad it was almost over.

Her office phone rang; she picked it up immediately.

"Chris would like you in his office ASAP." Chris's

assistant, Joanie, didn't mince words. "Warren Painter is on the phone." Joanie hung up without waiting for an answer, so Emily shot to her feet and covered the short distance to Chris's office.

Chris motioned her to the chair across from his desk.

"Warren, Emily just arrived. I've got you on speakerphone. Go ahead."

She looked at Chris, shrugged her shoulders, her hands out, palms up. If she'd been able to speak, she probably would have said something like, "What the hell, Chris? Why am I here?" But instead, she stared at him and listened to Warren.

"I'll get right to the reason I called. Emily, I want to apologize about Pete Shelby's actions the night of our annual gala. To apologize for what he did and for not believing you."

She blinked rapidly, trying to absorb Warren's news. Chris didn't seem surprised. Warren must have filled him in already.

"Yesterday, someone who works in our sales division came into my office and divulged how he overheard Shelby bragging to a regional sales exec about grabbing your, um, derriere, on the dance floor that night of the party." Warren's voice sounded tight, like he was forcing his words out through a sieve. "I just met with Shelby, and he tried to downplay what had happened. Again. I didn't buy it this time. I just sent Shelby packing."

Emily tapped her fingers slowly, first on one thigh, then the other, another calming technique Mandy had taught her. She was relieved at how effectively it worked.

"I'm sorry about Shelby's actions," Warren continued. "I wanted you to know he's been dealt with appropriately. And I'd like you to resume working on our account."

Emily parsed each word and noticed Warren didn't say anything about how he had embarrassed and demeaned her by taking Shelby's side. Didn't mention how unfair it was for him to kick her off the Clifton account in the first place. Now he wanted her back. Really? Chris waved his hand to get her attention.

"Please accept my apology," Warren said, "and say you'll rejoin the Clifton account."

Was he delusional? Did Warren really think she could go back to working on Clifton's account and act as if nothing had happened? Did Chris? She looked up from the phone. Her eyes met Chris's. She tilted her head and raised her eyebrows. What did he think?

"The decision is all yours, Emily." Chris's words came out softly.

"I understand if you need a little time to think about it," Warren said.

"No, I don't need time," she said, taking in a deep breath before continuing. "I could never work with people who didn't believe me. Trust is an important part of any relationship, work or personal. So, thanks, but no." She pushed herself up from the chair, but Chris motioned her to sit back down.

"Are you sure—?"

"I believe you have Emily's answer," Chris interrupted him. "Thanks for updating us, Warren. I'll talk with you soon." He disconnected the call.

Emily stopped tapping her thighs and tried to hide her anger. "Did you expect me to say yes?"

"I expected you to be honest."

"At least that still works for some of us." Tears stung her eyes. She wanted to say more, but she was operating on very little sleep and a whole lot of tension, so she folded her hands in her lap and waited for what she deserved. Nothing less would do.

"I owe you an apology, too. I was too busy trying to take care of a client and not lose the account. I'm sorry."

Her head bobbed up and down, and she debated whether to tell her boss what she had been thinking over and over again, early in the morning hours, in the middle of the night, whenever she allowed herself to remember how he'd forced her to take off a couple of weeks. With pay. Then he continued to pay her salary when she said she'd needed a couple more weeks to work with her therapist. He didn't support her in the beginning when it might have mattered most, but he did come through in the end, and that had to count for something. Didn't it? She'd worked for him for a decade, trusted him even if he didn't trust her. And it was only that one time he didn't believe her. Against his first and most important client.

One night when Emily couldn't sleep, she had tried to put herself in Chris's position. Tried to imagine being strong enough to tell the person whose account paid so many of his company's salaries and supported so many of his employees' families that he believed her. Even if he had harbored a hint of doubt. What would she have done in his shoes? Would she have made the same choice Chris had? She wanted to believe that, morally and ethically, she would support her staff. Truth was, it was easier to make such a decision in the abstract than it was when the elephant was in the room. Elephants were difficult to ignore.

"I didn't envy you, Chris," Emily said." I knew you were in a difficult position. But I wish you'd taken me at my word."

"I wish I had, too."

His words touched her heart, but the wound cut deep. More healing was needed. More changes had to be made.

"If I'm going to stay here—"

"You're thinking of leaving BAM? Emily, no. Please don't."

"If I'm going to stay here," she continued as if she hadn't heard him, "then we need to address the culture that permeates our society and seeps through these walls."

"I've had conversations with every account exec, and we

held an employee workshop about appropriate behavior in the workplace while you were on leave." Chris shifted in his chair.

"I heard, and those steps are important. But if you want women to feel safe here, emotionally and physically, if you want women to seek out BAM as an inviting and supportive workplace, we need to do more. Use what happened with Clifton as an example. People must understand you can't just apologize for what's been said; they shouldn't be thinking in such disrespectful ways to begin with."

"You're talking about a huge cultural shift."

"A shift in our culture, in our morals, in our ethics. I'm not trying to change the world, Chris. I'm not unrealistic. But we can change our little place in the world."

"That's also a tall order."

Emily realized she was still now squeezing her hands together in her lap so hard they hurt. She flexed them to get the blood flowing but more than anything, to help her think. She loved BAM. She loved working for Chris. Hearing Warren Painter admit Shelby was guilty of what she'd accused him of gratified her, but also threw her off-center. She was spinning and needed time to internalize this latest information.

She studied Chris's face and thought she saw more lines in the corners of his eyes, more bags underneath them. Life was aging a lot of people much faster these days, especially the two of them. This whole episode with Clifton had been hard on him as well.

"Who once told me, if it's not difficult to do, it's probably not worth doing?" Emily asked.

"You've gotten pretty smart," he said as they both smiled. "You've grown considerably, too. Changed a lot over these past ten years."

"That's nothing compared to how much I've changed in the last four weeks."

Their smiles disappeared.

"Where does that leave us? Where does that leave you?" Chris asked.

"Warren's call was a surprise. I need time to process it. Telling him I wouldn't return to the Clifton account was easy. I'm not so sure about the rest."

He opened his mouth to speak, but then reconsidered.

"We'll talk again on Monday." She stood, her legs barely holding her up, and walked out.

Chapter Fifty-Six

C hris wasn't the only one surprised to hear Emily was considering leaving BAM. She'd stunned herself that she'd even think about such a move. The words were out of her mouth before she'd thought them through, before she took in what leaving would mean, where she would go. That didn't make her words any less true.

Warren Painter had believed his own guy over her. That made sense from his perspective. So why hadn't her boss believed her over someone he didn't know? That bothered her. A lot. But enough to leave BAM? That she didn't know yet.

Back in her office, she returned to her work. When Martin knocked on her door, her arm flew into the air, and she almost toppled a glass on her desk.

"Sorry, Em. I didn't mean to startle you." He took a few steps into her office and dropped his voice. "I heard you and Chris talked with Warren."

She moved the glass to a safer spot, then told him about the phone call. Told him Warren fired Pete Shelby.

"What a jerk. I'm glad he got what he deserved." Martin spit out the words.

"And then Warren asked me to come back to the account." She looked at him without emotion and let the news hang in the air.

"And then you said ...?"

"I said what any self-respecting person would say." She paused for effect. "No."

"Just 'No,' or 'No, you SOB, you can't just apologize and pretend it never happened?' Did you tell him that kind of 'No'?" His playful smile warmed her and helped release some of the tension that lingered from Warren's call.

"I did say I couldn't work with someone who didn't believe me. Then Chris said goodbye to Warren and hung up."

"Wow, that took some courage."

"And then I pointed out to Chris that he didn't say he believed me either."

Martin's eyes circled the room while he thought about what she'd said. He raised his chin, then his eyebrows. "What does that mean?" He could barely say the words.

"I told him I had some things to think about regarding my future here, and I'd talk with him again on Monday."

"Em—"

She cut him off with a wave of her hand.

"I'm not seriously thinking of leaving BAM, but, you know, I'm hurt by the people who believed Shelby instead of me. And I want to work in a place where people respect others, no matter their gender, race, sexual orientation. You understand how important that is. I used to think BAM was that place, but now I'm not so sure."

"I can understand why you're struggling, and I don't blame you. Why don't you have dinner with Ramón and me? Maybe it would help if the three of us talk it over. You know Ramón is an excellent sounding board."

She tossed his offer around in her mind, and while the two of them were wonderful company, what she wanted most was to go home and sip a glass of wine before drifting off to sleep. That's the kind of Friday night that most appealed to her.

"It's a wonderful offer. But I need a quiet night at home."

"Understood. Do you want to walk out with me?"

"I still have a few more documents I want to review."

He lingered, hoping she would change her mind. "Okay, but remember, Stan Hester is still out there somewhere and it's getting late. Be careful."

She nodded, returned her gaze to her computer monitor, and got back to work.

Half an hour later, she'd finished her work and shut down her computer. Then she drank the last sips of water, and when she put the glass down, it hit her desk with a thump. It was loud, like when there's a quiet moment during an orchestra concert and someone sneezes. She tilted her head to listen but heard no laughter, no chatter outside her door. Was she the last person in the building? She thought about Stan and shuddered. Did the cops have him in custody? Probably not, or Detective Trench would have called her. Laura and Cara probably would also have called. She pushed her anxiety and disappointment that Stan was still on the loose aside, stuffed her laptop into her bag, and hurried down the hallway. Out through the front doors into a silky quiet evening. And an empty parking lot. Empty except for her car.

Emily was halfway across the lot when an engine roared to life. She saw headlights swing through the parking lot entrance. The vehicle was bearing down on her and she froze. She took a few tentative steps toward her car as the headlights drew closer.

A sharp pain of awareness pierced her temple. It had to be Stan. And she was out in the open. No place to hide and no one to help her. The other option was also unappealing: if she got into her car and tried to speed past him, she probably couldn't. She probably wouldn't even have time to start the engine before his car crashed into hers. He'd kill her in an instant. On the other hand, if she ran toward the building, chances were pretty good she wouldn't make it.

The time for weighing options was running out. He was getting close. Fast. She took one more step toward her car, waited another beat till he was closer to her, then turned and raced back toward the safety of BAM. Her heart pounded in her chest, matching the pounding of her feet landing hard and carrying her as fast as they could. Crashing metal and breaking glass shattered the quiet night. Stan must not have been able to swerve away from her car. She'd bought herself a little time.

She reached into the small pocket inside her purse where she kept her phone, but it wasn't in its usual spot. Was it at the bottom of her bag? Did she have time to find it? Did she have enough time to call 911 all the while trying to get back inside BAM? The car chasing her—she was sure now it was Stan—must have backed up after smashing her car, because the pavement in front of her was illuminated by headlights and the eerie vision of her shadow. He was coming for her again. She gulped air and tried to breathe as she kept running as fast as she could.

A flash of lights to her right distracted her. Was that another car? Did Stan change directions, circle around to get a better angle at her? How could he do that? She didn't have time to figure it out. *Hurry. Hurry!* Her mind screamed out the words she was unable to say. It was too dark to see beyond the lights, and right now, it didn't matter if it was another car or who was driving. The only thing that mattered was getting inside the building to safety.

Forget the phone. She found her ID and yanked it out of her purse, but the laminated tag slipped from her fingers. She grabbed the woven cloth lanyard just before it hit the ground. Lights were coming at her in two directions now, she was sure of it. And they were getting close. She ran for her life, stopped abruptly, and swept her ID in front of the blinking panel next to the front door.

The lights continued to blink red. She yanked the door. It didn't budge.

"Let me in!" she screamed. She flipped her ID over and scanned it again. The light turned green, she jerked the door open, rushed inside, pulled the door closed behind her, and kept running into the lobby.

Metal hit metal. Again. Horns blared. But she didn't hear the sound she feared most, BAM's glass front door shattering. She dared to look over her shoulder and saw two vehicles crushed together. She squeezed her eyes and tried to tell what color the other car was, whose it was. Certainly not a police car or she would see flashing red and blue lights.

Stan wriggled out of his car and tried to run away, but he struggled to put one foot in front of the other. And he was slowed from holding one of his arms with the other. He looked like someone trying to run while holding a fifteen-pound bag of potatoes against his chest. He wasn't going fast, but he was getting away.

She grabbed the phone off the receptionist's desk and punched 911 as fast as she could. While she asked the police to send help and tried to answer their questions, the driver's door of the other car opened. A man crawled out. Martin!

Martin yelled and cursed at Stan as he gathered his strength and went after him. Martin closed the distance between them, reached out, and grabbed Stan by the shirttail. Then he pushed him down on the pavement.

Emily wanted to run out and help Martin, thank him for saving her life, but she'd used up all the energy she had. Her legs collapsed under her, and she sank to the floor, the soft carpet cushioning her exhausted body.

Chapter Fifty-Seven

The once-still Friday night exploded in a wail of sirens that grew louder by the second. Several police cars roared into the parking lot, followed by an ambulance. Two cars screeched to a halt alongside the smashed cars in front of BAM's entrance. The others flooded their spotlights on Stan Hester, face down on the pavement. Martin, holding his side and gasping for air, knelt on Stan's back.

Men and women in blue streamed out of their cars, guns drawn.

Emily propped herself up on her elbows and stared in amazement.

"Don't shoot," Martin yelled, showing his empty hands to the approaching officers.

Officers holstered their guns and helped Martin to his feet. Paramedics jumped out of the ambulance and ran over, one assessing Martin's injuries and the other two kneeling down next to Stan. The cops stood over Stan, ready to arrest him, but waiting for the medical team to tend to his injuries first.

Emily tried to stand, but her legs refused to cooperate. It was as if they had pushed her to safety with all they had. She pulled herself up to a sitting position, hugging her knees to her chest, her body throbbing with waves of shock. Detective Trench banged on the front door and motioned Emily to let her in. She crawled to the door, raised herself up on trembling knees, and pushed the handle. Hard. Her body fell forward as the door opened. Trench caught her and carried her inside. Then, finally feeling safe, her tears came fast and unstoppable. She sobbed as the detective led her to one of the couches in the lobby.

"Are you hurt?" Trench ran her hands along Emily's arms, shoulders, and legs, and turned her head one way then the other.

"I'm not hurt," she managed to say between sobs. "But I was so scared. I was out there all alone in the parking lot. He tried to run me down. I thought he was going to kill me." Her quick breaths nudged her tears down her face. "Is Martin injured?"

"I think he's more or less okay, Emily. The paramedics are treating him. And Stan will be taken into custody. He's pretty banged up. Can you sit here a moment while I go outside and check on the situation?"

She assured the detective she wasn't going anywhere.

Detective Trench propped open BAM's front doors, and the evening air washed over Emily like a strong breeze coming off the cool waters of a mountain lake. Outside, a speeding vehicle careened into the parking lot. A door slammed, then Chris was at the front door, explaining who he was to the officer just outside. After showing his BAM credentials, Chris ran to her side and fell onto the couch next to her.

"Emily, my God, what happened? Are you all right?"

"I'm fine. Well, okay, more or less." She ran her hand across her forehead and rubbed her temple. "Okay, not really fine," she admitted. "But I'm not physically hurt. Did you see Martin?" She wanted so much to talk to Martin, to learn why he'd come back to BAM. How could he have known she was in trouble?

"The paramedics are checking him over. He doesn't appear to be seriously injured."

"He saved my life, Chris. I don't know what I would've done if ..." Fresh tears flowed down her face.

Chris draped his arm around her shoulder. "Go ahead, Em, let it out. You're safe now."

A short while later, Detective Trench and Martin walked into the lobby, Martin limping and grimacing in pain. Upon seeing him, her best friend who had saved her life, she pushed herself up off the couch, found strength in her legs, and flew into his arms.

"I'm so relieved you aren't seriously hurt," Emily said. "I was afraid he'd kill you. How did you know to come back?" She had so many questions for him, but mostly she wanted to feel his heartbeat against hers.

"Come on, let's sit." Martin led her back to the couch. Trench and Chris pulled up chairs to join them.

"When I left here," Martin said, "I passed a car on the side of the road. I didn't think much about it at the time, but the image kept coming back to me as I drove home. I stopped at a red light, and I couldn't shake a sense of fear." He shivered and shook his head. "I called Detective Trench. Then I made a scary U-turn in the middle of Main Street and sped back here as fast as I could." He stopped to catch his breath, and Chris handed him a bottle of water. Martin took a gulp and continued.

"When I approached BAM, I noticed the car was no longer on the side of the road. I'd just turned into the parking lot when I saw the car racing in your direction and you swiping your card to get into the building. I don't remember thinking. I stepped on the gas and aimed for the other car."

Emily stroked his cheek, the part of his face that wasn't red and puffy. "You were going pretty fast when your car rammed his. That must've hurt."

"I didn't notice at the time," he admitted, taking another swig of water. "I was aware of bouncing around in the driver's seat after I crashed into his car. I think my head must've hit the window, then I slammed onto the steering wheel. I'm not sure how I got each bump and bruise. I just knew when his car stopped, he couldn't get to you." He smiled at her. "I'm so glad you're safe."

"Did Hester get out of the car right away?" Detective Trench prodded Martin.

"I sat in my car and felt the adrenaline shooting through my body. I looked over at Stan's car just as the car door opened. He got out. Very slowly. I knew I couldn't let him get away. I took a breath, eased out of my car, and chased him, although anyone watching would have thought I was moving in slow motion," he said with a smile. "Stan wasn't moving fast either. I caught up to him without much effort and shoved him to the ground." He smiled at Emily. "Slamming my knee into his back is one of the best feelings I've had in a long time."

"How did so many police cars and the ambulance get here so fast?" She looked at Trench and asked a question that had been puzzling her from the moment BAM's parking lot had filled with emergency vehicles. "I know Martin called you, but I'd only been on the phone with 911 for maybe a minute."

"After Hester left Pep Boys yesterday," the detective said, "he went to the airport and rented a car. He used his credit card, so we knew what type of vehicle he was driving. We took some educated guesses he might try to track down you or Cara or Laura. We increased police patrols by Flagstone's studios and also around BAM. His rental car wasn't there when the patrols drove by BAM earlier. When Martin called me, I radioed dispatch to send help. Then when you called 911, we sent a couple more cars."

Emily was tired and eager to go home, wanted this nightmare to finally be over. But first, she needed more information. "What happens next?"

"Hester's in custody. He'll be charged with attempted murder for trying to run you over. In regard to the attack on Nicole, forensics found strands of her hair in Hester's car, plus that receipt from the Anchor Bar."

"What about the earring?" She was afraid to ask but had to.

"Nicole confirmed that's her earring," Trench said. "But she doesn't remember how or when she lost it. She said most of the evening after leaving the bar with Stan is a blur. Shortly after she got into his car, he offered her a bottled water. Nicole said she sipped less than half of the water and doesn't remember anything after that. Our guess is he drugged her. So, to answer your question, Nicole and her friends provided enough info on what happened that evening, we can still build a solid case against Hester."

Emily pressed her hands together. "I'm glad to hear that, and I'm so relieved Nicole will recover. What will Stan be charged with after what he did to Nicole?"

"We'll wait on all the exact charges until she identifies him in a lineup, but he's looking at sexual assault, perhaps attempted murder because of how badly he beat her. And then left her."

A pained look passed through the detective's eyes. Emily thought about all the sexual assault cases Trench must've investigated over the years, and she figured the detective had strong thoughts about Stan Hester and what he'd done to Nicole, to Laura, and to her. Plus women he'd hurt that the police didn't know about. Emily had caught a glimpse of Trench's emotions, not just a police detective helping a citizen, but one woman helping another.

Detective Trench glanced down at her notepad. When she

spoke again, her voice was softer. "We're also taking another look at Laura's claim of sexual assault. In light of the charges that Stan will face in Nicole's attack, Laura's word will carry much more weight than his now. I have no doubt that Stan Hester is going to prison for a very long time."

"And he won't be able to hurt anyone else. Ever again." Emily smiled. Stan would soon be behind bars. Churning emotions swept through her body; she struggled to find her equilibrium amid the lightness of relief that her nightmare was over, and the sobering reality she could have been killed.

"I'm definitely ready for that glass of wine," Emily said, looking at Martin.

"Yes, but my place, not yours," Martin said. "You're coming home to spend the night with Ramón and me. No arguments," he said when she opened her mouth to object.

"When the adrenaline and shock of what happened tonight wear off," Trench said, "you're going to need someone to talk with. Having someone try to run you down, try to kill you, is traumatic. You're going to need your friends tonight. We contacted Ramón and he's waiting out front for you two. You can go now."

"But what about the mess in the parking lot? Is my car totaled? Is Martin's?"

"I've got this," Chris said. "I'll stay here with the police as long as necessary. You can deal with car issues later."

Emily wasn't good at letting others take control, but tonight was an exception. She let Detective Trench lead her and Martin outside, where Ramón wrapped Martin in a hug after being warned not to squeeze too hard. Ramón hugged Emily as tightly as he could and tucked them both inside his car. The car door closed. Emily rolled down the window and called out to Trench.

The detective walked over and leaned down to meet her eyes.

"Thank you." Emily's voice cracked as she tried to get the words out. "Thank you for not giving up on me, especially when I got in your way."

"You're a little reckless and a lot stubborn, Emily Archer, but you're going to get justice against Stan Hester. We'll see to that." Trench started to straighten up, but she wasn't finished. "Oh, and we've dropped the charge against you for tampering with evidence. Your record is clear."

"Really?"

Detective Trench smiled. "Really. Now get some rest."

Emily called Cara on the way to Martin and Ramón's and told her what had happened.

"Oh, Em, that must've been so scary. I'm so glad you're okay. I have a hundred questions to ask you."

"Can they wait? I'm exhausted, but I wanted you to know I'm okay. Could you call Laura and tell her about Stan, that she doesn't need to worry about his threats anymore? I'll call you both tomorrow."

Ramón helped Martin out of the car and eased him onto the living room couch. Emily sat beside him, and they drank some wine and ate dinner. Then she kissed both of her best friends goodnight and crawled into the guest room bed, where she fell asleep the minute her head found the pillow.

Chapter Fifty-Eight

Emily had received a lot of hugs over the past several days. Mandy's was one of the best: warm and loving, protective and nurturing.

"I was so scared for you when I got your message and heard what had happened Friday night. I'm so grateful that monster didn't hurt you." Mandy held onto her for a moment longer, then stepped back but held her arms tight. "You said you weren't hurt, but Martin was?"

"Yes, he got banged up pretty good when he rammed his car into Stan's. Martin didn't realize how bruised he was until he tried to get out of bed Saturday morning and every muscle ached." She winced at the memory. "Nothing's broken, but it's going to take time to mend."

"Give him my best, will you?"

She nodded, and the women sat in their usual spots.

Mandy picked up her notepad. "Tell me how you feel about what happened, about Stan being arrested."

"I'm thrilled he's behind bars, of course, and the police have enough evidence to send him away for a long time. But

..." Her voice trailed off, as she searched for the words to explain the crazy thoughts swirling in her mind. "I thought I'd feel happier. Dance-in-the-streets kind of happy. Shout-from-the-mountaintops kind of happy. You know what I mean?"

She looked into the warm eyes studying her and thought about all the horrible stories Mandy must hear during therapy sessions, all the pain she saw on people's faces and in their tears. She owed Martin another big thank you for knowing she needed Mandy in her life. In some ways, for saving her life.

"What happened Friday night is raw and new," Mandy told her. "You haven't been able to process it yet. Would you like to work on that today?"

"Yes, let's." She grabbed the tappers a little harder than usual and let the images play out: Stan's car racing toward her, her hands shaking so much she couldn't get the security pad to read her ID card, and frantically calling 911 for help. They kept processing the scariest memories of the evening until she told Mandy her level of upset was about a three.

"That's good for now," Mandy said. "Let's work with some of the positive images from that night. Tell me those."

Emily's shoulders relaxed, and her grip on the tappers eased.

"There was relief when I realized someone was going to prevent Stan from crashing into the building. When it struck me I wasn't alone. That I'd probably get out of there alive, which I wasn't sure of for a while. Also, a jolt of jubilation when Martin tackled Stan. Relief, again, personified, when Detective Trench banged on the door, and I let her into the building." She thought some more. "And one last positive image, one of the strongest, of love and friendship with Martin and Ramón."

They used the EMDR protocol to process those images and experiences until she internalized the positive moments into her memories and emotions. Mandy paused the pulsing tappers and asked where her level of upset was now around Stan's frightening actions Friday night.

She laughed. "It feels like a one. How is that possible?"

"Keep letting these thoughts process, Emily, and you'll find the happiness you want. Write down your thoughts and emotions. Realize this ordeal is over. Don't rush it. Your sense of relief *will* come. Trust me." Mandy glanced at the clock and began wrapping up their session. "Are you headed into work now?"

"Yes." She told her about Warren's call and Chris's reaction when she said she might leave BAM. "I've decided to stay and work with Chris on creating a safer environment at BAM for women, people of color, people who are gay or those who identify as non-binary. Who knows where that'll lead? Maybe we can change the culture in other businesses."

"That sounds like a good goal. What about your journaling?"

"I have been writing," she said, "but I don't think of it as journaling. I'm not capturing my emotions each day. It's more like writing a personal essay, a very long personal essay, about what happened and how you and I used EMDR to reduce my painful reactions to the assault. Sometimes I think about sharing my experience, but I don't know if I can. It's way too personal to share with strangers."

"I understand," Mandy said. "Perhaps you could write your story as fiction, a short story or a novel about the trauma of sexual assault and the path to healing. Really focus on the healing part of it. That could be a gift to many women who've been assaulted or abused. Bullied or marginalized. Women and men."

"Write about it in fiction, huh? That's an interesting idea. I'll think about that." She picked up her bag and coat and thanked Mandy. "See you next week?"

"Absolutely."

That evening, Emily poured a glass of wine and picked up the bottle to take with her into the living room. She paused, looked at the half-empty bottle of wine, then put it back in the refrigerator. In the living room, she turned on the TV for company, surfed a bit, thought about watching a baking contest, but spotted an episode of *Jeopardy!* which might engage her brain more, and clicked on the channel. The big display of boxes, six categories across the top, and thirty boxes with dollar amounts filled the screen, then the camera cut to the first contestant. The name written on the lower part of the podium where he stood was Felipe.

Felipe. Emily reached for her phone, remembering Cara had texted her while she was driving home. "Felipe" had flashed on her screen before the message disappeared.

Emily grabbed her phone. Opened the app. Read the text from Cara:

Bumped into Felipe Santiago at work. Asked if he went to Central. No. He graduated Northeast High. In 2005. Asked if he played football. No. But he did go to games.

Was that it? Couldn't Cara ask Felipe about Angela? Wait. She spotted another text.

I mentioned that a neighborhood friend of mine dated a guy from Northeast High named Felipe. Her name was Angela. Did you know her? He thought for a moment, then said he did date a girl named Angela. They broke up after a few months. He never saw her again.

Emily's hands were shaking so much, she struggled to locate Lacey's phone number in the contacts directory on her phone. Then she tapped the number and groaned when the call went to voicemail. She almost hit the red button to end the call, then changed her mind.

"Hi, Lacey. Call me back when you get this message. I found someone you and Timothy should probably meet."

She and Lacey couldn't predict how Felipe would react once he learned Timothy could be his son, but Emily knew they had to help Timothy because not knowing what really happened to his mother was difficult enough. It wasn't fair to keep him from another potential piece of his past.

Emily thought about so many people suffering from PTSD, for all kinds of reasons, like Lacey agonizing about whether she could have prevented Angela's death. Then she remembered her conversation with Mandy and all the work she'd done over the past several weeks to ease the trauma of what had happened to her. Mandy told her Emily would never forget the assault, but thanks to EMDR, she wouldn't be traumatized by the memory, wouldn't wake up in a panic in the middle of the night. Processing the memory allowed her to recall it without reacting. Doing the work would also prevent her from being triggered when she heard about assaults on other women.

Her mind drifted to stories about other women, especially those in the news lately because of high-profile cases of sexual harassment or assault. Those women had found the courage from listening to others to speak up and name the men who'd attacked them. To try to seek justice even though the odds of being successful were often against them. What was it like to carry that burden for months, for years? To be haunted and pained by what had happened? Then to finally let it out in the open. Hopefully, these women were also finding the help they needed to heal.

Emily appreciated her own journey through a horrifying trauma to get to the other side, and how much stronger she was for having done the work.

Then she heard Mandy's words as clearly as if her therapist were sitting next to her.

"...consider writing your story as fiction, a short story or a

novel, about the trauma of sexual assault and the path to healing. That could be a gift to many ..."

She replayed Mandy's words over and over, then pulled
her computer onto her lap, and began writing.

Resources

You'll find many resources on websites and in books about Eye Movement Desensitization and Reprocessing (EMDR) specifically, and trauma, including PTSD, in general. Here are just a few that helped inform me and my writing.

The EMDR Institute, Inc. (www.emdr.com), was founded by Francine Shapiro, PhD. It's where therapists learn more about EMDR and where to take the training. You can search the site for an EMDR therapist in your area, and find the link to *Getting Past Your Past: Take Control of Your Life with Self-Help Techniques from EMDR Therapy*, by Dr. Shapiro.

The Body Keeps the Score: Brain, Mind, and Body in the Healing of Trauma, by Bessel van der Kolk, MD. This popular bestseller covers the understanding and treatment of traumatic stress.

The Body Remembers: The Psychophysiology of Trauma and Trauma Treatment, by Babette Rothschild, MSW, LCSW. "Packed with engaging case studies, *The Body Remembers* integrates body and mind in the treatment of posttraumatic stress disorder. It will appeal to clinicians, researchers, students, and general readers."

Waking The Tiger: Healing Trauma, by Peter A. Levine, PhD, with Ann Frederick. *Waking the Tiger* "normalizes the symptoms of trauma and the steps needed to heal them."

Acknowledgments

First, a big thank you to EMDR therapists the world over who are helping people from all walks of life overcome trauma. So many lives are better because of the important work you do, and the incredible way you help people put the pieces back together. A special thanks to Taka, Georgia, Dave, and Rebecca for helping me through difficult times.

In addition to my wife, Helen Huffington, MSS, an EMDR Institute Facilitator and Certified Consultant, Donna Knudsen, Psy.D, EMDR Institute Facilitator and Certified Consultant, helped ensure my EMDR sessions followed the proper protocol and that Emily's therapist never said or did anything a good therapist wouldn't.

Thanks to my beta readers: Renée Bess, Viv Lotz, Alix Stohl, and Donna Anderton, for your early feedback and direction. I also received useful advice from many talented authors during workshops and webinars. I could not have reached The End without them or my editors, Caroline Leavitt, Nancy Thompson, Jayne Lewis, and Sue Toth. Kudos also to my cover designer, Lynn Andreozzi for creating the perfect cover.

My path to publishing was aided by many, including the supportive members of the Women Fiction Writers Association (WFWA). More than a dozen of us formed the WFWA Indie Debut Authors Support Group. We've learned so much from one another and are celebrating each other's successes.

I am a member of Sisters in Crime, national, and the Mavens of Mayhem, upper Hudson River chapter. For a while, I was part of the Delaware Valley Sisters in Crime chapter, all wonderful people willing to share their knowledge. Another big shoutout to the Mystery Writers of America, their programs, and resources.

Thanks to the staff at Cabela's in Delaware for showing me the power of handguns. I needed to hold a gun before Emily could and their instructions were educational. To Women Organized Against Rape and Women's Law Project, both in Philadelphia, to the Pennsylvania Coalition Against Rape, and RAINN, the Rape, Abuse, and Incest National Network, some of whom walked me through the technicalities of the Pennsylvania law, thanks for your patience and information. Any mistakes are mine. Thanks also for the important work you do.

To my supportive friends and family—especially Cindy, Mark, Ben, and Will Rybaltowski, Diane and Chuck Combs, and David Boulden—my deepest thanks for believing in me. To my parents, I wish I could put a copy of my book in your hands, but in my heart, I'm sure you know what I've accomplished.

Thanks so much to my readers for sharing this journey with me. Not only thanks but big hugs to libraries and librarians. You've been a haven, a resource, and an asset to my life ever since I can remember.

And again to Helen, without whom I could not have found my own path to healing.

About the Author

JACQUELINE BOULDEN has been a storyteller for as long as she can remember. She's wanted to write a novel ever since she stayed up all night in high school to finish Theodore Dreiser's *An American Tragedy*. She wrote *Her Past Can't Wait* because she wanted to tell a story about healing from sexual abuse based on the success of EMDR psychotherapy. When not writing or reading, gardening or taking photos, she walks in her neighborhood with her rescue dog, who's teaching her how to speak Beaglish.

Visit www.jacquelineboulden.com and sign up for her newsletter. Follow her on Facebook (JacquelineBouldenAuthor) and Instagram (@jacqueline.boulden). If you enjoyed *Her Past Can't Wait*, please consider leaving a review on Amazon or GoodReads. It would mean so much.

CPSIA information can be obtained
at www.ICGtesting.com
Printed in the USA
BVHW061326021022
648427BV00002B/10